ESCAPING

SKELETONS

DL Havlin

and JC Havlin

Palm Pen Press, LLC
978-1-933678-35-1

PALMPEN PRESS, LLC

Dedication

Dr. Mary Custureri

a true lover and defender of the arts

~ ~ ~ ~ ~

Acknowledgements

I used to read acknowledgements with little or no appreciation and with less feeling for the author and those cited. No more! After my writing journey of the last 20 plus years, I truly know the value of those who vitally contribute to the success of any author on their quest to produce a worthwhile work.

My first major debt is to Robert Fulton, Ph.D., my patient, skillful, editor/muse. Babs Brown my faithful critic and alpha reader adds to my skills with every read, and to editor/authors Bev Browning and Veronica H. Hart who both have immeasurably improved my craft. A special thank you to agents Mary Sue Seymour and Anne Hawkins for encouragement at crucial points in my career.

I owe a second special thanks to my publisher, Taylor & Seale and to its editor-in-chief, Mary Custureri. Without her belief in my work and writing skills, *Escaping Skeletons* would not be in print.

The third special debt is to my 'beta' readers, past and present, who took the time to critique my work. Present readers Chet Collins, Tonya Player, Paul Owen, Judy Galinski, Sandra

Pirman, Jeanne Miller, Carol Robb, Gayle Marie Hackbarth Harting, Todd Sharp, Pat Cole and Andrew Schakowsky combine their criticism with suggestions and encouragement. Their backgrounds, including high school principle, teacher, editor, book store owners and managers, lit majors and seminary grad, (ages 28 to 64) help them provide invaluable feedback. Their comments such as "I hope you understand this for no one else will," "Provide alarm to wake reader when chapter 6 is complete," "Ya-da-da-da-da," and *"Bullus shitus,"* kept me on track; and "Written with heart and conviction," "I cried and I don't do that often," "Wonderful thoughts written in beautiful prose," "This is twelve on a scale of ten," fired my enthusiasm to write the next page, chapter, and book.

Finally, I reserve my largest, most heart-felt thank you for my loving wife, partner, do-everything assistant, Jeanelle. Without her support, encouragement, understanding and tolerance I would have abandoned writing long ago.

Chapter **1**
Pineland Florida, Randell Research Center

"I don't think so." Dr. Bill Wallace spoke to me gently, dispelling my high hopes of having made a major find. He saw the disappointment on my face. "Let me take a closer look, Chessie."

I handed the large clam shell to one of my idols. "Dr. Bill" was the type of archeologist I wanted to become. He was patient. He was unbelievably knowledgeable. He was excruciatingly thorough. He was eminently respected. He had the sleuthing abilities of Sherlock Holmes where antiquities were involved. I desperately wanted to become a female version of Bill Wallace.

"*Mercenaria Campechiensis,*" I said. "I bet this weighed five pounds when some Calusa harvested it 800 years ago. It's 12.4 centimeters across." I pointed to what I saw as evidence that the shell had been converted into a tool those many years ago before being discarded into the midden we were excavating. "See the crossing lines and wear marks on the exterior and that hole in the top?" I hoped for something that never happened—Dr. Wallace to be wrong.

"Your deductive reasoning is very sound. The marks

do look like ligatures were in place. But, look here." Dr. Wallace removed a small magnifying glass from his pocket.

"See these tiny lines? They're created by tiny roots that branched off larger roots that created those larger lines. The way nature wrapped those roots ... well ... it does look man-made." He held the shell up to the light and examined the hole. After a full minute of examination, he said, "Very interesting. I really don't know what to make of that hole. It's too tapered and not in the right place to be used as a hoe or scrapper. There aren't any signs of wear. See how sharp the edges of the hole are? You wouldn't expect to see that if a wooden handle had been inserted there." He looked at me and smiled. "I'm taking this with us to give it further thought."

Andy Tobin grumbled, "Why do the things she finds have some interest and mine don't?" Andy was Dr. Wallace's bright but flaky graduate assistant. Dr. Card had warned me about him before my month-long field trip as an assistant to Dr. Wallace at the Randell Research Center site. The young man was one large hormone gland.

Dr. Wallace's calm voice scientifically summarized his reasons. "Actually, Mr. Tobin, Miss Partin finds twice the items you do because she keeps her eyes and attention on the trench we're working in. You definitely won't find artifacts under Chessie's Tee shirt or in the rear of her jeans. What's there might pique your interest, may I add, probably futilely, but nothing located in either place is anything you can publish a paper on or write an article for *Archeology Monthly* about."

Andy was on Dr. Wallace's shit list. It was the doctor's assistant's job to keep a gas-powered pump working to drain most of the water out of the four-foot deep trench in which we sloshed around. He didn't do his job. It cost more than a half day of digging. Dr. Bill wasn't a vindictive soul, but he did expect others to be responsible. The dig was only a foot or two above sea level and only yards from the mangrove encrusted shoreline of Pine Island Sound. Randell is on one of Florida's west coast barrier islands. Pine Island is hot, buggy, but filled with archeological treasures. Inhabited for 11,000 years, the site served as one of the capitols of the Calusa Indian tribe that was the master of South Florida when the Spanish arrived in the early 1500's.

"Chessie, dear, Dr. Card called and asked me to get you back to the office as soon as possible." Lina Bunn, the Center's office manager, trotted up to the tent-covered dig. She was out of her office and perspiring profusely, two things she tried hard to avoid. I knew it must be important. "He wants you to call him now. I think he wants you to go back to Vero right away."

Chapter **2**

Randell Research Center Office

"What's up, Doc?" I tried my best impersonation of Bugs Bunny when Dr. Mark Card answered his phone. Usually, that would bring some type of a smart-assed response from my boss. He ignored my attempt at humor and leaped into what he wanted. "You alone?"

Lina Bunn grinned, "No, but I can go and take her off the speakerphone. Just a second." Lina pushed a button on her phone as she handed the old-style handset to me. She walked toward the door and said, "Tell him *adios, sayonara,* etc. ..." as she left the room.

"Now I'm alone. What's going on?"

"How quick, and I do mean quick, can you be back here?" Mark wasn't often flustered, but he obviously was at the moment.

"I still have a week-and-a-half on my trip." I was learning a lot, having a good time, and didn't want to leave early. "Dr. Bill wouldn't like it if I left now." At least, I hoped he wouldn't.

"I'll clear it with him. How quick can you be back here?" Mark's voice was urgent and insistent.

"What is going on? Did the low grade I gave to the Darnell boy get me in trouble?" My words flooded out.

"He deserved the 'F' he got. I don't care if his old man did pay for half the University's new athletic dorm. If they want to fire ..."

"Please be quiet and listen." Mark was upset. "Don't be so damned defensive. The EFU administrative people love you, okay? Now, just please listen! I know doing field work with Bill Wallace is a big deal. How about an even greater one? What about going to a foreign site that hasn't been worked before? One I've been personally asked to explore by our State Department? I get to take an assistant ... that would be you. All expenses paid. Is that worth considering?"

"Sure, I'm listening. Well, I'm more than listening."

"Good!" Mark sounded relieved. "Get back here as quickly as you can. They wanted us down there yesterday. You go pack, and I'll square it with Bill."

"Wait a minute, Mark! At least, tell me a little more about what we will be doing. Where is it? What kind of a find? What do the people paying for this want?" I've found things that sound too good to be true, generally are ... but, even more so!

Mark was silent for a few seconds. Either he was being super-careful in phrasing his answer, or I'd asked him something he hadn't considered. Finally, he said, "Chessie, this is one we're going to have to take on faith. The only gamble I see is a waste of our time. There is a degree of secrecy around this thing that is distasteful. Here's what I know, less one or two items I'm not supposed to share, at least, not now." I heard him take a deep breath. "You asked where. Okay, it is in Argentina. They haven't pinpointed the location other than we should pack for spending our time in a semi-tropical climate. That means we have to be going to somewhere in the northern part, probably in the eastern three-quarters of the country. I asked Phil Ford if we were flying into Buenos Aires. He said no. I'd guess we will go into Uruguay or Paraguay. That probably means jungle."

"Who is Phil Ford?"

"He is an assistant to the Under-Secretary of State responsible for this project." I didn't respond, so Mark continued. "It fits with what they told me about what we will be doing. Evidently, there are two archeological sites. One was built over the other. I do know there is interest in both sites. One discovery is potentially a new Indian civilization. According to Ford, the guess is pre-Columbian, but no one knowledgeable has looked at it. That excites me. The other portion of it is more modern. I'm guessing some type of cult and, since the US is interested, I'm thinking some type of settlement like that nut founded at Jonestown in Guyana. The US would be interested in fact finding before someone could twist what's found there into something sinister."

"Lots of bodies?" I asked.

"I can't say. When you see our preparations, you'll

figure that out."

"One of the secrets?"

"Yes. One of too many of them. But, that's the way it has to be." Mark had made his peace with walking into an unlit room.

"That's all you know?"

"That's all I can tell you before you say yes and the people running this check you out." Mark was fishing for my commitment.

I was close, but my pot hadn't reached boiling. "I know that my record is supposed to be expunged, and all, but governments have ways of not missing things like that. Is it going to be a problem?"

"Absolutely not! I already asked." Mark was three steps in front of the problem...as usual.

I looked for another reason to say *no*, though I didn't want to. "Mark, you know my recent experience with governmental agencies. Honestly, I don't trust them. Reagen was right when he said, the nine most frightening words you can hear are, 'I'm from the government and I'm here to help." With secrets involved, do we know what we're getting into?"

"This isn't the CIA or the FBI that we're talking about. They were involved in that, not this. It's the Secretary of State we're working with, at their request for God's sake! Get the conspiracy theory stuff out of your head." Mark was selling hard.

I countered, "If I remember correctly, the State Department had some small involvement."

"Yes, they have told me it was unwittingly. In fact, one of the reasons my name came up was that one of the people who ended up kicking the corrupt person to the curb remembered me from the Rooster Cocker, Harlan Mengel thing. They thought my expertise fit this situation."

I'd made up my mind, but I needed one more excuse to say *yes*. "Can you tell me anything else?"

"I can tell you something I observed but wasn't told. That passion you have for learning about poisons? I read upside down well. While I spoke to Phil Ford, he had papers in front of him that mentioned *curare* several times. That's about the most famous one there is. Might be a lot about it involved in this expedition." Mark dangled the right bait, though he didn't need any.

"Okay. You got your assistant. It will take me three hours to get out of here."

I heard Mark's sigh of relief. "That's great. I was told we'd have a meeting to provide us with more information as soon as I confirm my assistant's identity. I'll set that up. Is tomorrow too soon?"

"No. I think my boss will clear it."

Mark laughed. "Look, we can't tell anybody about what we're doing until the State Department guy tells us we can. That means nobody."

"I can't promise that. I'll tell Reading. You *know* him.

If I tell him that it's a secret, it will be."

Mark didn't hesitate. "Your brother is fine. He'd pry or trick the information out of you on where you're going, anyway."

Chapter 3
Chessie & Reading Partin's Duplex,
Vero Beach FL

"I didn't expect you home for a couple of weeks." My brother Reading, dressed in a pair of gym shorts that hadn't had time to settle in place, had an embarrassed look on his face.

"You have a friend in your bedroom?"

He nodded, grinned and said, "Mind heading to your room for a few minutes?"

I took a deep breath and put my hands on my hips. "How long do you need?"

"Oh, we're finished, just time to get dressed." We each headed to our separate bedrooms.

After I heard muffled voices and the front door close, I returned to the living room. Reading had added a tee shirt and flip-flops to his attire. I said, "Tell Emily, she has good taste in men, and tell her if she doesn't want people to know who she's sharing the sack with, not to park her car out front."

"I'll pass that along." He smiled and pointed to the clock. "If you want something to eat we'll have to go out. I haven't been cooking while you were gone and the 'fridge' is empty."

"Kind of wondered why you got dressed." I shook my head. "I guess we're looking at something fast, not gourmet."

"Why not gourmet? I'm dressed for Chick-fil-A. You can tell me what pried you out of the Randell Research Center while we chew." He snatched his pickup truck keys from the end table. "I'll drive."

~ ~ ~ ~ ~

Reading listened to me without interrupting. He does that well. Though he tried not to show his misgivings, a few signs flickered over his features as I spoke. They weren't pronounced ... I just know him so well. When I finished, he said, "Wow. That's something I didn't expect." He slurped his chocolate shake. "How long will you be gone? I'll ask Emily if she wants to bring some clothes over. She moved down to Ft. Pierce. It would save us both gas, and she's already on a first name basis with Wilma and Fred."

"Do our neighbors approve?" I didn't give him time to respond. "I don't know how long. I'd guess, but whatever I say would be wrong. You'll have to wait until I know before extending an invitation. There's supposed to be a meeting. This thing with Emily...getting serious?"

Reading's smile faded. He shrugged his shoulders, "She's good at what she does."

"What an ass! Does your *thing* do all your thinking for you?"

A little resentment and guilt shone on Reading's face. "Could be serious. So, now tell me what you didn't the first time you explained this diving board you're going to jump off of. Is the pool empty, or does it just sound that way?"

"I've told you everything I know. Mark says he'll tell me more as soon as I get approved by the guy running the show. And, there's—"

"Supposed to be a meeting." Reading shook his head. "When?"

"Tomorrow ... I'm not sure." That sounded stupid.

"You're serious. I thought you had developed more common sense. Don't go back to opening doors when you don't have the slightest idea of what's behind them." Reading shook his head. He likes to do that. He showed more than a little disgust. It offended me.

"All right, oh intelligent, infallible brother ... *where* did I go wrong? You know, I can ... change my mind. I don't think I will, but I can. What exactly do I need to know? What did I miss?"

Reading sighed. "Hey, you can do anything you want, but remember you're going to be in a foreign country. The sheriff and I aren't going to be able to keep an eye on you and pull you out of the *puuky* if you step in it."

"Since you think I can't take care of myself—"

"I didn't say that! Damn, Chessie, I just don't want you to get into something you can't get out of."

I tried to calm down before I spoke. "That's cool. So

give me some legit brotherly advice. What should I ask?"

Reading stared at me as he developed his checklist. When he started to tap his fingers, I knew he was ready. I raised my eyebrows, indicating he should start. He nodded. "To begin with, you need to do some checking on your own. When someone *doesn't* tell you something, there is a reason. I wouldn't believe fifty percent of what they tell me. Ask yourself why they might want you two down there, what there is to look at archeologically, who is really behind the trip, and most importantly, what are the things that could go wrong. Do your own research. Hasn't Dr. Card always emphasized that? Sounds like he needs to do some practicing of his preaching."

Reading's words reawakened my doubts. I tried to brush them away. "Reading, we are talking about the official US government here. You really think they would involve us in something shady and dangerous?"

"In a DC second!"

Chapter **4**

Dr. Mark Card's office at EFU

"You said tomorrow. It's tomorrow." Mark grinned as he spoke.

"I'll remember that when I get asked when I can be ready to go." Things were really moving fast. I figured that if it were like most issues involving the government, we'd be lucky to have the meeting in two weeks. Surprise! We would be meeting with Phil Ford in University President Jim Andrews' office in two hours. I was curious, "Why are we meeting with Dr. Andrews? They insist on that?"

"No, I did." Mark held up two fingers. "First, I have to give him a reason for the two of us being gone. Second, and this is the most important one, I want to have someone with clout knowing first-hand the US Government is in this. It will make it harder to explain if something happens to us. It's an insurance policy. Not quite Liberty Mutual, but it's something."

Mark's words told me he had some concerns about our upcoming adventure. "Reading told me I was about to dive into a pool without knowing if there was water in it. Sounds like you have second thoughts, too."

"Not really. The pool might not be completely full, but we'll be okay. I'm going to ask a few questions. See where it goes. But...I'm committed."

"Ask questions. That's exactly what my brother suggested." I peered into my coffee before I removed it from Mark's desk and took a sip. There weren't any answers there. "I must have passed approval, or we wouldn't be here."

"Chessie, one of the things I couldn't tell you ...you were approved before I called you. Why I couldn't, I don't know." Mark shrugged his shoulders, looked at his cup, smiled and said, "My cup's got a hole in it."

I looked at him quizzically. "So ... what else can you tell me now that I'm *approved*?"

"From what I know." Mark's laugh was nervous and short, "it's a lot of nothing." He got up from his desk, closed the door, and pulled his chair close to me before he sat down. "But, it is something. I know that we aren't going to be the only scientific people involved. I know Phil Ford isn't going into the field, someone named Mug MacAphee is the field leader. The name is all I know. We are supposed to let them know what we need to transport a minimum of forty skeletal remains, artifacts as large as a HUMV, and some things that possibly need to be sealed. I asked for details, and Ford claims he doesn't know any. He tells me that the Indians are Guarcuru. They lived on the marshes and plains in the Gran Chaco. Still do. That's in western Paraguay. But, he's told me to be sure to take boots I can climb hills with. A lot of things don't compute. He assures me we are going to be working in Argentina, but then he tells me we are flying into Asunción. I guess that makes sense. It's on the border." Mark took a breath. He tapped his fingers on his desk impatiently. Obviously, he was holding back something ... important.

"Okay. Mark, we've been together long enough for me to know when you're hiding something under the covers." I watched his face closely. Mark disguises his emotions fairly well, but for a few seconds his expression was that of a teenager caught stealing cash from mama's purse.

He nodded and slid even closer. I could remember a day when that would have caused a major hormone release. I batted my eyes involuntarily and thought, *Even a Corvette becomes routine after you've driven it a while.* Mark almost whispered, "They asked if I had had some weapons training when I went to Kosovo. Then Ford asked if you were, and I'll quote, 'a girly girl.' I told him you were in the Marines. His smile was as big as the Cheshire Cat. I asked why the interest in self-protection and weapons. The reasons he gave were contrived. First, he said we were going into very wild country. Jaguars. Snakes. The bastard doesn't lie well. You could read his eyes. He must not have worked for the State Department long. His second attempt was closer, but no cigar. Ford said there were still some Indians in the area that were unpredictable. He saw I wasn't buying, so he told me we're going into an area that has groups of bandits and paramilitary gangs.”

I pushed away from him in alarm. “Mark, are you crazy? What are you getting us into?”

He put his hand up and wiggled his palm at me. “Shush! Let me finish. At that point, I told him to put his head where the sun doesn't shine. That's how I learned that we are going to have first-class protection. There are eight private militaries going with us, and we'll get a military escort to the Argentina line. We'll get a small number of Argentine or American military to stay with us at the site. I asked why we just didn't go into Buenos Aires and pick up our military escort there. He laughed and said there were *issues*. Then he told me something that doesn't compute. He said, 'That would make it harder to get the heavy equipment to where you're going. We're sending it with you to make your job easier and quicker. It's 80% shorter.' I asked him what was going in with us. He mentioned two duce-and-a-half trucks and a backhoe. The trucks are for us and the equipment they think we'll need. There are jacks, lifts, lasers, jack-hammers, chainsaws, and every type of hand tool man has invented. Ford confided in me that all that equipment is what worries them. It makes us quite a prize for bandits and such. I asked him how we were going to move out any artifacts that we find. Ford laughed and said not to worry. He said Santa Claus will fly down and pick them up. You know how much I detest smart-ass martinets.”

"Why are we here?" I was astonished. It sounded like a lot of risk for nothing.

Mark smiled, "We're here because of what he had me sign at the end of our conversation. It was an agreement. Part was confidentiality; you'll have to sign one, too. Part was a statement that we are providing our skills and knowledge as archeologists, and," he smiled wider, "we get paid well. Very well." He waited for me to react.

I obliged. "How much?"

"A lot. I get $225,000, and you get $25,000 for sixty days of digging in the Argentine dirt and maybe dodging a bullet or two." He nodded as he watched my face. I make no attempt to hide my feelings. "And, my dear Chessie, if we are able to accomplish what they are hoping, Mr. Ford assures me there will be a bonus. A significant bonus."

I smiled. "That's why we're here!"

Chapter 5

Dean Dr. Jim Andrews' office

I didn't like Philip Ford within sixty-seconds of meeting him. His handshake was one of those mushy limp noodle types. His blue eyes looked like expressionless lumps in a livid white face that masked whatever the man thought. I couldn't help think he would make a great extra in one of the teenie-bopper vampire flicks. He seemed uncomfortable and avoided eye contact with me, so, naturally, I did my best to maintain pupil-to-pupil communication. He looked even more upset ... I loved it.

So did another stranger in the room who watched Ford and me with open amusement. What a terrific contrast to Dr. Andrews, Mark, and the Ford character. They wore suits. He had a pair of khaki cargo pants and a size XXX gray golf shirt that stretched to contain the man under it. His handshake was a bit like placing your hand in a vise, one that closed only tight enough for you to realize what your hand was in. He introduced himself. "I'm Mug MacAphee." He didn't have to say *I'm the leader*. You just knew he was.

I guessed Mug was forty, plus or minus a year. Describing him in one word ... that would be ... rugged.

He wasn't a huge guy like my 6'5", two-hundred-fifty-pound brother. He was built more like a fireplug. I'd say he was 5"11" and maybe two-twenty. His face was more pleasant than good looking. Several scars said *I'm a warrior*. His sandy light brown hair was cut in a fifties flat-top. What was impressive was his bull-chest and biceps that screamed they'd spent a lot of hours in a weight room. He might have been taller if he'd had a neck.

Dr. Andrews, "Andy" as everyone called him, was a giant mind in a smallish body. He ushered us to his conference desk where four of us sat. He remained standing, smiled and informed us, "Philip and Mug have discussed the need to keep information secret. I'll leave after I tell you that I'll approve ninety days of paid hiatus for both of you. It will start eight days from now. I'd appreciate if you would bring your teaching assistants up to speed and ... Mark you said you've talked to Dr. Wallace about getting instructor help from Gainesville. We should be fine. Congratulations. From what I've heard, this sounds like quite the adventure. We'll talk more after your meeting is complete. Good Luck."

We sat at the table like four stumps, inanimate and silent, as Andy left the room. As the door closed behind him, Ford went to Dr. Andrews' desk and removed the wire from his speakerphone. As he returned, Mark said, "Isn't that a bit extreme?"

Ford answered, "That's the protocol I've been given. I follow orders. It is important we all execute our responsibilities." He reseated himself, opened a briefcase and removed some papers. "Miss Partin, has Dr. Card explained that you are required to sign a confidentiality agreement? You will not be able to divulge what you see, do, or learn without first obtaining the written permission of the US State Department." He shoved the papers at me quickly and then stared at the table, not me. "Instructions for gaining approval are in your copy you will receive."

"Yep." I signed where the little tabs of paper said I should. Ford's eyes stayed focused on my pen, never venturing higher.

When I finished, I slid the papers back to him, and he quickly stored them in the briefcase.

"Can you tell me what I'm not supposed to be talking about?" I asked.

"You're going to be well paid, Miss Partin." Ford removed two binders, each containing a quarter inch of papers. He handed one to Mark and one to me. "Everything you need to know to get ready for the trip is in those booklets. I have a schedule that details when you have to be ready, the travel plans, and when we will arrive. There are also lists of things that can't be taken, protocols to follow when we are in each country we visit, and new and updated passports you are to travel under. That's about it."

"You didn't answer my question." I disliked Ford more each moment.

"I'm afraid I can't divulge that. What you've been

engaged to do is to investigate two overlapping archeological sites from significantly different time periods. You two are to analyze and document what you find, preserve what is of interest, and supervise the removal of pertinent items." He made eye contact for the first time since their conversation started. "Let me assure you that this is a legitimate scientific project that may have significant cultural and historical impacts."

"Are we going to be safe? Getting paid well doesn't mean squat if you aren't alive to spend it." Mark's tone was sharp. Philip Ford's condescending manner was annoying him, too. "Can you at least tell us what our government's interest is in this?"

Ford stared at each of us for a few seconds before returning his pupils to the papers in front of him. The silence was increasing the tension in the room. He finally took a deep breath and said, "Dr. Card, we've been over this. You agreed you were all right - with the secrecy portion of this opportunity."

Mark didn't appear willing to challenge Ford further, so I did. "Secrecy is one thing. Operating in a complete vacuum is another. I have a brother in law enforcement. One thing he always says is when someone doesn't want to tell you something, that something is what you most need to know. I have to conclude the reason you won't tell Dr. Card and me more about this expedition is that you wish to hide some bad stuff from us." I paused a moment.

"Is this likely to get us killed?"

"Absolutely not!" Ford burbled.

"Is it likely to get someone else killed or injured?" Mark was ready to become more aggressive.

"No, Dr. Card, no one will be harmed."

"Then why the interest in our ability to use weapons?" Mark asked.

Ford looked like a condemned man in front of his judge. Mug MacAphee spoke for the first time. "It's strictly a precaution. If I don't do my job, or at least, this part of it, you have a safety net. That ain't going to happen. I've never failed in an assignment yet, and this sure as shit won't be the first time. I'm here because I have three jobs to do on this wild-goose chase. One of them is to keep your butts from being bruised. I can assure you *they aren't going to be bruised*." He hesitated and glanced at each of us with his stony eyes. "I'm also providing men to do the muscle work for you. That's getting you and your stuff in, do what you tell me you want done at the site, and getting you out. My last responsibility is to safeguard what you find. *IF you find anything*. You understand I'm in charge. One of the reasons we are having this meeting is that I wanted to see if you two were going to be a problem. You aren't. That's good."

Mug leaned back in his chair, "I'll answer anything I can. Some things I can't." He turned his head and glared at Ford. Ford's mouth opened and closed instantaneously.

Mug had told Philip to shut up as clearly as if he'd said the words.

"Why are we really going to this site?" Mark asked.

"Because there is evidence that some important artifacts could be there. Both the US and the Argentine governments want to see if what is conjectured is true. I've been led to believe what's there could be exceedingly valuable. I have my opinions, but they're guesses so I'll keep them to myself. You will be there for archeological work." Mug grinned and added, "Next."

Mark asked, "Can you tell us what periods of time these are from, or something about them."

"I don't know enough about even one to give you info other than I've been told it's pre-Columbian. That doesn't mean shit to me ... I hope it does for you. I know about the other, and I can't tell you word one about that." Mug put his hands behind his head. "Next."

I asked, "What does poison have to do with this?"

Mug looked confused. "Poison? What in hell are you talking about?"

"Curare."

"That information and four bucks will get you a cup of coffee at Starbucks. What in hell are you talking about?" Mug looked at Philip who shrugged his shoulders.

"Mark saw it in paperwork Ford had in front of him when they had a previous meeting." I looked at Ford. "Surprise, some of us can read upside-down very well."

Mug leaned forward, glared at Ford again, and said, "Let me assure you that we don't have an interest in manufacturing curare. The poison doesn't fit *directly* into this." He emphasized the word 'directly' so that we wouldn't miss it. I immediately wondered why. Mug glanced at the sheepish-faced State Department representative and enunciated slowly and clearly. "Philip, please go over the travel dates and times with Dr. Card and Miss Partin." He looked back and forth from Mark to me. Mug laughed and said, "Yes, you two will be just fine."

Chapter 6

Chessie's bedroom

"What are you doing?"

I rolled over on my bed, being careful not to shove my laptop on the floor. "Why don't you knock!" I was in my bra and panties. Though I frequently strode around our duplex in that attire, it was still my choice to go on exhibition, not his.

Reading grinned. "I get it, privacy and all that. I'll try to remember. What are you doing?"

"I'm following your advice. Checking things out for myself. The meeting we had answered a few things, but it raised a lot of new ones and left a lot unanswered."

Reading's face turned serious, "Oh yeah, did your meeting turn out okay? How was the guy running the show?" I frowned. He added, "That bad?"

"I have as much faith in that dude as I would in a cow pie with a coconut for a head."

Reading laughed. "That is bad! Sounds like time to cancel your trip."

"Actually, the guy I thought was running the show isn't." I swung my legs out of bed and sat on the edge. "The man Mark met with and is doing the administrative part of it isn't the honcho for the actual expedition. I felt good about him."

"Names?"

"Philip Ford is the admin guy. Loser. At least, I think so. The leader is named Mug MacAphee. I liked him."

Reading sat down next to me. "Think those two will get along on your trip?"

"No worries. The lump of shit isn't going."

He nodded. "So don't waste time on the Ford man. What's this MacAphee man like?"

I thought for a few seconds. "The best way to describe his looks? Let's see, if you crossed a silver-backed mountain gorilla with a Marine drill instructor you'd have the image."

"He doesn't sound like Don Juan."

I shrugged my shoulders. "His job is to get us in and out safe and furnish muscle when we need it. We don't need a candidate for the Playgirl calendar. I like his attitude." I thought for a couple of seconds and added, "He strikes me as a no-nonsense type. Mug, if that's his real name, is probably a mercenary. Blackwater or something akin. He's scarred up. I sure wouldn't want to get into an alley fight with him."

Reading stood up, went to my desk, sat, and prepared to write. "Tell me his name again. I'll see what I can find on him...and spell it."

"Mug. I guess that's M ... U ... G. MacAphee. It's spelled capital M ... a ... c ... capital A ... p ... h ... e ... e. Just for laughs, the other guy's name is Philip Ford. Philip is spelled with one L. He works at the State Department."

Reading nodded. "You get a schedule?"

"Yes, we leave in eleven days and are supposed to be onsite in fourteen. They're saying they expect us to be done in sixty days. Andy Andrews gave Mark and me three months of leave, so I figure that's how long I'll be away."

"Learn anything else?"

I smiled. "Oh yes! We won't have to worry about the rent for a while. In fact, we can go talk to our landlord about buying this place."

Reading's eyes opened wide. "That much?"

"Oh, yeah!" I leaned toward the table. "I'm getting 125 pictures of Grover Cleveland!"

It takes something major to really excite my brother. "NO, SHIT?!"

"No ... shit!" I slapped my hand down on the bed.

"Let me thank you. It will take a few days to count the ways." We both laughed. He asked, "What are you checking out? Seems to me you have 125,000 reasons not to."

"I'm just doing what my omnipotent Bro says I should. I'm doing a little research. And ... I'm having less than no luck on where I decided to start."

"Can I help?" he said.

"Sure. I've been looking up curare. That's a poison that is mentioned in some of Ford's papers Mark got a peek at. When I brought it up, it seemed to upset them both. I thought I'd start there. I've looked up curare, poisons, Argentina, poisons in Argentina, Indian poison darts. So far, I haven't learned a thing."

Reading returned to the bed and sat next to me. He said, "Maybe it isn't poison. Try entering 'curare in Argentina.' It might be something else."

I tapped my laptops keys. The Internet took a few seconds. My eyes widened at the result. I recited what I read, "Teyu Curare Provincial Park." The next items I saw shot a jolt of electricity through me. I looked at Reading. "This is close to the Paraguay border. That's where we're flying into, and it's already an established archeological site. That's where we have to be going."

Reading scanned the screen. "I saw something about this on TV. They found a bunch of buildings and other stuff connected to the Nazi's." He grinned. "So now you know where and why you're going. The question is; what will you find?"

"They told us the site we're going to hadn't been explored before."

Reading nodded. "That means they lied, or what is more probable, something new has been found there, and someone in Washington wants to see what's there before anyone else."

Chapter 7

Vero Beach, Florida, Chessie's Jeep

"It is the same damned number." I was steamed. I answered and hung up within a second. "I wish there was some way I could get off the phone list I'm on. I get a robocall when I get up in the morning, and they continue all through the day."

Reading asked, "Aren't you on the state no-call list?"

"Yes, but either they don't know or don't care." "Is it the same number all the time?" I nodded. "I tried calling the number back, and it says it's unassigned. There are so many ways to scam numbers, returning a call is about useless. I want the satisfaction of finding out who it is and yelling at them. The bad part is it seems they call me most when I'm driving."

Reading thought for several seconds then said. "It's after nine. Solicitors have enough sense not to call. Does the call hang up right away, or do you have an open line?"

"Open line. I've tried insulting them. Whistling. Nothing makes them respond or discourages them." I turned into Publix's parking lot.

"Can you give me the number? I'll take it to the department's IT and communications officer. She'll have ways of finding out where it's originating that we don't."

There are some major advantages to being a captain in a Sheriff's office when it comes to snooping. My brother used his privilege sparingly, but he did use it.

"Gladly." After my jeep rolled to a stop in a parking spot, I removed my cell from my jeans pocket. "Let's see ... it's a 202 area code." I read off the rest of the number.

Reading scribbled the number on a tiny notebook that is his constant companion. "I don't want you to get paranoid, Sis, but we keep track of people in a similar fashion. You remember getting calls from this number before you signed up for your trip with Mark?"

My body stiffened as I finally made the connection Reading did so quickly. "No, I don't remember any."

"That's Washington, DC's area code." Reading rubbed his chin, a sure sign he thought he'd figured something out. "You need to call Mark and see if he's getting the same type calls. No, don't do that. Your phone might be tapped. Ask him tomorrow at work. I'll see if I can find out if these calls are coming from the State Department."

Chapter 8
Dr. Mark Card's office at EFU

"Yes, I have. But, Chessie, that's not something suspicious. I get a half dozen of those type calls every day. They're charities and sales calls—a nuisance, but nothing more. You need to stop looking for something sinister in everything that happens." Mark grinned. "You'll go crazy if you let little things like that bother you. If a car follows you for several blocks and turns when you do, you'll get hyper. It will drive you nuts."

"You're sure some came from the 202 area code?" I asked.

Mark nodded his head and looked disgusted. "Yes, I've noticed a few from there. It's probably a politician looking for a handout."

"It isn't me saying this, it's Reading. He says they do the same thing to track criminals." I put my cell phone on Mark's desk and readied it to push the speakerphone feature. "When he calls, you can hear for *yourself.*"

Mark's grin pissed me off. He obviously thought I was paranoid, obsessed or both. "Okay," I continued, "I know you think I'm batty about this. If he finds out the State Department is spying on us, will you agree we need to ask some serious questions?"

Mark's grudging agreement was sincere. "If someone is keeping tabs on us from Washington, yes, that's a red flag, and we need to find out more before bopping off to Argentina or wherever."

"I think I know where we're going. Reading figured it out." I hesitated, knowing that what I told him next could be met with skepticism.

"Where?" he prompted.

"A place called Teyu Curare Provincial Park. It fits all the clues we've gotten so far."

"I've heard that name," Mark said as he tried to fire the correct synapse.

"It's been in the news the last few years. There were some Nazi buildings—"

Mark cut me off. "Oh ... not the Hitler's alive thing! Spare me."

"Just saying. Look, Mark, the location fits. Should we discount what logic tells us?"

"No." His answer was laced with his returned skepticism...squared. "We can't sit here and wait for Reading's call with all we have to do before we leave." Mark impatiently tossed a couple of research texts on South American tribes and history into his open briefcase.

"Reading said he'd call by 11:30. That's five minutes. You can waste that much time."

Mark scowled.

"Please, for me." I knew where Marks buttons were hidden and I pushed one. A feminine pleading expression accompanied by the appropriate pleading words was a big red switch.

The scowl changed to resignation. "Okay, okay. Five minutes. If he doesn't call, we have to get back to work." He changed the subject. "Have you gotten everything on the lists they gave us? I know what the vitamins are for and the cornstarch, but extra shoelaces?"

"I'm not sure, but they may have ground leeches there, you tie the shoelaces around—" My phone rang ending the conversation. I said, "It's Reading."

Tapping the icon, I warned Reading, "You're on speaker. I'm with Mark."

Reading's first words were, "Does someone in your office have a phone you can use and call me back on?" Alarm showed on Mark's and my face.

Mark answered, "Yes, I can borrow Glenda's cell."

"Good, call me on my private number." Reading hung up.

Mark was back with his assistant's phone in a few seconds, and we were talking to Reading within a minute.

"So did you find out where the phone calls are coming from?" I asked.

"Yes." Reading answered. "Did you confirm Mark was getting the same calls?"

Mark answered, "Yes. I'm pretty sure I've gotten some

from DC."

"Are they from the State Department?" I asked.

I heard Reading take a breath. "No. They're from the FBI. I couldn't get a name, but our gal tracked them to the J. Edgar Hoover building. It's an unassigned block that's used exactly like I thought."

Mark and I responded simultaneously, "Oh shit!"

Chapter 9

Dr. Mark Card's office at EFU

"Yes, they agreed to meet the day after tomorrow. Ford sounded alarmed. When I told them about the calls and where they were coming from, he put together a bunch of four-letter expletives and Ford isn't the type." Mark shook his head. "It has to be a concern if the people sending us are that spooked. Maybe ... just maybe, we should pull the ripcord on this thing and bail out."

There was a knock on Mark's door, and Glenda entered. She placed her cell phone on Mark's desk and said, "There's a call from Chessie's brother for the two of you." She spoke to the phone, saying, "Mr. Partin, Dr. Card and your sister have the phone." Glenda left the room as though someone had threatened her.

"You two there?" Reading's voice came from the cell.

"Yes," I answered.

"I thought you should know this right away. Your tour leader isn't from Carnival Cruises. I did some background searches on Mug MacAphee. He had a great record when he was in the Army doing special-forces operations. He's been decorated four times. Now, Mug works for a private contractor whose biggest customer is the US Government. He's done some civilian extractions." Reading hesitated. I knew he was deciding if he should tell us something he'd discovered. He chose to tell us. "Rumor is your man Mug has been involved with a couple of successful assassinations. My sources told me he's great *IF* he's on your side."

Mark and I looked at each other. He reached his hand over his chest and ripped it away as though he was pulling the cord.

"Hello," I didn't recognize the full phone number, but it was a 722 area code call which meant it was local.

"Is this Miss Chesapeake Partin?"

I didn't recognize the female voice coming from the phone, so I asked, "Who is this?"

"A friend of yours. I'm sure you don't recognize
me, but I am your friend." "What kind of—"

The voice cut me off. "Shush, shush. Let me finish. Going to Argentina this time of year can be very cold. Winter is about to begin, and it gets cold as a mortuary slab. You don't want to end up on one of them." There was a click as the line disconnected.

I sat looking at the cell phone in my hand. As I watched, the phone number on the screen disappeared. The threat may not have been real, but the shiver that went through my body was. I started to leave my office to tell Mark about the call, but he entered and closed the door behind him. He had a strange look of anger and fright on his face.

I spoke before he could. "Mark, I think I just had a

death threat. I had a phone call from some woman telling me I'd—"

Mark completed the sentence's meaning, but with slightly different words. "… end up being returned to the US in one of the human remains containers." He walked over to me. Mark's fists were clenched so tight, his knuckles were white. His eyes said he was furious. Veins on his temple throbbed. He pounded his fists against the back of one of my side chairs. "You know, I'd pretty well decided I wasn't going. Well, that makes me want to go. If they think that intimidation will keep me from going … well, it won't. Screw them!"

I stared at him as if he was crazy. Not because I was surprised to hear he might decide to go anyway, but because I'd never seen him so enraged.

He must have misinterpreted my expression. He said, "Chessie, I can't possibly ask you to keep your commitment after this. I'll find someone else."

"Not so fast. Am I shook? A little. Am I going to fold my tent? Not yet. I want to see what Ford and MacAphee have to say. It is scary, but it's exciting, too." I smiled. It was a wry smile, but it was a smile. "I have an idea."

"Chessie, isn't it obvious that someone inside the government is fighting this whole thing? That's dangerous. What if one of the people sent to protect us actually is there to kill you and me?"

My smile faded. "That's what my idea is about." I

fervently hoped Reading could get a leave of absence from Sheriff McGill. I forgot that I had to convince my brother to be our bodyguard ... first.

Chapter **10**
Chessie and Reading's Duplex

"Two beers without asking for them and a ribeye, rare and marinated. So what do you want, Sis?" Reading is very hard to fool. He leaned back in his chair until it creaked. His expression was like the time a pick-pocket tried for his wallet and Reading was prepared for him. I hoped for better results.

I avoided a direct answer. "How are you going to keep busy while I'm away?"

"You're going even after all you told me?" He shook his head in disgust.

"How are you going to keep busy while I'm away?" I repeated.

He stared at me in amusement.

"Seriously," I asked.

"Go to work, come home, watch TV, sleep ... that kind of thing."

"Is Emily coming up to stay here?" I asked.

"No. She says she's not ready for that yet, but she'll take a rain check." Reading got a startled look on his face. "Oh, no! I'm not doing it!"

I felt I'd lost before I began. "Do what? I haven't asked you to do a thing," I said.

Reading swelled up like a weather balloon. "I am *not* taking any of your friends out. It took me six weeks to get rid of the last one. Remember Joanne Whittaker? No way!"

"I would never ask you to do that again. I promised I wouldn't." I tried to sound as if he hurt my feelings.

Reading wasn't fooled. "What do you want?"

I led into it slowly. "You know this business with the government providing the security? Given we know somebody is fighting to cancel the trip from the inside, I don't know if I can trust anyone. It makes me feel like I'm really vulnerable."

Reading's face was an unemotional mask. "You should 'cause you are."

"If we had one person we could trust ... completely, I think we'd be fine."

"Where are you going to find this protector? Remember, Lancelot is part of the King Arthur *legend*. The important word there is *legend*."

"We need someone who has military training, who is brave and strong, and whose integrity is unquestionable."

Reading smirked a bit. "Got somebody in mind?"

"You." I braced for shouts and laughter.

"Sure. Why not," Reading's face never changed.

"That was way too easy," I spoke what I thought.

"No. It is easy for me and hard for you." Reading looked at his plate. "Do you have an extra baked potato?"

"Yes. What do you mean hard for me?"

He grinned. "You will never in a million years get me approved for something like that."

"Don't bet on that," I said.

"I'll give you ten to one odds on that, and that would be stealing from you. They won't approve outside security for something like you're going to do."

I remained silent for a few seconds then said, "Go ahead and clear a leave of absence with McGill, just in case."

We both laughed, but for different reasons. I was happy. If I decided to accompany Mark, I'd have the best personal body-guard I could find.

Chapter 11
Old NASA Office building at Cape Canaveral

Mark's face turned red. His eyes had settled on one woman in the conference room where we were about to meet. Philip Ford had told Mark there were major concerns throughout the State Department administrative organization when informed of the phone calls. The people seated in the room were from Washington, Quantico, the MacDill Command Center in Tampa, and nearby Patrick Air Force Base.

I nudged Mark in the ribs as we sat down and asked, "You know that woman?"

"I sure do," Mark answered. It sounded like it wasn't in a good way. "Later."

Everyone was seated. An attractive woman dressed in a designer suit stood an introduced herself. "I'm Naleeva San Ettienne Y Marcos. My job as a special undersecretary is to advise my superior on cultural affairs in South America and the Caribbean. This project is part of my responsibility. Mr. Ford is assigned to me to coordinate its progress. We are here to discuss our project and obvious complications. Some," she hesitated a second before continuing in her Creole tinted English, "problems were expected." The woman's dark-brown pupils, her black skin, and the bright whites of her eyes accentuated their piercing quality. She surveyed the room, memorizing the unfamiliar faces present. "This project was to be done as quickly and with as low profile as possible. We will do our best to continue in that manner. I will introduce each of you and your purpose for attending."

She looked directly at Mark. "I'll start with the four most important. You are the people that will do what is very important work. Raise your hand when I mention you. Dr. Mark Card archeologist and head of East Florida University's archeology department." Mark raised his hand. The lady that he knew smiled as he was introduced.

"His assistant, Miss Chesapeake Partin." I raised my hand, though it looked like no one cared.

"Dr. Donald Dean." A very tall, very thin man raised his hand. He was handsome in a spindly way. His salt and pepper hair, rimless glasses, and Brooks Brothers suit made him look like an actor in a financial advisor ad. Naleeva continued, "Dr. Dean is a professor of bio-genetic engineering at Duke. He is an authority on the human genome." I wondered why he was included in the team.

She turned to an old man dressed in a shabby ill- fitting sports coat with leather elbows. It had to have been loomed in the sixties. "Mr. Elroy Cleggenhiest. Elroy is an antique dealer with special knowledge we require."

"I believe you all know or have spoken to Philip Ford." Philip raised one hand while staring at the other one.

"Marvin MacAphee, the administrative leader of our expedition." MacAphee raised his hand and said, "Don't any of you call me Marvin. My name is Mug." Naleeva added, "I wouldn't argue with him."

"Adelaide Kleist. Mrs. Kleist is a special advisor who will provide us with information if we require it. Her health and age will keep her from going. Thankfully Skype will allow her to view items on which she can lend her expertise." A very old woman raised her hand. She sat stiffly erect in the chair. I immediately thought of her as the dowager empress in *Anastasia*.

Naleeva reached the woman that Mark knew. "Alexa Lind is the interdepartmental coordinator for the CIA. She will see we don't stumble over each other's efforts." I heard Mark exhale sharply. I had no doubt their relationship was personal. Alexa could have been a face double for the actress Anne Hathaway.

I whispered, "CIA? I don't like that."

"Neither do I," Mark returned my whisper. I was sure there were more reasons Mark didn't want her involved.

Naleeva nodded towards her next introduction. "Mr. Steve Hansen is with the FBI. Special Agent Hansen is here because the problems we incurred are of interest to his organization." A strong looking man who looked like he should be playing defensive end on Sundays in the NFL waved one finger.

Mark and I looked at each other and shook our heads.

Naleeva took notice of our reaction.

She continued, "Captain Terry Thorn is your pilot. You'll be flying courtesy of the USAF." A smiling fellow who could have earned a living as a horse jockey as well as a jet jockey held both arms up.

"Miccolee Bertonarri from the CIA will join you after you've reached your destination." A black-haired girl of twenty-five nodded to the group. Naleeva told us, "Miccolee is a gifted interpreter. She speaks the eleven languages spoken in the area including Spanish, Portuguese, Italian, German, French, and six native dialects." The letters CIA made me uncomfortable though her appearance didn't.

The last man Naleeva introduced garnered my closest attention. He wore the uniform. "This is Technical Sargent James Garret of the US Marine Corp. He will coordinate all your needs that occur while you're on the site. Sargent Garret is assigned to the Marine base in Paraguay, and he'll be with you for the period of time you're at the site." Garret was a salty Marine. He looked like he was cast out of old iron.

Naleeva looked around the room. "I must emphasize the importance of this trip and its timely execution. Dr. Card, Dr. Dean, Miss Partin, and Mr. Cleggenhiest, you're tasked with unlocking the secrets that could exist where you will be taken or determine there is nothing of interest there. Two additional team members are already at your destination. You will also be joined by the two Argentine archeologists who discovered there might be important finds there. The rest of you are tasked to support and protect our scientific team. For some reason, we are not *sure* why there have been attempts to discourage our scientists from participating. We cannot allow this to happen. All of you are charged with the responsibility of seeing there are no repeats of these threats."

Hansen indicated he wanted to speak, but Naleeva shook her head and said, "Later you can make a statement if you want. I must tell you I won't answer any questions." She paused, took two deep breaths and quickly looked at each of us. She tilted her head to one side as she spoke. "I regret I cannot share what and why this program is so important. I will share why the secrecy is required. There are forces, both international and domestic, that may be embarrassed by this project. We didn't want these forces aware of our plans. That objective remains. The rationale is that the fewer people that share a secret, the easier it is to keep. It is obvious that has been breached. To what degree we don't know. We are taking steps to ensure this isn't repeated. All plans have changed from two days ago. The program will be accelerated. Now we'll discuss the details."

Chapter 12

NASA Office building at Cape Canaveral

"I think we've covered everything. I'd like to talk to Dr. Dean, Mr. Cleggenhiest, Miss Partin, and Dr. Card for a few additional moments." Naleeva smiled at the group. "The rest of you will leave."

I looked at Mark. He shook his head and looked surprised.

"I'm supposed to stay, too." Mug slouched in his chair.

"Please, will you all move to this end of the conference table?" Naleeva said as the last of the other participants left the room. She nodded to Mug.

He closed the door, removed an odd looking electrical device with an antenna on top from a backpack, and carefully circled the room. When he finished, he announced, "No bugs."

"If you think there is a lot of cloak and dagger associated with this trip, there is. When you arrive, you'll understand why. Now, I have to add more. All the schedules you just heard are changed as of now. You will be leaving in three days, not seven as we just discussed.

Our reason is we can't be sure that someone in the agencies that were represented won't leak our intentions."

I saw my opportunity. "Let me speak." I didn't wait for

Naleeva to approve. "I hope you understand. Just like you don't know whom you can trust, Dr. Card and I have discussed whom we can trust. You seem trustworthy. So did everybody at that meeting. But, I don't really know you or Mug. Sorry, but the tone of this thing is that we could have our lives on the line."

"You are correct, Miss Partin," Dr. Dean said, "Someone tried to run over me and my bicycle yesterday after I laughed at an anonymous caller."

"What will make you comfortable?" Naleeva asked.

"I don't know about the rest of you, but I want one person, a bodyguard, that I know will look out for us. My brother is a captain in the Indian River Sheriff's Department. He's tough, in great shape, and I know anyone trying to get to me or one of these other people would have to cut their way through him. That would not be easy."

Mark spoke up. "I know her brother. He'd be a good addition. And, if Chessie doesn't go, I can't get a replacement soon enough to go either."

"I'm for any additional protection," Dr. Dean said. Cleggenhiest nodded. Naleeva looked at MacAphee and held one hand toward him. He grinned, "I don't have a problem if he's as advertised and he passes the rest of his security check."

"What do you mean the rest of his security check?" I asked.

"We found out he was checking on me yesterday. His name is Reading, right?"

I nodded. "So we wanted to find out why."

"Can he be available that quickly?" Naleeva asked. Before I could answer, Mug said, "Leave that to me."

Chapter 13
The Partin's Duplex

"How much latitude or leverage do I have to change some of this?" Reading had read the plans and he looked as if he smelled a dead animal. One of the things I admire about my brother is how quickly he adapts to any situation he's thrown into. Twenty-four hours before, he was counseling me against going. Now, he was not only accompanying me, but he was also actively reviewing what we were doing, looking for what he saw as flaws. He was meticulous. Reading never saw a detail he didn't like. I knew if there was something wrong, he'd spot it.

It took MacAphee six hours to contact Benson McGill, secure leave for Reading, and have my brother join us. Reading met those of the research team that hadn't left. Naleeva and Mug reacted positively to him, or so I thought. Naleeva confirmed that when she decided not to introduce him to the other members who attended the meeting. It also told me she did not trust at least one of those people.

Mark was glad to see him. Reading had a chance to speak with Mr. Cleggenhiest and Dr. Dean. One fact Reading discovered was that Dr. Dean had looked for a license plate on the car which tried to run him down, but there wasn't one. Reading believed that indicated it was an attempt to kill him, not an accident.

I answered his question the best I could. "You have some leverage. Mark and I have told them we would back out if you didn't join. How much change they would let you make I don't know."

Reading rubbed his chin. "The way this is set up maximizes the potential of someone—" He shook his head. "Having the trip done on military transports, in government facilities, and having government security all sounds good until you think about the fact someone in the government is trying to destroy this project." He tapped his fingers on our kitchen table shedding nervous energy. "The plane they picked is an old C-130. The serial number means they probably pulled it out of the boneyard." He squinted his eyes and said, "Do you completely trust the Naleeva woman?"

"Yes."

"Once you get on foreign soil, it complicates matters for them. If someone is going to take a crack at scuttling this project, I think they will do it before you get to Paraguay. This says you are all going together and flying out of MacDill." He smiled. "You mind sitting in an aircraft cargo container for some time?"

"No." I thought about to what I'd just agreed. "You mean one of those big aluminum boxes you see on airport concourses?"

"Yes. I want you, Dr. Card and the others to spend

some time in one."

"What are you thinking?" I asked.

"If I can convince Naleeva to make a few plan changes, I think I have a way to ensure the four of you make it to Argentina and answer some other questions."

"What changes?"

"Move your departure point from MacDill to Orlando International. Load you and the rest in a cargo container, load the cargo container on the C-130, and not let anyone see inside. I'd be the only person with you when you load, and I'd be in it before you arrive to be sure it's safe. It's a public place, and no one will see how you're going to get to Asunción."

That was brilliant. "No one will know until we've left."

"Just the people that attended the meeting you had the other day."

"Why do that?" That sounded stupid to me. "You take all those precautions then toss them away?"

"Not exactly. Trust me ... we're getting to Paraguay safely." Uncharacteristically, Reading reached out and touched my hand. He is not the touchy-feely type. "You said you have a number to contact Naleeva; please give it to me."

Chapter 14
Orlando International Airport

Reading hoisted our luggage on to a baggage cart deep in the bowels of the Orlando International Airport. The team was all assembled in a quarantine room. Reading and Mug MacAphee were the only others present. A standard "igloo," the ground support lingo for a cargo container, was the only additional item in the room. Inside were four chairs, four cardboard boxes and a cooler. He spoke to Mark, Dr. Dean, and Mr. Cleggenhiest, "Is everything you want to go with us in this baggage cart?"

All nodded or said yes.

"It's time," Reading said.

"I don't know." Elroy Cleggenhiest was pale and perspiring. "I am a little claustrophobic. How long will we be in there?"

Reading said, "Don't worry. You won't have a problem." He glanced at Mug. "Okay, it's time to be sure everything is loaded correctly. You have everything covered on the tarmac?"

Mug nodded, "I'm on my way." He left through the only door into the room, a large electronically operated double panel.

Reading watched MacAphee close the door behind him. When the door's lock snapped, Reading said, "Load up. There are some clothes in boxes inside. Each box is labeled with one of your names on it. Chessie will explain what to do with them."

Mr. Cleggenhiest whined, "How long before we can get out from the plane?"

"You can't. We can't have anybody know whether or not you're on the plane. Remember aircraft have radios. Remain in there and stay quiet." They grumbled loudly, but Reading explained, "Chessie will tell you everything. I have to watch the door and be sure no one comes in." He looked at me and said, "Don't forget the lock."

I nodded and stepped into the cargo container and invited the others in by saying to puzzled faces, "Ladies come join me."

Chapter 15
Orlando International Airport

Reading walked to the gate where he was meeting Mug MacAphee. They would fly to Asunción on a commercial airliner. They waited in line behind me and the three nuns I was flying with to Paraguay.

I heard Reading ask if everything was loaded on the C-130. Mug said it was. Evidently, Dr. Dean did too. He laughed. I admonished him, "Sister Mary Denise, don't laugh so loud." Sisters Mary Martha and Mary Ellen chuckled then resumed a pious persona as we prepared to board the flight.

Reading asked Mug if the aircrew had been instructed not to disturb the container and if the C-130 was still stopping at MacDill for five hours. That gave us enough time for them, and us, to be there ahead of it. Mug said yes. I understood the reason for the very short layover between our flight from Orlando to Miami. The Aerolineas Flight would beat the C-130's arrival by three hours. That way Reading and Mug could be there to protect us as we arrived ... if we'd have been on it.

Chapter 16
Aerolineas flight 7651

I had new respect for women who decided to devote their lives to the church. The habit I wore was hot, and the material scratchy. I felt confined. I was sure the three men seated around me were more miserable than I. That gave me some type of perverse enjoyment.

Our flight attendants were so obliging to us, it was embarrassing. I wondered what they would think if they discovered that all four of us were imposters. Particularly, the three men in church drag. One attendant whispered to another that she'd never seen an uglier group of nuns. 'Mary Denise' Dean asked how much longer our flight was. As I answered, the flight attendants chattered excitedly. One pointed at Mug and Reading seated ten seats behind us. Within seconds a slim brunette hurried down the aisle with a slip of paper. I watched her hand it to MacAphee.

His reaction was immediate. I heard his angry voice, but he was too far away to hear the words. I saw him slam his fist into the seat ahead of him. Reading and Mug were having a heated conversation. Suddenly, they both stood and started walking up the aisle toward me. I quickly turned so my eyes were directed to the airplane's front and dropped my head low so my face couldn't be seen.

I felt a tap on my shoulder. Reading said, "Beg your pardon, Sister. My friend has just been informed of a great loss. Do you have a Bible we might borrow?"

"No, I'm sorry," I said, keeping my head down as I spoke. A sense I didn't realize I possessed told me they were bending over me.

Reading pressed lightly on my shoulder. "Look up."

I swiveled my head and looked up into Reading's amused face, and MacAphee's confused one.

"My friend just learned about an air crash that he had friends on. Could you say something to comfort him?" I knew Reading must have determined MacAphee wasn't part of the conspiracy against us.

Trying to look as pious as possible, I muttered, "May the Lord give you relief."

Reading leaned over until his mouth was next to my ear. He whispered, "You could do better, Chessie. He doesn't have gas pains." I did my best to choke down my laugh, but enough escaped to draw looks from surrounding passengers. They varied from puzzled to indignant. Reading said softly, "Someone will meet you at the gate. Go with them." He straightened and said, "Thank you, Sister," and led the astonished MacAphee back to their seats.

Only then did the fact that someone had tried to kill us jolt my brain.

Chapter 17
Silvio Petti Rossi Airport, Asuncion Paraguay

As Reading promised, a man met us at the gate. He led us to a private room where our clothes waited. The most remarkable feature of the trip was the relative lack of communication among the four of us. Even Mark's and my conversations were minimal. Maybe it was our perceived need not to speak to preserve our disguise. Maybe we all were in a state of introspection because of the rapidity of what was happening around us. Probably it was because the shocking events stunned us into silence.

This ended when we changed clothes. Dr. Dean was the first to mention what was in all our thoughts. He said, "Has anybody but me thought what in the hell have we gotten ourselves into? I'm sure I'll wake up, and this whole thing will have been a bad dream. My arms are sore from pinching them and I know I'm as awake as I'm going to get."

"How in the hell I agreed to this ... I guess we all are candidates for the Nobel stupidity awards," Mark said. He looked at me and added, "Sorry, Chessie."

"You didn't twist my arm." I looked at the other three. The least phased was Cleggenhiest. He looked unconcerned. Elroy saw me staring at him.

He smiled at me and said, "It would scare me more if I were as young as the rest of you. I'll die soon anyway. The money I'll be paid will just go to my great- grandchildren sooner if they are successful. Besides, there is only one reason they would want me here. I am an expert on antique clothes from the mid-Twentieth century stemming from central Europe. I am also a Jew. If you can't see why that makes me happy to be a part of this, you have no sense of history."

"You're convinced this whole thing has to do with the story of Nazis escaping to here?" Mark asked.

The old man just laughed.

"Good hunting and good luck," Dr. Dean said. "The only thing I want is a way back to the States as quickly as I can find one. Who's going with me?"

Mark and I looked at each other. I shrugged my shoulders. "We're here now. Downing that plane takes our accidental deaths off the table as a way to get rid of us as far as I can see. Too many coincidences won't pass in something like this. They don't want publicity for whatever they're hiding. That makes us safer. I have faith in my brother and MacAphee. I'll stay if Mark does."

"I'm not going to let them run me off. I'm curious now. I'll stay." Mark looked at Dean for an answer.

"I can't believe I'm saying this: I'll stay, too."

~~ ~~ ~~

"May I call you Chessie?" Naleeva San Ettienne Y

Marcos asked. The woman had pulled me aside from Mark and the rest. I was as confused about what the reason might be as they were. She clarified that in seconds once we were alone. Naleeva had taken me to an office deep in the center of the Silvio Petti Rossi Airport.

"Certainly."

Naleeva smiled and said. "And I prefer if you call me Nali. My parents called me that as a child, and I've always used it with *friends*."

Nali had just asked me if I would be proceeding with the trip and I'd answered with a firm 'Yes!' She walked to a couple chairs, sat down, and said, "Please join me." As I sat down, she added, "I want to express my thanks to you for suggesting your brother be added to our expedition. What a great addition. His idea to create the illusion you were on the freighter and send you by commercial jet instead was brilliant. When he called me to suggest that, I honestly didn't believe it was necessary. I see how right he was to not take the chance."

"My brother doesn't leave anything to chance that he has control over." I smiled. "Mind if I don't tell him you think his idea was brilliant? He'll be scratching his head out three feet from his body."

Naleeva looked confused but quickly caught on. "Oh, you think his head will get big! I'm sorry, I've already told him." She smiled again. "Reading does not seem to be a man with an ego problem."

"You said the magic word ... man ... that inherently means he has an ego issue."

She laughed at my joke.

"I will be speaking to all of you in a few minutes. Hopefully, I can convince everyone to continue on. I assure you that my superiors are fully aware that the threats were completely serious and all precautions will be taken to be sure no more threats exist." Naleeva nodded to me. "May I count on your assistance to help me keep them from quitting?"

"Yes, but I don't believe that's necessary. They all said they weren't going to back out." I saw relief spread across Naleeva's face. I understood why she elected to share her nick-name with me. This project was terribly important to her and she was doing all she could to build bonds to ensure success.

"Good! I assure you that everybody involved will redouble their efforts to see to the safe and successful conclusion of what we are setting out to do."

"That's good to hear." I wasn't completely honest with Naleeva. It occurred to me that if everybody redoubled their efforts, someone might be redoubling their effort to kill the project ... and us.

Chapter 18
Highway 1 in Paraguay

"This country looks a lot like Florida and Georgia," Reading said. Eight of us were packed into a HUMV. We left the hotel we stayed at in Asuncion after getting a night's rest. I don't sleep well in strange beds and the added apprehension that was in all of our minds meant it was truly rest, not sleep. I was periodically dozing off, but Reading's observation aroused me enough to take a prolonged look out of the window.

The land we'd traveled was flat to gently rolling farmlands and pastures. Far to the east, the outline of large hills broke the level horizon. "It does," I agreed. Cane fields, cotton, and peanuts were familiar. The large amounts of acreage we passed that was planted in soybeans were different. Braham cattle grazed on grasslands. "How far is to Encarnación?" I asked.

"You have about 120 kilometers left. That's seventy-five miles. This is a decent road, and we ought to make it in less than two hours." Sargent Jim Garret sat behind the steering wheel. It was one of the first words he'd uttered since he'd greeted us in the morning.

"I haven't noticed many paved roads," Dr. Dean observed.

Garret nodded and grunted his agreement.

"When you get outside the large cities like Asunción and Encarnación there aren't many. That makes travel a problem, especially in the rainy season. Most of the roads are either sand or clay. If you don't have a four-wheel drive or a horse, there are no guarantees. The roads are mud ruts for a third of the year." Mug pointed to red clay side road. "That's what eighty per cent of the roads are like down here."

The conversation died. My belief was the danger we were in was a weight that encumbered us all, but none wished to discuss. What good would come from talking? We'd made our decision. We'd agreed to be hyper-vigilant. We'd agreed to have each others' back. My thought was that discussing it further would just increase my apprehension and accomplish zero.

We bounced along in silence. It was about to drive me bonkers. I don't like silence. Speaking to Sergeant Garret was as fruitless as speaking to a stump. Cleggenhiest and Mark couldn't stay awake. Dr. Dean hadn't been responsive to any conversational overtures. Reading didn't have anything to discuss we hadn't thrashed about a hundred times before. Mug was awake, but his stares made me feel like a steak, and uncomfortable.

The eighth person in the HUMV was a Marine corporal from Chicago assigned to provide us protection. She wasn't happy to be involved and let that be known by what she didn't say. After another fifteen minutes, I thought I'd give it a try, anyway.

I asked, "How do like being stationed in Paraguay?"

She shrugged her shoulders, continued to stare straight ahead, and mumbled, "It's okay."

"I was in the Corps for four years. Know what it's like." I hoped to establish some type of common ground.

"Uh-huh." She continued her forward stare.

"What do you do down here?" I figured I'd find something. I didn't.

She slowly turned her head and shifted smoldering eyes at me. "Stand guard-duty, keep my bunk made, eat, sleep, and sit on my ass. No, it isn't dangerous down here. No more than the Southside of Chicago. Yes, I like being a Marine, as long as it doesn't include babysitting—"

"Corporal Cole, shut your pie hole!" Sergeant Garret found something to say. "I have one more thing I want to hear from you before I put some duct tape over your mouth. Understand?"

Corporal Harmony Cole's eyes returned 'front' as she said, "I apologize." If there was a shred of sincerity in the two words, I didn't hear it. At least our mini-spat woke Dr. Dean and Mark and they returned to their professional form.

"Did anyone tell you whom you will be working with down here?" Dr. Dean didn't wait for Mark's answer. "I was told I'd have someone from Universidad Austral. They have a first-rate Biomed department. No name. He is supposed to be a DNA expert."

"I got three names from Naleeva. All of them have some connection to the University of Buenos Aires. Wait a sec." Mark pulled out a vest pocket-sized notebook that he always carried. "Their anthropology group is outstanding, according to President Andrews from my university." He tilted his head to the side and grinned wryly. "I guess it's okay. The only person I know about that graduated from there is Che Guevara."

Sergeant Garret showed his first unsolicited emotion ... a disgusted grunt.

Mark continued. "Okay, the person who made the initial discovery is a gal named Migdahlia Macias. She has some connection to the area we'll be in. Misiones is the state or whatever the proper terminology is. Her specialty is religious artifacts. Dr. Eduardo Rialto is a senior professor of archeology. He has a background in native people. The last one is an Ida-Marie Argello. All I know about her is her name."

"Sergeant Garret, Mug, do either of you know anything about these people?" Dr. Dean asked.

Garret grunted and shook his head.

Mug said. "I met the Macias woman. She's damned smart. How she got involved is a good question. She doesn't normally do fieldwork. How you get from religious records to bones in the mud ... you make a guess."

Mark groaned. "Damn, an amateur in the field. I hope

she didn't louse up the site."

"She didn't." Mug farted and grinned. "Huevos Rancheros do that to me. Oh yeah, she put rope up around the site and got the local police to protect it. Right away, so she says. I talked to the guy in charge. He says she was a real bitch about it. Anyway, she was sharp enough to scout out any trails leading to the site and get them restricted."

"If she's an amateur, she must be a good one," Dean remarked.

Mark turned to Mug and asked, "You know what we're going to see, don't you?"

Mug grinned and pinched his lips together.

"Come on, Mug!" Mark pleaded.

"You can wait for an hour-and-a-half. Naleeva and the rest of the crew will be waiting at a hotel. You'll learn more then."

Mug laughed. "Yes, you will."

Chapter 19

Hotel Casa del Corazón, Encarnación, Paraguay

What would be our team was assembled for the first time. After the introductions, it was obvious our team would take some time to function as one. We separated like opposite poles of a magnet. Mark, Dr. Dean, Mr. Cleggenhiest, and I found one side of the table and our South American compatriots the other. The tension set at the electric level. I had expected some professional rivalry, but not what I sensed. Resentment flooded the room. I wondered if that flood would wash our "team's" goals away.

Names and faces don't always go together. I know that. Try as I might, I can't resist trying to visualize a person's looks based on their name. My attempts to peer into the looking glass were perfect ... perfectly wrong.

I'd visualized Migdahlia Macias as middle-aged or up, with proto stereotypical Hispanic features, hair, and skin, nerdy and bookish. It was my biggest miscalculation. Migdahlia was athletic with a tall, slim build, had pale blue eyes, strawberry-blonde hair and tanned skin that contained freckles. She looked more like a supermodel than a librarian. A young supermodel.

Eduardo Rialto. My vision of him was tainted by the

archaeologists I knew. Mark and Dr. Bill had a serious side tempered with a laid-back, informal style. Rialto was twenty years younger than I anticipated. He wore a suit and tie, looked 'starched,' and his body language was defensive to the extreme. Under his $400, form-fitting suit, his body was cut and muscled like that of a boxer. I found out later he was an amateur fighter, light-weight, and played soccer in Spain. The contrast to Mark's cargo pants, tee shirt, and relaxed posture were glaring.

Rialto's assistant wasn't the young grad student I had assumed. The woman was a female clone of her boss. Her biceps, triceps, and shoulders were products of hours in the weight room. Her hands and fingers were calloused like those of my Marine martial arts instructor who owned a black-belt in Karate. Ida-Marie Argello's black hair, deep brown eyes, mirrored Eduardo. I had the feeling I wouldn't want to have a disagreement with her in an alley. The cliché didn't cover my concern. My desire was to avoid a confrontation with her at all costs.

The previously unknown was Dr. Dean's counter- part, Petro Beltran. Suave, yes, that was a one-word description. Petro was almost as tall as my brother and built much like him. He looked like someone I'd seen before. It took me a while, but I figured out the likeness. Beltran was a ringer for Caesar Romero, a movie actor I'd seen on old movie channels. I stared too long and hard. His smile told me he had formed an opinion of me and my interest. My face reddened, and I looked elsewhere. It was the lone thaw in the icy room.

Naleeva and Mug were the only others present. Naleeva frowned. She sensed the tension and the trouble it could breed. Mug grinned. Strife wasn't a problem for him. He was confident he'd get his part of the job done. Strife among the "egg-heads," as he was to call us, was something he'd handle. Naleeva stood up and said, "Shall we discuss what we are all here to do?"

I wondered ... how long before the explosion.

Boom! It was instantaneous.

"Wouldn't it be more honest to ask what these people are here for?" Eduardo stood as he pointed to our side of the table. Derision covered his face and motions. "We are working on Argentinian land, Argentinian artifacts, and with *our* people's past and history. We don't need the Colossus from the North to tell us how to do what we can do as well for ourselves." His English was tinted with a heavy accent that I thought was emphasized for effect. He looked at Naleeva and snorted with disgust. "Why are you even here? You are not a scientist. Your name may be Hispanic, but everything else is Yankee."

Naleeva and Eduardo's eyes clashed in a mini-war before Naleeva said in Spanish, *"Por favor, Senor Rialto. Trata de no ser un hombrecito."* Anger welled up in Eduardo, but Naleeva didn't flinch. She continued in English. "We are here at the request of your government.

That is the Argentinian government. That should be enough for you to understand the answer to your questions. However, I will provide some more. One artifact Miss Macias found is made of chert found in Florida. Another is a copper piece made from ore that comes from Michigan. There may be more. Our interest should be obvious. It is also a locus site. Dr. Card is experienced in research design for sites where more than one archaeological find is included. In this case it may be three. We are providing ground penetrating radar and other electronics that will speed up the task and improve findings to supplement what you have. All kinds of site equipment like additional survey tools are here ... with us. Oh yes, we are paying all ours and your costs." Naleeva extended her hand and raised her eyebrows inviting a response.

Eduardo eased back into his chair. He was silent, but his anger hadn't diminished. Migdahlia showed only mild displeasure, but Ida-Marie's face was a storm cloud. Beltran's expression was entirely different. I thought he looked at all of us like mice in one of his Biomed experiments. His countenance displayed amused contempt. Our side universally looked shocked and defensive. I'm sure I didn't look any different.

Mark suggested, "Maybe a short break would be in order? My coffee needs liberating."

Naleeva nodded. "Ten minutes. Be back promptly. We have lots to do."

Eduardo beat everyone to the door. Things weren't starting well.

Chapter 20
Hotel Casa del Corazón,
Encarnación, Paraguay

"I understand how they feel," Mark said. "If there were some way for us not to be involved ..."

Naleeva shook her head. "There isn't." She barely smiled as she stated her opinion. "It will get better when you are on the site. The scientist in all of you will come to the top. There may be some friction, but you will work it out. I won't be there, that should help."

The five "Yankees" stood talking, waiting for the others to return.

I asked, "You won't be at the site, Naleeva?"

"No, I may visit, briefly, but, no, I won't be there."

"Why did you say it will be better because you won't be there? Is it cultural? The macho-man thing?" I wanted to know if my guess was right.

Naleeva nodded.

"Do you think they'll come back?" Dr. Dean said. "Everyone, but Beltran, looked furious."

Naleeva smiled. "They will come back. I'm sure Rialto is on the phone with his superiors. They will explain it in a manner he will accept. Maybe *comply* is a better word."

"Let Mark spend some one-on-one time with Professor Rialto. He can sell bikinis to Eskimo women in the dead of winter." That sentiment came from a person who entered the conference room. Alexa Lind, the woman who introduced herself as CIA during our meeting at Cape Canaveral, strode across the floor to us. She saw the thunder-cloud forming on Mark's face, and she quickly added. "Relax, Mark. I won't be where you're going. I'm here as a tactical back-up, just in case you need it."

It was Mug's turn to look upset. "I don't need you meddling in my business."

"I sincerely hope we don't have to get involved." Alexa's voice was full of sarcasm.

"You won't," Mug said. They stared at each other like a couple of sailors at a bar preparing to fight over a girl.

Naleeva's voice broke the joust. "They're back."

"The very heart of developing research design plans is to know the questions for which you intend to find answers. There is no reason to excavate if we don't know what you want to learn." Mark was becoming frustrated. In the space of two hours, Eduardo and Mark had become allies. I watched Naleeva play them like a musical instrument, or so I thought. She used the basic tenants of their profession to drive them together.

Eduardo spoke passionately. "This is foolishness. What knowledge we hope to gain about the Guarani and Guarcuru is clear. Was this a shared settlement? Was it a slave camp? It would change many thoughts about the two tribes' relationship. It is important to learn." He paused.

"The reason for the first overlap is clear. Was the site an established mission outpost in the late 1500s? This would tell us much. It would add to our knowledge of the era and prove the Spanish tried to penetrate deeper into Guarani territory than believed." He tapped the table with his index finger making a loud noise. "But ... this third issue ... you say it is 'recent.' You give us no real information, and all you can say is that it must be our primary concern. Ruins of buildings are built over the other sites. Who built them you ask? Go to the old records."

"There are no records. That's why we want you to determine who built the buildings and what they were." Naleeva looked annoyed. She added innocently, "And anything else that might be connected to them."

Migdahlia said, "I'm the only person who has seen the buildings. They are much like those built at Teyu Curare by the National Socialists who escaped from Europe. Is the question whether these buildings were built by them? I think we all know that is true. Why not admit it?"

"Because if we do, all types of speculations will erupt." Naleeva took a deep breath. "That could be very embarrassing for both our countries."

"Why should we care? Why should you or the United States care? That happened over a half-century ago." Migdahlia was very emotional. I wondered why *so* emotional.

"There was a belief that the Western Allies helped

some of the Nazi leadership to escape to here and other South American countries in return for the technology they possessed. The United States was the prime suspect. Most of these Nazis came to Argentina. Peron was pro-Nazi. The truth is, we don't know to what extent Nazis came here. We know it was in the thousands. Some were high-ups. Mengele, Bormann did. But, we don't know who most of them were." Naleeva looked disturbed.

"Hitler?" Mark asked.

Naleeva shrugged her shoulders. "There is much evidence to point to his death. But the body the Soviets claimed was he was never authenticated. There are as many tales of what really happened to the remains as there are people willing to pay for the story. Just within the last few years, a DNA test proved the piece of the skull the Russians said was from Hitler's corpse turned out to be female."

Mark smiled. "What you want us to find out is if there's evidence that a Nazi settlement was located on the site, if anyone was buried there," Mark looked grim, "and if possible, who it was."

Naleeva nodded.

"I ... no, we," Mark looked at Eduardo, "can do the research design."

Eduardo said, "Yes."

"Can I see all the records and data you have from your work, Miss Macias?" Mark asked.

"Professor Rialto has them," she said.

Eduardo nodded and said, "They are in my suitcase. I'll get them for you when we leave."

Mark stood. "We need to see the site first. When can we leave?"

Chapter 21

In a truck convoy on Ruta Nacional 12, Argentina

"That was about one-tenth as red-tapeish as I thought it would be." Reading stretched his legs out as much as the HUMV would allow. When we crossed the Rio Parana, the bridge ended on Argentine soil. Our entry into the country had obviously been eased. That is an understatement. We popped into and out of Posada, the largest city in Misiones Province as quickly and easily as a bar of soap escapes your hand in the shower.

"They never even looked at my passport photo. Naleeva certainly had everything laced up in advance," I said.

"We went through there as slick as a greased pig." Mug had replaced Jim Garret behind the wheel of our vehicle. That made me curious.

"What happened to Sergeant Garret and Corporal Cole? Not that I'm pining for their company, but I thought they were assigned to escort us." Garret was Mr. Quiet and Corporal 'Sunshine' was as friendly as a shedding snake ... at least toward me.

Mug laughed. "They'll be around. Let's just say they'll get to where we're going by a different route."

"Why all the cloak and dagger? It seems like everybody

and their brother knows we're here." Reading asked what I was thinking.

"The sticky door called diplomacy. If our military comes waltzing across the border, a dozen reporters will make up a dozen plots the U.S. is using to subvert our Latin friends. Naleeva has jumped through the right hoops to get this pulled off. That's with both governments and some private people as well. All the trap doors are locked." Mug looked in the rear view mirror at the other passengers in our vehicle. "Even if someone called to leak what we're here to do to the press, they wouldn't have any success." He grinned at one of us in the rear. Reading sat next to him in the front seat. I knew it wasn't me, and I was equally sure it wasn't Mark. That left Eduardo, Migdahlia, and Ida-Marie. My money was on Eduardo.

Mug changed the subject. "Look your last at big- city comforts. That was the city limits of Posada." He looked at his watch. "We have to kill some time. It's about 130 kilometers. The last half will take three times more to travel than the first half. That means we have," he calculated the time in his head, "about four hours to kill." He saw the look on Reading's face. "It's okay. Our greeting committee won't be in place if we get there earlier."

Migdahlia said, "May I suggest we visit the ruins of San Ignacio the Jesuit mission? They are only a few kilometers from our route. It was built in 1696, but the mission was founded much earlier and moved about. The Jesuits abandoned it in the 1760s. It was so large that over 3,000 Guarani were sheltered there, and it became a commercial center. Most of the missions in this region of

Argentina, Paraguay, and Brazil were destroyed in an uprising in 1817. The jungle reclaimed the San Ignacio Mission until 1897, when it was gradually cleared. Today it is a protected national site."

Mark said, "That sounds good." He looked at the rest of us. We nodded. Mark asked Mug, "That doable?"

"Miss Macias, is there room to park the rest of our convoy without creating a problem or causing a lot of commotion?"

"Yes, I know the park manager very well. It will be okay. He'll park us in a remote place, so we don't attract attention."

I asked, "Migdahlia, you seem very familiar with the missions. Is that part of what your archeology work centers on?"

"Yes, I was looking for early sites of other missions when I found what we are going to study."

"I'm real curious, Miss Macias," Mug said. "That's wild and dangerous country. Naleeva told me you were out there by yourself. You must be one tough lady. Why did you pick that particular location to hunt? Jim Garret had snake, and spider anti-venom serum ordered for his grunts. He says the place has a lot of both. Rattlesnakes, Fer-de-

Lance, and Crossed Vipers. Banana spiders as big across as a grapefruit. He also says that area has some dangerous two-legged vermin. Outlaws. Some people that just don't like strangers. Wasn't it risky for you to be there by yourself?"

Migdahlia took a breath before fudging an answer, "I wouldn't go back alone."

"How did you say you decided to search that area?" Mug was interrogating her!

"I didn't."

"Oh. You must have had some reason." Mug was relentless.

"I found a reference in old church records." Migdahlia's face showed anger mixed with guilt. That was hard to figure. She snapped, "Why do you do what you do? It's dangerous."

Mug smiled. "Because people pay me very well to do it."

~ ~ ~ ~ ~

The old San Ignacio Mission ruins were spectacular.

Mark and I could have spent several days investigating them. We both filled flash drives with pictures, made notes about the architecture, and scribbled down information Eduardo and Migdahlia provided as we toured the grounds. We left after three hours. I couldn't help noticing that Mug attempted to isolate Migdahlia, while she did an artful job of avoiding him for those three hours. I wondered what he had in mind ... business or pleasure.

"That is the road, off to the right," Migdahlia said after we passed through a small agricultural town named Santa Pipo. The red clay farm road looked like one of a thousand I'd seen in South Georgia.

Mug warned us, "I hope your kidneys are insured. The first half isn't bad, but the last part is rugged." He waited for the little convoy of three HUMVs and three trucks to accordion together before giving final instructions to the drivers. We were going to plunge into rolling farmland with some formidable looking hills in the distance.

When Mug opened the vehicle's door, he informed us, "By the time I get back, have your cell phones, I-pads, anything you can communicate with, out, turned-off, and ready to give to me for safe keeping. All communications go through me from now on." The grumbling and grousing were immediate, but he said, "That's the way it is," without an apology.

As we waited for MacAphee to be sure all the vehicles were in four-wheel drive mode, I looked around. I saw a bridge we would have crossed if we'd continued on Route 12. The sound of flowing water told me there was a river I couldn't see behind a solid wall of banana trees. The clay road was graded and appeared well-used. A field of soybeans would be on our right as we drove into wild country. The beans stretched endlessly toward a forest a great distance behind the planted area. Ditches on either side of the road were lush and green with a few puddles scattered in low spots attesting to the frequent rains the area received. Cumulus clouds with "dirty bottoms" floated over us, a few looking as if they would soon be emitting rain. I felt I was back in Florida as the hot sun streaming through the HUMV windows baked my torso and arms. A swarm of mosquitoes gathered as we waited for Mug. Yep, just like Florida.

$\sim\sim\sim\sim\sim$

"The easy part is behind us." Mug pointed in front of the HUMV. The clay road ended abruptly. It was replaced by two muddy ruts that entered the jungle. Weeds covered the trail, but someone had recently taken vehicles over it. The foliage was bent and crushed where the vehicles and large wheels had rumbled through. Water filled the ruts, and slick mud had the impressions of mud tires' thick treads pressed into them. The hills were no longer in the distance; we were at their rugged base. Rock outcroppings were exposed on hillsides around us.

As we started into the thick tree canopy, Reading said, "We have company. Somebody has been driving back here very recently."

"Yep." Mug's wrestling match with the steering wheel started and would continue for eighteen kilometers. "That's our advance team. I hope they have done what they're supposed to do. If they didn't finish, we might be spending the night sleeping in our vehicles. That won't be fun."

"What are they doing?" I asked.

"Remember all those little creeks we crossed back a ways? From here on those creeks either have bridges that aren't in good shape or don't have a bridge at all. There are three we can't ford. Our people are building temporary bridges."

~ ~ ~ ~ ~

We had crossed two of the three prefabricated bridges spanning streams that cut through the valleys. The third and final bridge was ahead of us. For the first time, we saw the "advance team." Three men dressed in park ranger uniforms stood in front of the fragile-looking structure that crossed a deep ravine. It was at least twenty feet down to the water that rushed over rocks and boulders. The late afternoon light made our three helpers look sinister until they approached the open HUMV window. One was Corporal Jim Garret wearing a park ranger blouse and striped pants. Out of uniform? That was interesting.

He said, "Mug, we have a problem. I'm not comfortable sending a deuce-and-a-half over the contraption until I reinforce it some. I think the HUMVs will be fine. I'd just get the passengers out and have them walk across."

Mug examined the narrow steel pans forming two metal ruts across the roaring creek. I don't know what he thought, but I didn't like the idea of walking across them.

He wasn't enthusiastic. "I can get mine across. I don't know about my other drivers."

"Don't worry about that. I'll get Corporal Cole to drive them. She's good. Before you all get out." He peered into the back seat at Migdahlia, "Miss Macias, did you get over to this creek when you were here?"

"I got to it, but not here, and I never crossed it." Migdahlia's face admitted she'd screwed up. "I guess I crossed it, but not here."

"Did you use this road to go back to the place you camped?" Garret seemed agitated.

"No." Her answer had a flat tone. I thought she was avoiding something.

"Well, it's a damned good thing you didn't." Garret looked at Mug, shook his head and said. "You and your people be *real* careful over there, or someone will be digging you up a hundred years from now. There's a short rock road that starts about 200 meters from here, and it goes a quarter of the way back to where Migdahlia camped. When we got there, something didn't feel right. Why build a road there? I looked around. Guess what; there's an old pillbox off to the side. It's covered in the jungle now. That made me twice cautious. Glad I was. Up the road, there was a big-assed crater in those cobblestones. I've seen enough mines explode to know that was what I was looking at. Good thing we had a couple of metal detectors you guys are going to be using. We found nine old Model 42 Teller mines. I sure hope we found them all."

Reading said, "Tellers? Those are old German mines aren't they?"

"Yep." Mug answered. "What did you do with them?"

"Dug them out. Only two were still operable. The detonators deteriorated to the point they wouldn't function. I put all of them in a box and stored it a long way from where we will be camped. I'll show you when we get settled. We don't want anyone wandering there by accident."

Chapter 22
Archaeology site, Misiones Province, Argentina

I didn't need Mug, Garret, or Reading to point out that the stone road had been made as a defensive strong point. Whoever built it, selected a perfect location. Steep rock outcroppings flanked both sides. The road was three meters wide and was about 150 meters long. The machine gun emplacement overlooked the road on top of one of the outcroppings. The holes that the mines had been removed from were evident. They had been laid in a pattern that would have been nearly impossible to miss unless you knew their exact location. Sergeant Garret' s words, "I hope we got them all," pounded through my brain as we eased up the steep grade and over the places the mines had been removed from. Sergeant Garret, Mug, and Reading decided to examine the road and pillbox. Corporal Cole took over the driving duties in our HUMV.

Our HUMV reached the end of the stone road and drove onto a large relatively level piece of land covered with second-growth trees and underbrush. Migdahlia said, "The clearing where I camped is maybe 300 meters ahead." The area was grown over, and light had waned enough that we didn't see the clearing until we entered it. Tents sat in neat rows on one side. The other side was a supply dump.

The clearing had been drastically enlarged to accommodate our convoy. I wondered if they had considered they could be destroying what we were there to study.

Cole pulled the vehicle up to one of four larger tents and said, "This is the women's tent. I'll get your gear to you in a few minutes."

"You already have our tents set up?" I asked, more as a thank you than a question.

Corporal Cole looked at the three of us seated in the rear. "We wouldn't want you *ladies* to break a sweat before you go beddy-bye." The sarcastic whine said as much as the words. "The mosquitoes are bad, so be sure you keep your netting closed and fastened. I wouldn't go out more than you have to after dark. The latrine is over there." Cole pointed at a shed erected fifty yards away. "Be careful if you have to get up. We killed a six-foot-long Fer-de-Lance here when we cleared this place."

A swarm of mosquitoes was assembling outside the HUMV door as I swung it open. The gray light made every undulation of the soil suspicious. Migdahlia followed me. Ida-Marie didn't slide out of the HUMV immediately. She was leaning over Cole with her mouth close to our driver's ear. After a few seconds' delay, she joined us on the ground. The HUMV pulled away.

"Let's get out of these bugs!" I waved my arms wildly

to chase them away. As I tugged on the zipper to our tent door, I heard Migdahlia ask Ida-Marie, "What did you say to her?"

"I told her if she talked to us in such a manner again, she would do so without teeth."

Chapter 23

Archaeology site, Misiones Province, Argentina

"Inside the tent." Mug's voice penetrated the canvas as if it weren't there. "You all okay in there?"

"We're fine," I answered.

"I see you found the lantern. There are flashlights under each of your cots. You all have a couple bottles of water next to the flashlights. Just remember, what goes in must come out."

We laughed as a response.

Mug added, "Chow is at 0700 in the morning. Hope you gals have pleasant dreams."

Mug's steps brushed weeds outside making a fading noise that told us he was walking away. Before it became silent, a big cat's scream reminded us of where we were. Ida-Marie put her hands up and pointed in the direction of the sound. "That Jaguar sounds hungry."

I shook my head and said, "Migdahlia, you are one brave girl. I'd have been petrified to be here by myself."

Migdahlia remained silent, and Ida-Marie laughed. "What's funny?" I asked. "I do not, for one second, believe Migdahlia was here alone. I know her. She is a good scholar and archaeologist, but she prefers Argentinian steaks to Argentinian snakes." Ida-Marie put her hands on her hips and stared at Macias. "You were here, but tell me you were alone without looking away."

Migdahlia didn't answer. Ida-Marie smiled. I realized there was a lot the rest of us were unaware. Migdahlia was keeping secrets. Ida-Marie *was not* your proto-typical scientific assistant.

Chapter 24

Archaeology site, Misiones Province, Argentina

"Wake up. You have a half hour to get to the mess tent." Migdahlia's face was two feet above my eyes. It took a second or two to realize I was awake and wasn't in Vero Beach. When I moved, my back reminded me I was lying on a camp cot. Unzipping my sleeping bag, I swung my legs out and saw Migdahlia pull her jeans up to her waist. My brain still was clogged with sleep fuzz, and I shook my head to clear it. Ida-Marie had added to my miseries, and I looked for her. Her bed was made, and she was gone. The woman had snored so loudly the tent walls vibrated. After two hours of holding my pillow around my head, I had finally fallen fell asleep in spite of the noisy air-compressor sleeping in the cot next to mine.

"Better hurry, Chessie." Migdahlia's voice snapped me back. I watched her step out of the tent and zip it part way closed. It was time to concentrate on why we had come all the way to Argentina. There was time to worry about cloak-and-dagger motives later. That's what I told myself ... and I hoped I wasn't lying.

~ ~ ~ ~ ~

I stood alone outside the large tent that served as our mess hall and meeting room and really examined my surroundings for the first time. Our base camp was located on what appeared to be a plateau. An area of one to two acres had been mowed. Long grass, weeds, and saplings stood in piles at the edge of the cleared area. Four large tents and eight pup tents formed a line on one side of the clearing. The opposite side of the camp seemed like a huge supply dump of crates, equipment, and a newly built pole barn scattered at random. Our trucks hadn't made it across the bridge. At least they hadn't made it to camp yet. The jungle formed walls on all sides of our camp. A hundred yards behind our tents, a large promontory rose another hundred feet above the site. Its sides were covered with heavy vegetation, the final twenty feet of the peak being hidden in dense vines.

Looking past the confines of our camp, I saw mini-peaks of the hills stretching in both directions—the spine of a hill complex. I was to learn a river gorge, the Nancaguazu, was visible to the northwest. Some of the surrounding hillsides had exposed sheer walls of mostly red-tinted rock. The site sloped gently to the southeast. Behind the supply dump stood the latrine, a shed with a canvas roof. On the south edge of the clearing, I saw what I thought were stone fences like those I'd seen in New England. Then I remembered our visit to the ruins of the San Ignacio Mission and realized I was looking at one of the three sites we were to excavate.

"Good morning, Sis." Reading scared me. He got within an arms-length without my realizing he was there.

This was the first time I'd seen him since we had separated at the bridge. His pants were damp to the thighs, and some perspiration crept down one temple.

"Looks like you've done some exploring already. Find anything interesting?" I asked.

"Mark and I took a walk. We found some items of interest." Reading pointed to the stone structures I'd noticed. "We started down those ruins. It's a rectangle about sixty by a hundred feet. A few more rock foundations stand inside. One of them is built around an artesian spring. You know Mark—he never speculates, but he says he guesses this is the site Migdahlia was trying to find. And found. He was concerned that our military friends had disturbed the area close to it. Mark said the pictures and notes Macias took were excellent, and he couldn't see where it had been messed up...his words, not mine. He was making notes and talking about how he wanted to lay out the site for doing the digs. The first thing he wanted you to do was some probabilistic sampling. I have no idea what that is, but you're going to do it."

"It's taking statistically based samples. I'm sure he'll take some non-probabilistic samples as well. Did he say he wanted to start there?"

Reading shook his head. "I asked that. Mark said *no*. He had Macias' notes with him and wanted to look at the rest of what she found before making that decision. We walked a couple of hundred yards farther." Reading pointed to a copse of trees that rose above the surroundings. "That spot is elevated. Some boulders have formed a circle, maybe seventy feet in diameter, and about six to ten feet higher than the ground around it. Mark was excited for two reasons. First, he didn't think it was a naturally occurring structure. Second, he was able to find carvings on one of the stones that Macias took a photo of. The carving was stick figures. One he got excited about was two groups of figures that definitely were carved to look different. Another was of a woman with a big cat eating her. It looked as if she was tied up and people were watching. Creepy."

"It sounds like that's an exciting find." The whole area had been reclaimed by the surrounding jungle, probably for hundreds of years. I was sure Mark and Reading had to push through heavy underbrush to find the area. "Is that where you got so wet?"

"Not really. Migdahlia's notes are really good. She even made a rough map of a trail to get there." Reading frowned. "Remind me to ask you to do me a favor." He pointed to the promontory. "The cover over there is a lot heavier, and there aren't as many big trees to shade out the underbrush. We got our morning shower climbing around there. That's the third area, and, Sis ... that's the area Macias wrote the most information about and took the most pictures. You see that?" He pointed to the vine-covered peak. "That leaf cover hides an observation tower.

It's built out of stone. There are a bunch of buildings and tunnels built on and in that high spot. Mark and I counted ten." He paused. "There's an Iron Cross mounted next to one building opening."

"A religious artifact?" I asked.

"No. It's not that kind of cross. It's the German military's symbol. This is some type of Nazi refugee camp. I'd bet on that. Teller mines. That strong point is guarding the entrance. When Mug, Garret, and I went poking around in that pillbox, we found what was left of an old ammo box.

"Garret says the printing was in German and that it was what the Nazi MG-42 machine gun used. What this place was used for and what happened here is what we need to find out ... not who built it." Reading held up one finger. "Before I forget, there was one picture in the folder that Migdahlia was pictured in. Mark asked about it, and she claimed it was a selfie. I guess it was close enough if your arms are five feet long. That favor I asked for, I want you to see if you can find out if she was up here looking for the mission or really looking for those buildings. I don't think she was here by herself."

"You aren't the only one." Reading stared at me questioningly. "Ida-Marie all but called Migdahlia a liar last night

in the tent. She said she didn't believe Migdahlia was here alone. I had the feeling both of them know a lot about this spot, and this trip, and what's going on than the rest of us."

"I wouldn't limit to those two. I have some suspicions that—"

"Reading, Chessie, Mark wants to get us all together to talk about getting started. He wants everybody in the mess tent in ten minutes." Mug's summons ended our conversation. There were more questions in both our minds than answers.

Chapter 25

Archaeology site, Misiones Province, Argentina

"Don't look so damned miserable. You're making me feel bad," Mug shouted at me.

"You haven't seen my really miserable look, yet. It will bring you to tears." I tried smiling, though the sun was doing its best to roast me as I stood holding a survey rod while Mug peered through a digital theodolite. Mark had put every person in the group to work as soon as he finished his outline of how we would proceed. Most of us were assigned to one of three survey groups designated to plat the grid system Mark wanted.

"You can move in a few minutes." Mug bent over the tripod, bumping it in the process. It almost fell. He cursed. "I'm going to have to run those readings again! Shit!" He adjusted the tripod and made sure the plumb bob was hanging freely and in the correct location after it touched the ground.

"You are graceful, Mug. Was your father an elephant?" I dug the spurs in a little.

"Yes, and my mother was a gazelle." He finished, being sure he was in the right spot. "I just want to help you get sunburned quickly."

I was glad Mark wasn't around to worry about whether

the surveying was being done correctly. Normally, Mark would have had one crew do all the platting. Mug had talked him into working off a central point and have three crews dividing and marking the site with survey stakes, using little-colored bits of plastic ribbon attached to each. They were sprouting up like spring tulips. Mark had allowed himself to be convinced that changing his normal method of surveying a site would be okay. This told me the pressure level the time constraints placed on him. Mug, Ida-Marie and I constituted one of the teams. We were working in the area where the supposed mission ruins were.

As Ida-Marie shoved stakes into the ground where Mug instructed, we heard excited shouting from the jungle, past where Mark and his team worked. They had taken what was believed to be the Guarani Indian site. However, the shouts came considerably farther in the jungle than where they were positioned. We all looked in that direction.

Ida-Marie said, "Wonder what they found?" She had a strange smile on her face.

~ ~ ~ ~ ~

"You all need to know this." Mug stood at the head of one of the long tables in the mess tent. Everyone at the base camp had assembled.

"Two of Sergeant Garret's soldiers were scouting the area. They found partly buried skeletal remains. We don't know much about them except they aren't archaeological in nature. I've notified Naleeva and asked her to contact Argentinian authorities to see how we should proceed. As of now, none of our plans has changed. Questions?"

"Are we in much danger?" Mr. Cleggenhiest asked. "Obviously, there is some. Isn't it time we are told what we are really here to accomplish? I think we all know what it has to do with. Though I was told not to discuss it, my expertise is in World War II artifacts, specifically German artifacts. Why else would I be here?"

Mug took a deep breath and held it for a couple seconds. "Naleeva is coming in by chopper to talk to you all. She'll be here tomorrow. Are you in any immediate danger? No. I don't think you will be in the future." Pausing, he pinched his eyes before saying, "... unless we find what we hope we won't." MacAphee saw our confused and angry faces and took another breath. "Okay, okay. Yes, you are all here because this is a Nazi hideout. That's about all we know for sure. We want to know a lot more. That's your job. What we do know is that this spot was kept a closely guarded secret. High-ups in the Nazi hierarchy came here. Some very important event occurred at this spot." He hesitated. "This is my opinion, and nothing I know is fact. I believe no one who knows what happened ... wants the rest of the world to know what it was."

"Or, who it happened to!" Migdahlia sounded agitated. All eyes turned to her as she got up, ran out of the mess hall and disappeared into the tent I shared with Ida- Marie and her.

Reading and Mark walked out of the tent with me as we headed back to our work assignments. "You think you'll see her this afternoon?" Reading asked Mark. "She's on your survey crew."

"She'll be there. None of us would be here if she wasn't desperate to know what happened in this place. Who knows? Maybe she does and wants the rest of the world to know." Marked nodded. "She'll show. She'll take any crap that comes her way and not back off or complain."

I grinned at Mark, "You like her don't you?"

"Yes, she's smart and tough like another lady I know."

"Thank you, Mark. Compliment accepted," I said.

Mug yelled loud enough for all to hear, "Everybody, let's get back to surveying. I have nothing else to offer you but bugs, sweat, and more sweat."

Chapter 26
Archaeology site, Misiones Province, Argentina

When I returned to the tent after showering, I found Migdahlia Macias sitting on the side of the bunk. Her head was down, and her shoulders slumped forward. The tee shirt she wore topped a pair of cut-off jeans. I looked at her dejected posture and decided to try cheering her.

"Women like you sure make it tough on me. You could fall into a concrete mixer and come out looking like you're ready for a prom. I work at it and still look like an abandoned car." I got a smile, so I continued, "How did you make out with the survey you're doing? I think we'll finish ours by noon tomorrow."

"We will finish tomorrow."

She looked at me in a way that prompted me to say, "What is going on inside that brain of yours?"

She blushed, staying quiet for several seconds, but looking very serious. She finally said, "I was thinking how different you are from the way I thought you'd be when I first met you."

"In what way?" I asked.

"Oh, it's not just you. Your brother and Mark are so nice. So is the old man. I had an idea you would be like the American tourists that we see in Buenos Aires." Macias looked embarrassed and stammered, "Not that I hate Americans. It's just the—"

I finished her sentence for her, "How the ones I see act. Migdahlia, the people you see in Buenos Aires are the money people. New Yorkers and LA hot-shot elites. They aren't like the rest of us; they just tell everybody they are. I'm as comfortable with most of those folks as I am with a room full of snakes."

"You didn't ask me about what I said in the mess tent. Everyone but you and your brother wanted to know. I'm sure you were curious. Why didn't you?"

I looked serious, "If you wanted me to know you'd have told me. Besides, did you tell all those people that were pumping you for information the truth?"

A faint smile formed on the girl's beautiful face. "No."

"So, if and when you want to talk," I said

Macias' eyes opened wide, and she pointed to the closed tent flaps then her ear. She said, "Is that you, Argello?"

The tent zipper screeched its unique sound, and Ida-Marie stepped inside. She looked at both of us like we were scraps on her dinner plate. "You two conspiring against the world?"

"No, just you." It was plain that Migdahlia didn't trust the woman. Neither did I.

Ida-Marie laughed. "I won't sleep well tonight. One of you might slither out of bed and try to slit my throat." She rubbed her feet on the canvas tent floor making a scraping sound. "Hear that? I'll listen for the rubbing. You might want to tune into that as well. You never can tell who or what is lurking about." She was trying to intimidate us.

I reached under my bunk, fumbled around in my duffle bags for a while, found what my fingers wanted, and removed my 9mm Glock. I held the automatic in the air for her to see. "Ida-Marie, that is good advice. You never know what kind of varmint might be wandering around." I checked the chamber and slid it under my pillow. "I'm not that good with a blade, but I shoot expert with what's under my head."

Argello laughed. "I'll remember that. Sweet dreams."

Ida-Marie kept us awake for part of the night. It was her snoring, not her words that did so. Before I fell asleep, I stared at the ceiling and listened to the jungle's night noises. One of the thoughts that passed through my brain while I tried to get it inactive enough to fall asleep was that I believed Macias was about to tell me her secret right before she caught Ida-Marie eavesdropping. I hoped I hadn't lost the chance to find out what it was.

Chapter 27
At the Archaeological Site.

Mug, Ida-Marie and I sat cross-legged on the ground while Mark checked Mugs numbers. Our survey crew must have done well. No scowl formed on my boss' face as one always does if he encounters mistakes. Mark's no better at controlling the expression of his emotions than I am. After ten minutes of sampling, he grinned and said, "Looks good. We'll get this drawn up." He joined us on the ground. "If the plat drawing goes well, we can start sampling tomorrow. Chessie, we'll do stratified sampling here. Rialto said he wants to do simple random samples on the area in the grids outside what he believes was a fortification or a ceremonial Guarani site. That structure might have had several uses. He'll use judgmental sampling there. Since Migdahlia found what has been verified as a Guarcuru artifact there, it could be a very significant site. Our guess is that the structure will be so different in content than its immediate surrounding, it won't fit into a statistical analysis."

"Who is doing the German site?" Mug asked. "You platted it. Are you going to be lead on that?"

"That was the plan. I talked to Naleeva about the bodies we found. She froze everything until she gets here today."

Mark reached for his water bottle. "That's completely different. Everything is different when you're working in and around large buildings. Working in there is going to be dangerous." He looked at me. "I know you haven't been in that area yet. The buildings are partly built into the hillsides. They're semi-military in design. Some of the supports were wooden. The termites have eaten most of them. They could be death traps. You saw the mines, so that's a possibility." He paused and said, "There's a large number of snakes. I saw a Fer-de-Lance and a Boa on one trip in there."

"What are the structures made from?" I asked. "Evidently, not wood."

"No. The substrate here is basalt. Most of the structures are built from native rock, I imagine out of a quarry somewhere close. There is a moderate to deep soil covering here. They probably found an exposed spot like some of the rock hillsides we saw coming in. There was concrete used as well."

The thump, thump, thump of helicopter rotors made us all look up. Mug pointed to the craft. "That's one of ours. It's a CH-E46."

"It looks like a Huey to me," I said.

Mug grinned, "Close enough."

We rose and walked toward where the chopper, and Naleeva, were about to land.

~~ ~~ ~~

A gentle tropical rain dropped on the mess tent roof. I saw there wasn't the usual lightning and thunder accompaniment as a good omen. Mark sat on one side of me and Reading on the other. It was as if they were trying to protect me from an unknown danger. I wasn't living in fear, far from that. I was excited. My sixth feminine sense told me we were about to become part of history. I wondered if Mark and Reading were transferring their fears to me. Men do it sometimes. That allows them to concentrate on "protecting" and buries the fears they experience.

Naleeva was chatting with Migdahlia. Naleeva's face was serious, sometimes grim. I wondered what that meant for us. She wasn't in a hurry to address us, that was clear. Naleeva reminded me of Dr. Bill Wallace. She appeared so composed, in spite of what must be a monumental mess for her. Obviously, major stress existed with the problems she handled. The woman didn't show it. Her posture was great, and she exuded confidence that those around her absorbed. At least, I did. The pose she took when talking to Macias reminded me of something. It nagged at me until it occurred to me that Naleeva was Venus de Milo in ebony. I thought about that and concluded, "not really." Maybe it was strength combined with femininity that I saw in Alexandros of Antioch's sculpture that made the mental connection.

Migdahlia sat next to where Naleeva was standing, and

I saw Naleeva was ready to talk.

"Let me have your attention." She waited for the table to quiet. Everyone involved in the project assembled at the two long tables. Sergeant Garret, Corporal Cole and six other Marines sat with Mug MacAphee and his seven mercenaries at the "second table." Most of those were men I hadn't met. Our table seated Mr. Cleggenhiest, Dr. Dean, Dr. Rialto, Ida-Marie, Dr. Beltran, Mark, Reading and me. Joining us were five individuals who flew in with Naleeva. If I had a reason for concern, they were it. Three we knew. Alexa Lind, Miccolee Bertonarri from the CIA, and Stan Hansen from the FBI had been in meetings before. The other two were complete strangers.

We learned they were members of the Argentinian Department of the Interior. Both looked bored. Mark whispered, "Suits." One of the men looked familiar: I knew I'd seen a picture of him somewhere, or of someone who was his twin. He wore round-lensed glasses on his round face. He was obviously the cheese, and his companion the mouse. They never spoke except to each other in my presence, and I gathered that most of that was the mouse sucking up to the cheese.

Naleeva spoke. "A combination of what has happened both here and leading up to our trip leads the State Department and me to believe that I must explain to you the importance of what you are doing here, and why the mission MUST remain secret. I also need to make you aware of danger you may face so you can be prepared for it." Naleeva removed a thick envelope from her briefcase and slid a file folder from it. She said, "I'm going to tell you about a classified project called, NILREBELTTIL. You are that project."

Chapter 28

Mess Tent at the Archaeological Site

"You have all signed non-disclosure agreements, and it has been emphasized that nothing you learn can be divulged without government clearance." Naleeva circled the tables with her eyes, taking all the time needed to do it. "Let me underline that importance. Seven people have been killed so far...that have had involvement with this project. You know of the three on the cargo plane. You, and we, suspect the two corpses found here are victims. You don't know about a woman who provided information for Miss Macias' research has been found poisoned, and that pilot Tracy Thorn... some of you met him ... was found hanging in a motel room. He removed himself from the flight just before it took off."

Everyone exchanged concerned glances. Maybe *I did* have something to fear.

"I know that all of you must be apprehensive. Let me assure you we are making certain that there will be no future threats from the outside. Now let me explain what NILREBELTTIL is about." Naleeva opened the file folder that was in front of her and turned a few pages. She looked up and said, "NILREBELTTIL is to prove or disprove myths or facts that the US and Argentine government are very concerned with. I will condense this as much as possible and provide you with what you need to know. I'm sure one of you will decipher the anagram name of this project. NILREBELTTIL backward is LITTLEBERLIN."

Naleeva allowed the whispers to subside. "All of you are aware that after the Second World War, many Nazis escaped Europe and ended up in South America. Large numbers of those came here to Argentina. Places like Teyu Curare, just miles from this site, have been discovered and have been verified as being locations the Nazis built to relocate."

"That we know. You may know there are those who believe Hitler did not commit suicide. Many rumors were fueled by pictures supposedly of him and Eva Braun, that he escaped and lived in Argentina...that Peron sheltered him ... and that the United States helped facilitate his escape in return for the internment of top German scientists. Though every rumor has been examined and disproved, it still exists. I say every rumor has been disproved until now. Miss Macias cannot be disproved. Her DNA is directly traceable to that of Eva Braun and possibly to Adolph Hitler."

All eyes turned to Migdahlia who returned the stares forcefully. Naleeva raised a hand. "I don't want one unkind word spoken of Miss Macias. She is not her sister, brother, mother, or grandfather's keeper. Let me add that she doesn't know what happened here and is unsure of her parentage line. That is the what and why she was trying to discover something here. Without her cooperation, we wouldn't know anything about this. She is a brave woman."

Naleeva nodded her head. "This is *the rumor* we hope to prove false. That this site was, or was to be, the home for the Führer. That an American covert operation helped Hitler escape to a U-boat in the Baltic Ocean, then to Palma in Majorca and then to the Argentinian coast and ... to this place. An error was made. And ... when that error in judgment was discovered, another American black op rectified the mistake. They killed everybody here. There are no records in any government files to make us believe any of that is true. But you have to ask, is there a deep state, and would they do such a thing? There *would be no records*. I and many others think the answer is ... we have to look."

Mark asked, "What happens if we find the rumor is true?"

"As long as you never discuss what we find, nothing." Naleeva wasn't smiling.

Reading murmured, "I hope the government doesn't believe that two can keep a secret if one is dead."

"If that happens, if we find something horrible was done," Naleeva paused and took a deep breath, "History will change and who knows what else. I can promise you this: you will be protected as long as you remain silent."

"I can second that." Alexa Lind nodded and added,

"With the provision that Naleeva mentioned. Keep your mouths shut."

Naleeva frowned slightly, took a breath and said, "I've asked Miss Macias to give you limited information about how she found out about this place." She sat and looked at Migdahlia.

Migdahlia sat, silent for several seconds. I watched her fight unsuccessfully as moisture puddled beneath her eyes. She rubbed her forearm over them and started a tale I'll never forget.

"I will tell you what I may." It was obvious she was very reluctant to speak of her past. "Since I was very young, information about my parents, grandparents, and great-grandparents was kept from me. Maybe that is why I have been so determined to discover it. I was kept from seeing them except on a couple of occasions. Only once was I able to meet with my grandmother in private and that was a secret meeting. She lived much of her life in Paraguay and the last of it in Brazil. That was because of her connections to a political figure, Alfredo Stroessner." At the mention of the name, the South Americans straightened in their chairs. Stroessner was the violent absolute Paraguayan dictator notorious for atrocities. Migdahlia continued. "My mother's maiden name was Stroessner. Her mother was Emma Ava Fortunado, and I was not told what her mother's name was. That woman, my great- grandmother, was never discussed in my presence and I was warned when I was nine to never ask or speak of her. That made me curious for life.

"My mother was hospitalized, and I had occasion to go through her personal papers. I did not know where my grandmother lived until I found her address in them. I met with her secretly. She told me about my ancestors. Even with just the two of us in her room, I could see her fear just discussing her past with me. She claimed that her parents had been killed in 1961 in an isolated spot that no one was allowed to enter or leave. Grandma Emma gave me information about the spot being the sight of an old mission that predated the larger ones like San Ignacio. She told me how to find it in old mission papers. The place was where the first Jesuits who came here, dealt with the Indians. It was then Grandma Emma whispered in my ear, 'Child, your great-grandmother's name was ...' She paused, too frightened to mouth the words. Grandma compromised when I implored her for the name. She whispered, 'Eva H.'"

Migdahlia sighed. "She told me that soldiers came and attacked where she lived when she was sixteen. There was horrible fighting, and everyone except a half-dozen was killed. She, her brother and four other girls survived. A young officer saved them from being shot. The girls, were taken to Paraguay and left with a family. That is how she met and married Juan-Lopez Stroessner. Her bro—"

Naleeva quickly interrupted, "You can't discuss that."

She shook her head sternly to be sure Macias understood.

"Anyway," Migdahlia continued, "she provided me information about whom to see to find the old church records. She had done the same thing. Emma said that nearly cost her, her life. I found the old documents. They used compass readings from the Mission ruins at San Ignacio, San Carlos, and San Javier and the buildings at Teyu Curare to fix the location. That is how I found this place.

"I came here to find out what I could about my past. I found so—"

Naleeva shook her head.

Migdahlia took a breath. "Three people, my friends, came in with me. I found this was the right place and that it was rich in early Spanish and indigenous people artifacts. I knew I would need help and these finds could help me acquire it. Then ... then ... we were chased away. I ..."

Macias looked at Naleeva who shook her head.

Migdahlia started again, "Two stayed so my other friend and I could get away. They did not return. That is when I contacted Eduardo, he contacted our government, and this is the result."

"That is as much as she can tell you." Naleeva returned to her feet and pointed to the high ground a hundred meters behind the tents we slept in at night.

"You can understand the international embarrassment

and the propaganda that some middle-eastern countries and others would make of this. There are a lot of ifs. It is up to us to find the honest answers. It is up to others to determine what is to be done with what we find. It is up to all of us to keep whatever we learn here as a sacred trust."

"Do you really believe that this many people can keep a secret of the nature you're asking?" Mark stated what I and several others were thinking.

"I believe they can ... given the proper incentives." Alexa Lind spoke and stood with a calm ferocity that was frightening. "You've all signed papers that would create great, very great, financial peril for you if you violated the terms. I would like you to consider what harm you could cause if you run your mouths. No one can—"

"That's enough Lind!" Naleeva shouted. "Sit down and shut up!"

The two crossed stares that were high voltage lasers.

Mark looked at Alexa and said, "You don't have to worry. Remember, I've worked with you before and I know what you do for a living. Everybody will know. Maybe deplore you, but they'll know."

The high voltage shifted. If either dropped eye contact, one might have fried the other.

"Enough! We have to see this through, and we won't do it at each other's throats. Alexa, Mark do you both understand?" Naleeva said.

"Oh they will," Mug said. He looked at Alexa. "Alexa

has worked with me in the past. She knows what I can do to keep things ... let's just say going right. Isn't that correct, Alexa?"

Alexa's eyes dropped to the table. Mug had punctured her balloon. The hot air exited, and some fear entered where it left.

Chapter 29

Mission Ruins at the Archaeological Site

"Here comes Mark." I watched him stride across the camp area. The energy in his stride meant that his meeting with Dr. Rialto, Dr. Dean, and Naleeva had gone very good or very bad. Mug and Ida-Marie stopped cutting back weeds from the first area we planned to work, and we watched him smile as he approached.

"Good news?" I asked.

"Yes and no, mostly yes." He waved his hand over the old mission site. "Change of plans. This will be our second site. All of us will be working on Little Berlin. That's what we've agreed to call it. Naleeva didn't like that; she wanted the anagram. Too politically sensitive she said, but we told her she could call it what she wants in her reports. Besides, that's the only argument she lost."

I said, "If she won all the arguments, why aren't most of the news good?"

"You know you can agree once-in-a-while." Mark grinned and pointed to my biceps. "Chessie sometimes you don't need to arm-wrestle the world. Naleeva said she realized she was taking away some of our prerogatives. Other than starting and finishing Little Berlin first," Mark savored saying that, "We proceed how we want, and we have complete control over the site. If we run out of time before we can get to the other two sites, she says she'll get everything set up for a return visit. One that's less stressful. Mug's people and most of the Marines are available to hump and haul. The only other conditions are that if we make a major discovery, we freeze work, notify her and she may, or may not, come to see it. If we need to communicate with the outside world, we do it with Mug present."

Mug bowed.

"Naleeva told me she wanted to see you, Mug. She's getting ready to leave."

Mug handed his grass-whip to Mark and said, "Second shift, or do we move now?"

"We move now."

~ ~ ~ ~ ~

The rainstorm reduced to a light drizzle. Most of the expedition's company watched Naleeva's chopper warm its engines as Alexa, Hansen, the two Argentine officials, and Naleeva climbed aboard. Miccolee Bertonarri sat at the table with us. I wondered why. An interpreter? We didn't have the need, at least I didn't see one. I figured her major impact would be to make our tent crowded. The aircraft sat there for several minutes. When the sky brightened, and the drizzle became mist, the rotor blades beat the air, and I thought our governmental anchors were cut free. I was happy to see the alphabet leave ... CIA ...

FBI ... DOS. We could get started.

Reading, Mug, Mark and Eduardo decided to see if the rain made the site too wet to work. They emerged from the woods shaking their heads. I noticed that Reading had something dangling from his hand. It was a large snake. When he got close enough, he shook its tail, and it made a familiar rattling sound. He said, "They have them down here, too."

I checked the other ladies' reaction.

Migdahlia squirmed and looked worried.

Ida-Marie smiled and asked, "Are you going to clean him?"

Miccolee passed out.

I was glad I brought snake boots. Over the next few days, much of our time would be spent removing brush and weed cover from Little Berlin. If we were going to encounter snakes, it was a good possibility that would be the time.

Reading left his souvenir lying outside the tent. Mark and he sat beside me. I asked, "Well? Are we going to get wet?"

"No. Looks to me like there's still a lot of rain upstairs." Mark pointed skyward. "It rains in the afternoons, threeish or fourish. We'll get an early start tomorrow." Mark saw the disappointment on my face "Don't look so disgusted. You'll get a chance to find a Rosetta Stone next time you dig."

"I haven't seen what it looks like over there." I waved my hand in the proper direction. "Curiosity and all that jazz."

"I'll walk you over if you have nose trouble," Reading volunteered. He grinned and looked into the sun's glare that appeared like magic to make a liar of Mark. "Weather's changing just for you."

"I'd like to go with you," Migdahlia suggested.

"Sure," Reading said. "I'll meet you in a few minutes. I want to put boots on. Wait for me at the trail you came out on."

Migdahlia trotted back to our tent while Reading and I took our time walking to the woods. I wondered why Migdahlia was interested in seeing what she already knew well or if she had another reason for accompanying us.

Chapter 30

Little Berlin at the Archaeological Site

Entering the heavy jungle that covered the Little Berlin site underlined what I already knew—nature reclaims what is hers and she does it forcibly. I calculated that the site had been abandoned for sixty years or more. With the exception of the usual sprinkling of huge tree trunks that survived for hundreds of years in a virgin wilderness environment, it was difficult to visualize the woods was once a grass lawn.

Trees twelve to sixteen inches in diameter were everywhere. The fact they were so uniform in size was the primary evidence of the area's second growth status. Underbrush was also heavier than I anticipated. Weeds and saplings screened one's your vision in all directions. A jaguar could have been waiting twenty feet away and we wouldn't have known it. Water dripped from the leaf canopy above that shut out most light, making it perpetual twilight.

"The old entrance is ahead." Migdahlia pointed at a mound of leaves fifteen feet in front of us. She used her "walking stick" to lead the way. The walking stick was an aluminum tube an inch in diameter with a two-inch long pointed piece of steel installed in the end. The top of it was wrapped in tape half-way to the "spear-point." It was where she grasped it. The stick was six feet in length and doubled as a formidable weapon.

"I found it from my grandmother's description," she said.

"Yeh. I see it. Mark and I walked past this and didn't realize what it was." Reading unslung the shotgun he carried on his shoulder. He called the gun and its shells filled with #8 birdshot 'snake repellent.' Mark used the barrel to expose a column of rocks stacked waist high. I got my first look at the most common material used in constructing the buildings and structures in the old Nazi compound. Rocks, they looked to be sedimentary, were carefully interlocked to form a two-foot square column. None was more than six inches thick. The person who did the work certainly had a master stonemason's skills.

The remains of metal brackets were bolted to the column's top. I pointed to the rusted wreck. "Looks like there was something mounted on it."

"There was. A metal arch was over the path." Macias shoved her walking stick into a thicket of vines, saplings, and brush. It clinked against the column's companion. "Hear? The other side." Migdahlia motioned to the path's right. "There is supposed to be a rock-lined fish pond over there. I never found it, but we should be careful. If we fell in it, we could get hurt."

"We don't need that." Reading moved to the far left portion of the trail and led us toward the buildings he said were near. "Another fifty yards and we'll be in the surveyed area. Most all the underbrush is cut down." He carried his shotgun rather than shouldering it. Reading said, "This is where I killed that snake this morning. Keep a close watch. I heard another one, but never saw the damned thing." That kept Migdahlia's and my eyes focused on the path and its sides.

"Here we are." Reading stepped into the cleared area. Orange, blue and yellow ribbons fluttered from the stakes that marked the grid and Mark's sampling spots. The complex that the removal of underbrush revealed caused me to suck in my breath. I heard Migdalia murmur, "*Este es grande*! It looks so different with the weeds gone."

"Impressive isn't it?" Reading said. "Even with just half the brush removed."

"That's an understatement," I said. What I was looking at was part residence and part military bastion. There were several buildings above ground, built on a natural rock outcropping that sloped upward at a forty-five- degree angle. Arroyos divided its sides into numerous rocky passages. Rock walls augmented what nature provided. The building built on the promontory's peak poked out of the jungle and was covered with huge-leaved vines. It looked as though it was twenty feet higher than its surroundings. Massive rock walls were everywhere, all built in interlocking layers ten feet high. I could see where wooden gables and roof structures had been attached.

Nothing was left but a few pieces of rotting timbers.

The promontory was one mass of tunnels. Many of the arroyos ended in large rectangular openings. One large enough for a big truck to enter had heavy iron hinges mounted at its sides. Stone structures that looked like fences wound between the buildings. Circular structures built into the walls puzzled me for several seconds until I noticed openings built into them. They were gun embrasures. The structures were gun emplacements.

When we were fifteen yards from one of the walls, Reading said, "You been inside any of these?"

"Just one. It was frightening, and I knew I needed more help." Migdahlia pointed to a building at the base of the tower. "They chased—" Migdahlia's eyes widened as she realized she spoke without realizing she had divulged something. It was something she didn't want the others to know. Not until they experienced "it."

I looked at Reading, and he returned my stare. He asked Migdahlia, "Do you have something you need to tell us?"

"I had one thing to tell you, and now I must make it two." Migdahlia swiveled her head around as though she expected someone to be lurking. "You were told a lie by Naleeva because she was told a lie. It is *not sure* that my DNA is from Hitler and Braun. It shows that there is some relation. When I asked Dr. Rialto to come back here, and he heard that the possibility exists, he said that would be a strong lever to get approval and money to come here."

"Why are you telling us that and not the rest?" Reading asked.

"Because I trust your sister. I know you are here to protect her. I want you to be sure I do not disappear or ... something. I tell you this because I intend to stay very close to your sister. It would not be fair if you didn't have this information."

I knew the look on Reading's face. He was pretty sure that Migdahlia wasn't telling the whole truth, but he'd accept what she said and eventually find the whole truth. I knew she'd just become a whole lot safer.

I asked, "What is the second thing?"

Migdahlia dropped her eyes and stayed silent.

"Number two is?" I prodded with a little edge in my voice.

She looked embarrassed. Migdahlia took a big breath and spoke haltingly. "I am ... a person of science. If you told me what I will be telling you, I would find it hard to believe." She hesitated then blurted out, "This place is haunted by the ghosts of the people that died here. My grandmother told me not to come here for that reason. I did not believe such things and I laughed at her. I am so sorry now." She walked to a low spot in the wall and pointed over it. Her finger aimed at a stone stairway that descended into the ground. A door opening was at the bottom. Dark and foreboding, the outline of stones on the floor was the only thing visible in the semi-blackness. It *was* evil looking. "There are several of those entrances around these buildings. I went in one with my friend. We walked around the room. It was empty except for an old rusted gun lying on the floor. We bent over to look at it. There was a noise. When we turned, there was a skeleton standing against the wall where there was nothing a second before. We ran away and never went back. There were noises that night. Someone took all of our food. We saw shadows in the buildings. We left. I know you don't believe me. As I said, I wouldn't."

Whether Migdahlia really experienced what she claimed, or not, I shivered. There is nothing like hearing a ghost story on the spot it occurred.

"We'll take a look at that tomorrow." Reading's eyes scanned the sky through the leaf canopy. "We've got another storm coming in, and I don't want to get caught out here in it."

"Please don't tell the others," Migdahlia implored him.

Reading glanced at me and I nodded, "We won't."

Macias mouthed the word "thanks," remained pensive for several seconds and then made her decision. "I must tell you the one last thing. Before what we saw in the building, we found a skeleton. It was far from the compound. It had boots on. Hobnail boots. I decided to take it back with us. I took pictures, marked the location and put it in a locked collection box. When we fled, it was one of the few things we took with us. I found I had lost the key. The lock had to be cut off. No one opened the box until then. The skeleton was gone. It had escaped."

Chapter 31

Mess Tent at the Archaeological Site

Reading and I sat alone. Mark, Mug, Eduardo, Dr. Dean, Dr. Beltran, Sergeant Garret and Migdahlia were making their final plans to begin the excavation. The only other people in the tent were two of Sergeant Garret's soldiers cleaning up.

"What did you think about Migdahlia's little talk this afternoon?" Reading asked.

"She's scared, and she's looking for a safety net ... anywhere she can find one. Wouldn't you?"

"Yes, she's scared, but I wonder if she intended for us to deliver the message to the others," he shook his head, "I don't know what to think. Something didn't compute with me."

I thought for several seconds and tried to determine how I'd react if I were in her situation. "I don't know if I'd want people thinking I'm something that Hitler spawned. The best she can expect is universal distaste and suspicion. The worst, I'm sure some will want to shorten her lifespan. That what you were talking about?"

"Yes. I kind of wondered why she even opened this ... Pandora's box. She had to know what was likely to happen. Migdahlia is either having one hell of a case of buyer's remorse, or there is something else." Reading stared past me. "Here comes the crew."

Mark, Mug, Migdahlia, and Eduardo left their seats and headed for us. Dean and Beltran remained seated, laughing at the others' jokes, I supposed. Garret slipped out the mess tent door into the steamy evening air.

"We got some instructions from Naleeva." Mark waived a printed copy of an email. "She wants us looking for graves around Little Berlin. *First!* That makes my decisions very easy, though I don't like them. We now have five sites. Tomorrow we'll be using the GPR units in these areas." Mark spread five large drawings in front of us. He tapped his finger on them. "Chessie, when we get back we need to get Andrews to buy us one of those Auto-Ranger set-ups. We just fed all the readings it took and stored it on a computer and wham! These CAD maps were complete in minutes. We have two GPR sets so—"

"I forget all of us don't know the jargon," Reading interrupted. "Sorry. GPR is ground penetrating radar. Okay, of the five sites, these three are cleared enough to use the equipment." He pulled one from the stack. "Two GPRs means two teams. Eduardo, Mug, and Chessie have this sub-site. Chessie, you keep the notebook, take pictures, cross-index the printouts from the GPR. Eduardo, you're the lead, and you run the GPR. Mug will be your team's gofer."

Mark pulled the second map from the stack. "I have the

second site. Migdahlia, you have the record keeping and Reading, will you be the gofer?"

"Sure."

"Thanks, Reading." Mark pointed to the maps. "I'm using GPS numbers to locate. The Datum Points are heavy steel stakes with red ribbon on them. The three yellow stakes mark the position of the tripod legs when you set up. One thing you probably would figure out in a few seconds. The indicator on the drawing for datum points is an "X" with two circles around it. An "X" with a single circle around it marks the outside confines of the site."

"Record everything! Just because we've been mandated to work these areas first doesn't mean we are going to compromise good excavating procedure. If someone comes back a hundred years from now, I want those archaeologists to take our notes and set up from them." Mark rubbed his chin. "In one of these areas, there is supposed to be a graveyard. In another, there is supposed to be a mass grave for a battle that is rumored to have happened here. What the radar sees is a guess. The graveyard means that coffins were probably used. A mass grave probably means skelctal remains. Under any circumstance, look for areas where the natural soil structure has been disturbed. Those are the first areas we need to look at."

"Do we have to clear the weeds and brush from the two remaining sites?" I asked. I wasn't looking forward to dodging snakes in the extremely heavy growth covering Little Berlin.

"No. Sergeant Garret's people will do that, and they'll also finish up the surveying on them. Most of that has to be done." Mark smiled at us. "Questions?"

Heads shook. "What time?" Mug asked. "I'll roll my people out and have the equipment and tools on the sites and ready to go."

"See you all in the mess tent at 5:30."

Chapter 32
Berlin Site #2

"There's nothing here," Mug said. He impatiently carried the latest data strip from the Ground Penetrating Radar unit Eduardo carefully pushed over every square centimeter of Grid Locus E20 to E25, N40 to N45. I recorded the findings on the printout in the site notebook, noting three shadows that might be of interest.

The entry was: Site: Berlin #2, Grid location: E20 x N40, Day/date: May 13, 2017 / 9:08 AM, Weather: Overcast, hot, winds low to moderate. Datum level: + 287 meters MSL, Datum point: – 27.37 Lat X – 55.90 Long Collection boxes: None, Collection bags: Recorder strip from GPR Collection containers other: None, Notes: Three inconclusive areas of radar returns of an unidentifiable nature. E22/N41 – E24/N43 – E24/N44. Crew: Dr. Rialto, MacAphee, Partin. Entry by: Chessie Partin.

I looked at Mug when I completed my entry. He was bored, impatient and disgusted. I laughed at him and said, "You only find King Tut's burial vault in every thirtieth grid block. So, you have," I faked counting squares on the map, "nineteen more."

A chainsaw roared a hundred yards away. The jungle was so thick that Sergeant Garret's team and what they were doing was completely shrouded from our view. Mug looked in the direction of the noise. He asked, "Do you need me here? All I'm doing is walking these sheets to you. You don't need me for that."

I thought about that for several seconds and answered. "You aren't here to work; you're here to protect us. You think we need protection right now?"

Mug shrugged his shoulders. "Not really, but if I left and something did happen, I'd be in a world of hurt." He shook his head. "I guess I'll remain the Maytag repairman while we finish the job. I'm not used to sitting on my butt."

"You're not. You're standing on your feet." I enjoyed his disgruntled face. "Think of it as an important task. You're keeping the floor of the jungle from floating up."

"Funny."

Eduardo shouted, "*Madre de Dios*!" He pushed and pulled the radar unit over the same area. "We have definitely found something."

Mug and I sprinted to him. I asked, "What is it?"

"Starting here," Dr. Rialto positioned the unit, "The earth has definitely been disturbed. See the changes? Now watch this." He moved the unit ahead a little more than two meters. "See that. I've seen that before. It is either a very large pipe or a number of fifty-five-gallon drums buried end to end." He tore off the record strip and said, "I'll start over. I want you to mark the areas I tell you with green and orange tipped stakes. They'll mark where the disturbed ground starts and where whatever is buried here is located."

Mug was relieved to be able to do something. "I got that."

"I'll be sure the information all gets on the site log." I added, "Can you figure how deep it's buried?"

Eduardo concentrated on the screen and made a few adjustments to the controls. "The tops are about 140 centimeters down." He moved the radar unit forward another meter and said, "There is another row." Dr. Rialto stopped the unit and told me, "Be sure to make this note: The objects buried at the identified marks are all within disturbed strata, are symmetrical, suggest being man-made, and this suggests relatively recent interment."

I nodded. "If we excavate should we put the back dirt in E15/N40?"

"Yes. Also reserve E10/N40. There wasn't anything in there." Rialto examined the area we'd just discussed. "Chessie, make a note to ground tarp everything we put back dirt on."

I scribbled notes on the log site record as Eduardo pushed the unit and Mug marked locations of the mysterious objects beneath the soil. They continued and found that buried cylinders extended into the surround grid blocks both north and east. The recorder strips showed them plainly.

"Something different. I'd guess it's a box, maybe thirty

by ten centimeters." Eduardo placed a note on the recorder strip. It isn't buried deep. Twenty centimeters, maybe a little more." He examined the readings. "It's buried outside the area of disturbed strata. It could be something entirely unrelated."

I was busy making log entries, filing specimen bags, and cataloging them when excited shouts came filtering through the jungle from where Sergeant Garret was clearing brush.

"Wonder what's going on over there?" Mug asked.

"A snake. Maybe the ruins of a structure or a skeleton." Eduardo went back to operating the GPR unit. He added, "We'll find out at the mess tent during lunch."

Chapter 33
Mess Tent

"I thought I was dead." A private from Sergeant Garret's squad was filling the rest of us in on the excitement at Little Berlin, Site #4. All of the personnel in the group with the important exceptions of Mug, Mark, Eduardo, and Sergeant Garret were circled around the shaken soldier. The four leaders were huddled at the opposite end of the tent.

"I'm walking along, and I step on this little bump and ... wham ... I heard a pop behind me, turned, and I'm staring at this metal canister that popped up. I knew what it was. I waited for it to explode and for the angels to come."

Migdahlia asked, "What was it?"

"A Bouncing Betty," Corporal Cole said. "That's a World War II anti-personnel mine the German's used. It's about the size of a coffee can, has a charge that launches the damn thing four feet in the air. It's full of ball bearings, and it explodes. Fred was lucky. We all were. Those damned mines have a wide killing radius. The detonator was rusted and didn't work. Sarge is telling your buddies he wants to freeze all work until we can do minesweeping on all five sites and the paths to them. We got careless. We might not be lucky next time."

"What do we look for?" one of MacAphee's men asked.

"Your Bible," Corporal Cole snorted. "I thought you were professionals. They're buried below ground and covered with a thin layer of dirt. The trip mechanism is on top. You know you've stepped on one when the blast kills you."

Cleggenhiest spoke to the group in general. "That convinces me. If you want to find me, I'll either be in my tent or here. Anybody going to join me? I have three decks of cards, and I'll play bridge or poker ... your choice."

Chapter 34
Mess Tent

"How many did Garret's people find?" I asked.

Mug stopped setting posts to support the large tarp that would protect us from the sun, and the excavation we'd be starting under it from the rain. "Seventeen."

I whistled. That was a large number for the relatively small percentage of the land the five sites constituted. "Where did they find them?"

"Everything was on #4 and #5." Mug straightened up, put his hands on his hips, and bent backward. "They found five more of the same type mine Private Carter triggered there. On Site #5 they found four of the big mines. Tellers. The rest were Bouncing Bettys." He leaned on the posthole digger he was using. "Garret hasn't finished #5, yet. The side by the cliffs is going to be hard to do."

"Cliffs?" I asked.

"You haven't been on the other side of those buildings? The whole complex was built on the edge of a steep slope. It drops down two hundred feet and at a very severe angle. I'd guess 60 degrees or more. Half-way down it drops off in a sheer wall of red rock. Dr. Card said its basalt based. I don't know what that means, but ... At the bottom, there's a creek. That creek cuts a half-circle around the high ground. Whoever picked this spot had a military eye for picking great defensible positions. Three men with pea-shooters could defend the whole back of that building complex."

I was more concerned with stepping on something that would convert me to hamburger. "You think Garret and his people got them all?"

"Mines? Yeah. Garret hand-picked his soldiers. They're good. Besides they're going to be surveying some of those sites before we get there." Mug shot his hands into the air simulating an explosion.

"You have to go any deeper?" I asked.

"One more ought to make it deep enough." Mug drove the posthole digger three feet into the ground. He spread the handles, removed the scoop of soil from the hole and placed it in my wheel borrow. "That will do," he said. "How long will it take to get me enough dirt to pack around the posts?"

"Not long to run it through the screens. If I find something, that's different. We'd have to determine if we want you to dig a different hole to preserve the area where we've made the find." I pointed to the series of three screens every bit of excavated earth would have to pass through. "It will probably take fifteen minutes for me to sift through it and get the dirt back dirt to you."

Mug nodded and trotted over to get the four, three- inch pipes that would serve as supports for the tarp, while I pushed the wheel-barrow to the screen boxes.

~~ ~~ ~~

At Berlin Site #2

Mark hammered the last stake into the ground marking the trench where we would begin to dig. It would be seven meters long, and two wide dug to an unknown depth when we were finished. Mug's men would be put into service as "day laborers" hauling dirt from the pit to the area we designated as the back dirt storage area. None of them were happy about their new duty. One grumbled, "That four-pound shovel is twice as heavy as my six-pound gun." They did their job, if grudgingly. Migdahlia, Reading, and I manned the screen boxes looking for artifacts. Mark, Eduardo, Ida-Marie, and Mug did the actual digging. Excavating a site is both exciting, and in its way, glamorous while being tedious, boring drudgery at the same time.

The screen boxes were set up ninety feet from the excavation and back dirt tarp another forty feet from us. Within an hour of starting everyone learned and was performing their tasks smoothly, or so it seemed to me. Within four hours we had a respectable pile of dirt building, but we hadn't discovered anything of interest.

Once I settled into the routine of searching the soil for a treasure someone had left behind for me to find, I put the danger from mines, snakes, and two-legged vermin out of my mind. It is what I do. It is what I love.

The loam did not break itself down into screen-able particles like the sandy soil I was familiar with in Florida. It needs gentle assistance.

Reading operated the shaker with Migdahlia and me took turns assisting him. One of us was always searching the screen looking for some bit of the past we'd uncovered. Migdahlia finally found something. She carefully removed a bit of metal from the screen. It was perfectly round, two or so centimeters in diameter and thin.

She examined it, gently removing the dirt from the object. Migdahlia smiled. "It's a coin." She gently rubbed, stared hard at it and exclaimed, "It's an American Quarter! It has a date of 1956." She carefully placed it in a clear plastic baggie that served as a specimen bag.

Within thirty seconds she excitedly announced. "There's more. They seem wrapped in something." She gently prodded the clod and abruptly halted. "Stop shaking the screen."

I could see four discs that were probably coins partly exposed in the wad of "earth." Migdahlia prodded the clod gently. It resisted her effort. I noticed that some of the dirt held together in a flat sheet. We both recognized what we were looking at simultaneously. "That's cloth. That's change from someone's pocket."

The material was so rotted it disintegrated in our gloved fingers as we tried to salvage it.

"Move your hands away and move out of the light."

Reading was taking pictures. He is a fast study. He asked, "What do you think you've found?"

"Someone's pants, I'd guess. The question is: where is 'the someone' who was wearing them." I looked at Migdahlia. "Are those coins from the US also?"

She gently examined two of them. After several seconds she said, "Yes, both are American nickels." Reading said, "Uh-huh." He had his manure munching grin that means he's figured out something others haven't.

"What have you found?" Ida-Marie asked as she approached us.

Migdahlia didn't answer so I said, "Coins and an old piece of what we believe is cloth."

She nodded and said, "Oh." She put one hand up and told us, "I'm here to help you. Your boss thinks I'm too careless using a spade."

I looked at her suspiciously. Mark could always find something for someone to do at a dig. Labor was in short supply. He'd gotten rid of her for some other reason. "You can haul the back dirt to the tarp," I said.

She nodded, but she didn't appear pleased.

After we put our find in a specimen bag, I walked over to the excavation to tell Mark what we found. He was in the pit measuring the depth of some type of find at the bottom. Eduardo was taking pictures and making notations in the site log. Mark brushed away dirt from a curved surface. "It's a steel drum." He carefully removed dirt from the metal. "I'm surprised this isn't rusted worse than it is." Mark looked at Eduardo and asked, "What do you think? Deepen the trench at the end of the drum and go down five centimeters lower than it is?"

"Yes, right here at the end. We can open it and see what is inside." Eduardo thought about what he said for a few seconds then added, "We need to find a way to be sure there isn't oil or some dangerous material inside. It could be anything from oil to explosives, mines or ammunition."

"Agreed," Mark was focused on the metal drum. "There's something printed on it" He bent over to get a better look. "Chessie, hand me a trowel and a brush, please."

I selected the two tools Mark requested and handed them down to him. He was trying to find the end of the drum. Mark handled the trowel with the care a surgeon handles a scalpel. The dirt he removed was meticulously transferred to a bucket. He found what he was looking for after he removed ten centimeters of the earth covering the drum. "Here's the end, right where the radar said it would be. The other two rows are next to this one." Mark pointed to either side. "I want to remove enough soil around them, so we have room to work." He bent over and brushed the soil away from the printing and read German, "*Achtung, Ol Enhalt!*"

I said, "Well, we know they had oil in them at one time. I wonder what's in them now. There's no reason to have buried them here or in the way they been arranged if they contained oil."

"We are about to find out." Mark was scooping earth from where the opening was. "Eduardo get pictures of this and note that the drum covering was non-metal. This looks like it was plywood at one time." The rotted material was carefully removed and placed in a specimen container. "Hey Chessie, would you get a flashlight for me."

I found one in the tool pile and tossed it to Mark. He was busy removing enough material to shine a beam of light in and see what the drums contained.

"Thanks," he mumbled as he exposed an oblong hole big enough to put two fists through. Mark clicked on the light, bent down to look inside, and directed the beam in the hole. After several seconds, he straightened as if an electric bolt shot through him. He murmured, "Holy shit!"

Chapter 35
Little Berlin Site #2

We stood around the precisely dug pit edges staring at what we'd found. All earth down to several centimeters below the bottom of the drums had been removed. The reason they weren't deeper was evident. Part of the pit's floor was rock. The end of each drum had been removed and carefully preserved. They were in containers at the edge of the pit protected by the tarp keeping us and the pit dry from the gently falling afternoon rain.

No one thought about the rain or the red rock that was the pit's base. All stared at the contents of the three open ends of the drums. They were clothed skeletons. For as far back in as the flashlight beam would penetrate, a jumble of cloth, bones, and skulls filled the steel tubes that served as burial vaults. We took turns climbing down the ladder, getting on our knees, and gazing into the mini caverns. When my turn came, I became queasy. It surprised me. The last three years had exposed me to human remains in all conditions and settings. This collection of bones couldn't be more gruesome than those I'd viewed. Still ...

I peered into the darkness that the flashlight beam chased. What it exposed made me exhale. For as far back as you could see, bodies had been shoved into the cramped space. The drum bottoms had been removed, so they formed a continuous "pipe," I counted a minimum of six drums placed end to end. I said what I was thinking. "Why take the bottoms out of the drums?"

"I would imagine they needed more room. They cut the bottoms out to be able to get more bodies in the space available." Mark pointed to the center drum. "When you look in there you'll see that the bottom isn't cut out. The way the body is laying in it, I'd guess it was dumped in there and transported here. Notice how this center line of drums is higher. It is almost wedged between the other two rows. Why? I'd bet it was the last put into this burial site, probably after the others were placed here, but not covered."

Sergeant Garret had already confirmed that the uniforms were those of U.S. Marines. I stared at the cloth of the shirt covering the skeleton closet to the opening I was looking into. The corporal's stripes were clearly visible. I shook my head. "What happened here?" I asked.

"That's what we're here to find out," Mark said. "I have an idea, but we have a lot of work to prove it." He knelt down next to me. "Look at the skull closest to you and look in the teeth."

I squinted at a small rectangular piece of metal forced into the teeth. I recognized it immediately. I'd worn them ... dog-tags!

Mark told me what I already knew, "That's the way

they identified bodies that had to be buried in the field and recovered later." He said, "Now, look at the skull in the center drum. No tag."

I moved in front of the middle drum and whistled. "Did you notice what's on his collar? Depending on whether those oak leaves are silver or gold we have a major or a lieutenant colonel. No one was expecting to come back and dig him up." I shook my head. "Why? Why go to the effort of field marking most of the bodies and not identifying an officer?"

"Like I said, that's what we're here for," Mark replied.

As I climbed up the ladder, Reading had a concerned, serious look on his face. I started to ask him what he was thinking, but he mouthed, *not now*, before I got a word out. "How long have they been here?" I asked anybody who'd answer.

"After 1955," Mug said. "We checked one of the serial numbers on the tags through Naleeva. She says that's when it was issued. Some details on the uniforms, the material, all agree with that." He took a deep breath. "That reminds me. Naleeva upgraded the importance of not speaking to anyone outside of this camp about what we're finding." He shouted, "Keep your mouths shut! Everybody impressed? Naleeva said I have to check everybody's gear for hidden cell phones, I-pads, or wood piles for sending smoke signals." He paused. "She's frigging serious. She says the last thing we need is someone from the outside poking in this. We don't want any of us leaving here in a body bag."

Migdahlia was crossing herself as she climbed the ladder. What she had seen in the pit had shaken her. There were tears in her eyes, and I put my arm around her. We walked away from the group. I said, "This is no different from other digs you've been on. I know you have a personal connection, but remember these are things now. What made them people left. What you see is when they died."

"I know that." She looked at me and shook her head. "Most all my work has been in research libraries, and I've done very little fieldwork. It ... it ... affects me more than I can tell you. These men buried here certainly do! I don't know how I'll react to—"

There was nothing for me to say to her. But, by what she told me, I'd learned that she expected to find more bodies. Many more bodies. To these bodies, some of them, she expected she would have a direct connection.

Eduardo asked Mug, "Did Naleeva give you any directions?"

Mug shrugged his shoulders. "Do what you're doing, but do it as fast as you can."

"We need to get the backhoe in here if we are to do this fast. Arm and shovel power will take a week or more just to excavate. Even then, we can't use the equipment close to the discovery. We must do much of it by hand to preserve the integrity of the site." Eduardo Rialto's voice rose as his doctorate, and sense of scientific discipline emerged.

"I'm sure she doesn't want you to break your own rules. Keep your rules, but execute them *fast*." Mug wasn't smiling.

"How long will it be before you can get the backhoe in here?" Mark asked.

"Garret's checking for mines in the area he'll have to cut through." Mug pointed toward the location of the mess tent and the low sound of a growling diesel. "Corporal Cole is on the 'hoe and is cutting a road right behind him." He saw Mark and Eduardo's concerned faces. "She's got instructions to go around anything that remotely could be like what you're looking for and to stop and come get you if she does stumble on something."

Mug's assurance didn't do much to allay their fears or help their disposition. Mark grumbled, "Okay people, let's get back in the hole and dig and do our thing."

Chapter 36
Little Berlin Site #2

"Be careful," I cautioned Reading. Mark had entrusted me with exhuming the object that had been detected several meters away from the burial site. The last thing I wanted to do was screw up.

"Hey, you can man the shovel and I'll supervise if you'd feel more comfortable." Reading spoke good-naturedly, realizing I was feeling some pressure. Digging up whatever was buried a couple feet beneath us could be an extraordinary piece of the puzzle we were working to put together. He removed a spade-load of dirt and dropped it in the wheelbarrow. Reading's movements were slow and deliberate as he sank the spade into the earth a couple of feet from where the stakes marked the position of the "box" or whatever the shadow on the recorder strip turned out to be.

Reading reached into the wheelbarrow and removed something after dumping a spade-full. He held it up so I could see it. "Something for your collection bags. One brass cartridge, .45 caliber. It was in the top six inches of soil and about a foot away from what we're looking for."

I removed a bag from the "toolkit" each archeologist carried with them. The empty casing was filled with dirt.

"That from a sidearm?" I asked.

"Could be, but I'd guess it was from a sub-machine gun. Probably an M-3, that was a standard issue back then." Reading looked at the rear of the brass. "It has to be cleaned up to tell what weapon it was fired from. I'm sure some firearms expert can do it."

I nodded as I 'bagged and tagged' the casing.

The grunting of the backhoe drew my attention. Corporal Cole was the operator. Her curses were louder than the machine labor pains.

Reading grinned. "Your buddy must have hit another rock outcropping."

"She's not my buddy." I looked at the woman shouting instructions at a couple of hapless privates assigned to do her bidding. For some reason, Corporal Cole had taken an instant and deep dislike for me. The harder I tried to break the invisible barrier between us, the more distant she'd become. Regardless of her feelings about me, I couldn't help liking her. She was her own person and very competent in every task she tackled. I admire those qualities. I wrote her dislike off to either the black/white thing or boob envy. She wasn't overly endowed.

The pile of back dirt that had to be screened grew so large so fast even three screening teams couldn't get close to keeping up. Mark and Eduardo gave up trying. The excavated material that they felt had a low chance of hiding some artifact went directly to the back dirt pile. There was still enough soil they felt needed checking to keep two teams shaking screens and fingering any suspicious items caught in them.

Reading's voice brought my thoughts back to what we were doing. "You want to get a picture of this?" The spade-full of soil he was dumping on the ground had exposed the corner of a solid object in the hole he was digging.

"Take one more shovelful out, but be sure not to damage whatever that is," I said.

"Your, *whatever* is an ammunition box."

He was correct. After checking the line level on the string, I made measurements documenting distance from the data plane and the distance below the soil's surface that the box had been buried. I wrote in my site notebook and spoke at the same time. "Thirty-eight centimeters. That's too deep for natural coverage based on the topography. It definitely was buried here."

I recorded my findings in the site notebook. Site: Berlin #4, Grid location: E20 x N49, Day/date: May 18, 2017 / 9:08 AM Weather: Sunny, hot, winds low.

Datum level: 226 meters above sea level/38 centimeters below the established surface, 114 centimeters below the plane.

Datum point: E1/N1 GPS 23556 code A Collection boxes: One – Serial# 109 Collection bags: One – Shell casing from fired bullet (recovered from back dirt) Collection containers other: Notes: One object preliminarily identified as an ammunition box. Pictures taken – Identification #s begin with prefix E23/N49. Box unopened. Notified Dr. Card for further instructions.

Crew: R. Partin, C. Partin. Entry by: Chessie Partin.

I carefully removed the rest of the dirt around the ammunition box using the rules Mark had established for the items extraction. Nothing was visible in the back dirt. After snapping pictures from every conceivable angle, I lifted the box out of the excavation. It was badly rusted.

"Reading, would you go find Mark and ask him if he wants to look at anything before I put this in the specimen box and seal it?" I held the box in latex gloved hands.

"Sure." Reading sauntered off.

I stood watching the rest of our team. All were totally immersed in their work. At least, those I could see. The abandoned backhoe acted as a screen between where Reading and I worked and the rest of our group. I walked around the machine to see if I could find Mark, but he wasn't in the area. Sighing, I returned to the hole. Even though the ammunition box wasn't terribly heavy, it was tiring. My hands moved to find a more comfortable position. When they did, the rusted hinges broke, the box fell to the ground, and the contents spilled from the container.

I said, "Shit!" and kneeled to put what lay in heaps around the box back where it had tumbled from. Its contents registered on my mind for the first time. The largest pile was a conglomeration of bead chains and small metal plates. Dog tags! I feverishly counted. Forty-two, a whole platoon of men! Snatching them off the ground, I returned them to the box along with two leather pouches and a Kabar knife, then slapped the lid on the best I could. I looked around and sighed with relief. No one saw my disaster. I looked next to the box. One lonely dog tag and chain lay on the ground. My fingers snatched it up, and I was about to put it in the box when a strange sensation invaded me. Instead, I debated whether to put it in my pocket. Why? I thought of an old comedian's favorite saying my father used to mimic, "The devil made me do it." I slid it into my pants with the conviction it was the right thing to do though I had no idea why.

I stood shifting from foot to foot waiting for Mark and Reading to arrive. My emotions lit my face like a neon sign, and I was sure 'guilty' would flash on and off as soon as they looked at me. My pupils focused on the broken hinges, wishing I had laser vision capable of welding the lid shut.

"What you got?" Mark's voice made me jump. He added, "Didn't mean to scare you."

I tried to sound nonchalant and officious at the same time. "This is the object that was on the GPR sheets you asked me to excavate. It's an ammunition box. The hinges are rusted through." It doesn't work. I sounded ridiculous and winced at the sound of my own voice.

Mark chuckled, "I'm sure you did everything by the book. You've done this in Florida. Doing the same thing here isn't different." He assumed I was concerned with something I wasn't. Fine! I was relieved and smiled.

"Do you want to open it?" I asked trying to sound totally innocent.

"No. Put it in the specimen container and seal it. Naleeva wants to be involved in opening any items that fall in the cloak and dagger category." Mark looked at the hinges. "The lid's in really bad shape. Put it in a big plastic garbage bag and then put some tape around it to make it secure."

"No prob—" I never finished. A loud explosion shattered the mid-day jungle noises. It came from an area adjacent to the buildings. It was an area I didn't believe we had entered.

"A mine!" Reading shouted and ran off to see what was happening.

Mark started away, snapped his fingers and turned back to face me. "Can you take care of that? Wrap it, do the recording, and get the boys to take it back to camp."

"Sure." I was sure. *Sure* no one would ever know I'd bungled handling the artifact. I whistled as I pulled a large black garbage bag and a roll of duct tape from my toolkit.

Chapter 37
Mess Tent

"Everybody is accounted for." Mug smiled like the Cheshire Cat. "No casualties in our contingent, but there is a wild hog that has as many holes in him as a block of Swiss cheese."

Everyone sitting around the tables looked relieved.

"That was a loud bang. Was it one of the big landmines?" Dr. Rialto asked.

Mug shook his head. "It was another Bouncing Betty." He spoke loudly, so the rest of the tent's occupants would stop yakking. "Yo! Listen up! Evidently, there are mines sprinkled all around this place. Don't go to any place that hasn't been cleared. The area where old Porky blew up was on the far-left side of the tower and the buildings outside of Berlin Site #4. Stay away from there."

Mug sat down with Mark, Reading, Migdahlia and me. As he did, Migdahlia abruptly excused herself and left. Mug lifted his arm and sniffed. He said, "I need a shower? The beautiful Miss M seems to think so."

He and Reading watched the female's tantalizing curves cross the clearing to the woman's tent. Reading was watching for a different reason. I know my brother ... it had been a while. Mug stopped trying to figure out what was spinning in Migdahlia's pretty head. He shared some things he learned on his pig burial patrol. "I'm sure that where I just came from is going to be added to Little Berlin Site #5. There's a graveyard over there, a fairly large one. The gravestones are elaborate." Mug looked around to see if anyone was close enough to eavesdrop. "The text is in German, and the decorations on them are circa Berlin 1939. There are a couple of mausoleums some with portions built underground. I recognized three names that are household types. Krupp, Richter, and Kleist."

"We need to get over and see what's there." Mark looked around the room for Eduardo. "I have to find Dr. Rialto and tell—"

"I already have, and I've talked to Garret about searching the area for mines. We need to give him some parameters, but..." He leaned closer to us. "Chessie, has Migdahlia ever told you for sure how many people were with her here?"

"No ... not definitively. She said something about having a friend that came with her, and she mentioned that two men stayed behind to be sure she got out safely. But, I'm not sure that was everybody."

Mug stared at me, Mark, and Reading for a few seconds as he decided whether to share his last piece of info. He took a deep breath. "I assume the two corpses were the two that 'stayed behind.' The third person came out with her. Well, when I was over by the graveyard, I found a spot where another mine had gone off. Granted, there wasn't much left. Wild animals and insects did away with most of it, but I found another corpse over there. It still had remnants of flesh on some of the bones. Off a few yards, I found a skull. I'd say male judging from the size and what was left of the clothes. Makes you wonder, doesn't it? Either way: if she had more company or if more company tried to have her."

Chapter 38
Little Berlin, Site #2

"Anyone want to guess how many?" Mark solemnly stared at the three fully exposed lines of fifty-five-gallon drums.

"There are eleven drums in two lines and eight in the other." I could see Mug allotting space for bodies. "Thirty, maybe thirty-five."

Reading nodded, "That's about right if the only things in those drums are skeletons."

Garret said, "I figure a few less."

It remained quiet for several seconds before I said, "Forty-two."

Everyone in the group standing on the edge of the excavation looked at me. "That's pretty exact," Mark said.

I shrugged my shoulders and my face flushed. "Woman's intuition," I mumbled.

The big moment had arrived. We would begin removing the drums and bodies from their resting places. The two doctors had derived a method of removing the burial chamber as nearly intact as possible. Large cradles were built around each set of two or three drums. A beam and hoist system was erected over the pit. Each two or three barrel section would be lifted, records made, and the barrels moved to an area where we would examine and catalog our finds.

"How many remains storage boxes did they send?" Dr. Rialto asked.

Mug looked at a clipboard. "Says here 125." He pointed to a stack of white plastic nested containers. "I had the crew bring fifty."

"You ready?" Sergeant Garret and four of his Marines wanted to begin the process.

Mark said, "Ready, Eduardo?"

Eduardo lifted his head from behind the large video camera he was using to capture the images of the vault's removal. "Yes, ready."

Garret nodded. Hands and arms strained as the multiplying force of the pulley system lifted the first load upwards. After the drums separated, Mark said, "Stop. Now move them apart about six inches." He wrote his observations in the site log while Eduardo filmed and Migdahlia snapped photos. Reading, Ida-Marie, and I would soon be assisting separating the skeletons, placing each in its own collection container, and identify the clothes and any other personal belongings that accompanied each. We'd place all these in collection bags. Naleeva's top priority; we were to be sure to identify the remains by the dog tags wedged in their dental work.

One of those tags would read: Wilson, Bernard T O pos 124-44-3256 USMC L Catholic. Its mate was hidden in a zippered compartment in my makeup case. Regardless of my personal curiosity, our serious work was about to begin.

Chapter 39
Little Berlin, Base Camp

The "dead weight division" of our field team was finally getting to work. That's the title Mug MacAphee had invented for Doctors Dean and Beltran and Elroy Cleggenhiest. Up to the point where we started recovering human remains, all three kept mold from forming on the decks of cards that kept them occupied. Once the collection boxes began flowing to the base camp, Mug erected "the laboratory tent" a twenty-foot square that housed a wide assortment of scientific equipment and its own generator.

Somewhat reluctantly, the three gave up their poker and hearts games and went to work. It didn't take much time to see that both Dr. Dean and Dr. Beltran were experts in their field. In Donald Dean's case, his capabilities weren't confined to genetics and the human genome. His anthropological knowledge approached that of Mark and Eduardo. He found a few mistakes we'd made when we separated the remains and rectified them. We also found that all but one of the mistakes were made by Ida-Marie. Mark and Eduardo shifted her task to be part of one of the shaker screen crews.

When Mark asked Eduardo whether Ida-Marie always

was lax in executing her work assignments, Eduardo's answer surprised us. We'd assumed that Ida-Marie and Eduardo were a team like Mark and me. Eduardo told us, "I don't know. I've known her from our university system and been on some field work trips with her, but she normally works with another archaeologist. My assistant had been scheduled to come, but said she had personal problems and was replaced thirty days before we were to go." The conspiracy theorist in me concocted several far-fetched scenarios. The one truth was: Ida-Marie wasn't as dedicated as the rest of the team members to maintaining archaeological process integrity.

When Ida-Marie was removed from digging, Reading stepped in to fill the gap when Mark asked him. He did admirably. In several ways, Reading's temperament is better suited to the tasks we had to perform than me. He is very patient and disciplined. I've had to learn to adapt those traits when in the field. His attention to the smallest detail fits the work well. Within two days he was a functioning field assistant. Most importantly, Reading did things precisely as instructed; something Ida-Marie was incapable of doing. Since immediate outside security threats to us weren't apparent, Reading's stated purpose for being on the trip had lessened. I knew he could be counted on to resume his original role in an instant.

It appeared our danger from the world outside Little Berlin had ceased. Two of Mug's men and two of Sergeant

Garret's Marines acted as camp security, guarding the base camp and the road to our site. There was no activity. The only excitement was the fleeting glance of a big cat, probably a Jaguar. Landmines were the biggest danger to our safety. We were sure exploding death was scattered around us. Anytime any of us ventured into the woods the threat weighed on our minds. Garret and two of his men were busy clearing the Berlin Site #5. He had removed over sixty mines and was only 40% complete.

After the last drums and the remains they contained were removed, we discovered equipment that had been used by them was buried underneath. It was a mishmash of all sorts of things from K-ration container remains to a 50 caliber machine gun. All were standard US materials. The discipline of meticulously exhuming this find settled into the routine of squared ditches, multitudes of photos, detailed and complete site log entries, and sore backs at the end of the day.

We were nearing three weeks on site. It was evident our time schedule was entirely inadequate to do much more than do a sampling of what lay hidden at the other sites. Mark estimated we had a week left on Site #2. Past clearing and platting the other original four sites, virtually nothing had been accomplished. The discovery of the cemetery added another site, one that was sure to have priority in the eyes of those paying for the expedition.

With the routine came a measure of boredom. With

boredom came some changes. Miccolee Bertonarri emerged from the isolation of the ladies' tent, her books, and her love affair with her cot. I'm sure it was sheer boredom that drove her out of the canvas. To date, Miccolee and Elroy Cleggenhiest were unnecessary additions to our crew.

The five female expedition members found themselves generating increasing interest from the twenty- three males. Relationships began to form. One of Mug's men who spoke several languages showed interest in Miccolee. She was seldom seen; leaving the tent was still a rarity. Migdahlia sought out Reading when we weren't working, and this left me looking for Mark. Ida-Marie split her time between Dr. Beltran and Sergeant Garret, though neither seemed overly enamored. Corporal Cole and one of Mug's men spend increasing time in the mess tent. Love definitely was in bloom. Maybe not love. Sometimes a little lust is inevitable.

It was my curiosity on a day ending our third week at Little Berlin that triggered some discoveries and reactions that ended everything routine and almost ended our lives.

Chapter 40
Little Berlin, Base Camp's Mess Tent

Jim Garret swished his fork through his reconstituted mashed potatoes. He looked forlorn. "This is a plain insult to a boy from Idaho." Reluctantly, he plopped a fork-full in his mouth, frowned, and spoke around the wad of white revolting his taste buds. "First thing I do when I'm on leave is to order me a big baked 'tater."

Garret sat with Mark and me as we inhaled our lunch. "It's prime rib for me," Mark grinned. "We all have our favorite things we miss when we're away." He changed the subject, "How is clearing the mines coming on Site #5?"

"Almost done. I've moved over to the cemetery." Garret grimaced and shoved another load of mashed potato into his mouth. "We haven't found much except in one small area. All the paths in and out are cleared. So are ones leading from the buildings to Site #5."

I asked, "Is it safe to go over and look? I've only seen a small part, and that was before the rest of the brush was cleared."

"Yes, as long as you stay inside the areas marked with the steel pins with blue flaglets on them. Everything is clearly marked. Paths have a green ribbon in their middle."

He thought for a second. "We haven't done much inside the buildings. They could have been booby-trapped, so I'd stay out until we check them."

"I'd like to see the rest of buildings and Mug told me there were cliffs and a stream on the other side. He said it was a fortress." I hoped he'd volunteer to take me.

"He told you right." Garret frowned and shoved his empty plate away from in front of him. "Sorry, Chessie, I have to finish up clearing what's left of the cemetery site. Mark's been over there. Get him to take you."

"I'd love to, but I have to stick around here until Naleeva calls. She left word she wants a progress report this afternoon." Mark tilted his head toward the Sergeant. "Do you think she'd be okay by herself?"

"Sure. Mines aren't a problem anymore so long as you stay in the marked area." Garret hesitated then added. "Two things you need to be careful of over there. We killed three snakes, a Fer-de-lance and a couple of jungle rattlers. Watch where you're stepping. You also have to be real careful around the edge of those drop-offs behind the buildings. The rain has turned that area into slick mud. You fall back there, and you won't stop until you hit the rocks 200 feet down. You know where the path starts, right?"

I nodded and said, "I think I'll take a stroll over there. How far is it, Sergeant?"

"As the crow flies, four or five football fields. Staying on the cleared paths, twice that."

"You need me for anything, Mark? I'll be back in two or three hours." I looked at the sunshine. I was sure it would turn to rain late in the afternoon. "Definitely less than two hours."

Mark grinned, "Be careful. Say, you can do something for me while you're there. Take a camera with you and take some pictures of the buildings and the land behind them. I want to show them to Naleeva. If she calls early, I'll join you over there."

"Okay. I'm going to throw a camera and a few other things in my backpack and then head to Site #5."

Mark nodded and smiled. I wondered if I should add a blanket to the camera, bottles of water, and the 9mm automatic I planned to take.

As I started to leave the tent, Garret said, "If you decide to go to the cemetery, stay away from the areas marked with red stakes. There are areas there that our detection equipment sounded off, but we couldn't find anything. It's best to avoid that spot." Garret got a strange look on his face, one I couldn't read. "Anyway, it's spooky over there, Chessie."

I couldn't tell if he was trying to frighten or patronize me. I'm sure I bristled perceivably. "Don't worry Sergeant. I'm not your typical helpless kitten out in the rain."

"Believe me; I'm sure you're not." Garret leaned back in his chair. "I'm just saying there's something about that area that makes the hair on the back of *my* neck stand up.

It takes something major to do that."

Chapter 41

Little Berlin Site #5, at the buildings

I stared in awe. Since the rest of the underbrush, vines, and saplings were removed, the full extent of the complex was revealed. It was huge with the additional trees and brush removed. The buildings were all built around the outcropping. Most were ruins, the roofs having deteriorated decades ago. The same stonework that made the walls circling the buildings was used to erect the buildings. It made sense. The slabs of rock were the closest available substantial building material. I was sure we'd find the quarry the rock came from a short distance away.

The sun filtered through the leaf canopy overhead. It created a crazy patchwork of light and shadow patches on the ground that presented the illusion of life when the gentle breezes fanned the leaves. The crawling "creatures" added another factor to a scene that was foreboding and threatening enough already. The threat of mines kept my eyes glued to the ground, making sure I stayed in the "cleared" area marked by blue flagged stakes.

I approached one of the openings in the stone fence. Instead of both sides being vertical, one looked as though a giant had taken its fist and smashed the pulverized rocks inward. It didn't take much brain strain to figure what happened. Some type of explosion hit it. I wondered if RPGs were in use in the late 1950's. A bazooka maybe? Part of a steel latch mechanism still remained on the opposite side. The explosion had blown away the gate barring access to the courtyard area. The opening drew me as certainly as a ticket to a Brad Paisley concert would. I looked inside before I stepped through a portal into a violent past. A massive hunk of rusting steel sat on a cracked and crumbled concrete pad. After a minute's study, I was able to identify it as a large generator and a diesel motor. Several yards away, rusting sheet metal had been the generator's fuel tank. I swiveled my head 180° and quickly found what I was looking for ... the ruins of what had been light fixtures. This enclave had definitely been designed as permanent.

Several seconds elapsed before I summoned the courage to step inside. I remembered Mug's comment about the hair standing up on the back of his neck. His comment about the mystique was an understatement. As I took my first few steps inside the compound, I thought of Migdahlia ... here ... without the task force of people that were back in camp. What a gutsy woman ... no, person. My respect for her doubled in that instant.

The ground beneath my feet was a stone paved walkway. To the far left, as Mug said, was the cemetery area. Even from two hundred plus meters the red flags on tall stakes were visible and fluttered their deadly warning.

A shudder passed through my body. The walkway split at a "Y," one trail leading toward the cemetery, the other toward what was a major entrance to the buildings. My feet made the subconscious decision to take the house path. As I approached the rock stairway, my mind suddenly informed me I could be walking the same stones Adolf Hitler had stepped on six decades ago. The thought was mixed with revulsion for the man's deeds and excitement that I could be standing in history's path. The slabs of rock forming the stairs created a wide surface to step on and a uniform height I guessed at fifteen centimeters.

The steps led to a large stone porch that served what I visualized as a double door, probably a "front entrance." The building had been two stories, and part of the upper portion on the second floor was a crumbled heap of ruined material piled on the floor inside the building. As I stood staring into the ruins, I became aware that someone or something was staring at me! Involuntarily, I stepped back, spun around and looked for an intruder. I didn't see a thing.

"Get a grip, Chessie," I told myself. Garret's and Mug's warning not to enter the buildings or wander in areas not yet cleared of mines flashed in my mind like a neon sign. I backed away from the opening like plague resided inside. For the first time, I noticed that the other side of the porch provided my first glimpse of what lies behind the building complex. I walked over to the porch edge and gazed at a spectacular view.

The porch was forty yards from the drop off I'd been warned about. A jungle-covered miniature mountain rose from the valley that disappeared under the rim of what was a canyon. I'd been told steep cliffs were behind the buildings, and below that, the boulder-strewn Nancaguazu River. The mountain sides were lush green. It appeared to me the growth was virgin covering. Palm trees mixed with hardwoods. One spot was light red colored with large areas of tan where a steep drop exposed the rock base. I decided to take a closer look.

Rocks formed a staircase identical to the one I'd climbed on the opposite side of the porch. It led to another stone path that wandered toward the rear of the buildings and valley below. I walked along it, captivated by the scene unfolding in front of me. The view made my surroundings less threatening, and the tension in my body lessened. My focus left any potential threats and centered on the painting nature provided. I could understand someone picking this place to live.

The path ended at a stone bench built, I'm sure, as a place to enjoy the view. The river was visible, roaming off to the left and right, but the area immediately behind the buildings wasn't in view. I hesitated. The warning about slick mud, coupled with being uncomfortable with heights, kept me from taking the first step onto the grass and weed covered soil. After debating whether to go further, I took one exploratory step. The ground was wet but felt secure beneath me. Curiosity won. If I stayed a couple of steps from where the edge of the drop-off occurred, I was sure I'd be safe.

I gingerly picked my steps and covered the remaining forty feet to what looked to be the drop-off's edge. A step-and-a-half from the sharp drop, I halted and looked down. It was as described. The height was dizzying. The slope dropped away at a severe angle and, at a spot seventy or so feet down, disappeared.

The sheer face of the cliff was below. A mild case of vertigo tried to disorient me, but I stayed rock stable. I could see some curves in the river below that weren't obscured by the cliff edge. Imagined or real, I fancied I heard the faint brushing sound of the rush of waters. Suddenly, the distant roar of a big cat came from the gorge below and made the view surreal. I tried to spot the Jaguar or Puma.

"Aaahhhhhh!" I screamed as I felt someone shoving against my back. I tumbled forward, over the edge, and immediately began sliding face first and face down. The soft mud and slippery weeds acted like the snow on a ski run. I desperately grasped at clumps of grass, weeds and tried to dig my toes in the mud to slow my skid to the cliff and death.

My hands found something that arrested my progress. The rest of my body arced around and when it stopped, I was facing up the slope with my arm stretched from a two-inch diameter sapling that my hand had a true death grip upon. I looked up. No one was at the top of the slope. I tried to use my toes to push up my body up the slope to take the strain off of the arm that was keeping me alive. One toe found nothing but space. I was that close to the cliff's edge.

Using the toe that was in contact with the earth, one arm pulling against the sapling and the other arm that used my hand to claw into the mud, I worked my body to the point my shoulders were even with the tiny tree that was my savior. At least, both toes touched soil when I pointed them downward. I put my face down for several seconds ... breathing hard, giving thanks I wasn't dead on the rocks below, and wondering, what next?

Chapter 42

Little Berlin Site #5, on the side of the cliff

My heart rate slowed, but it certainly hadn't returned to normal. Reading referred to things like what had just happened to me as, "Oh, shit!" moments. I looked up at the crest of the hill, hoping I'd see a familiar face and fearing I might see a strange one. I briefly considered screaming for help, but I quickly realized that if the person on top realized I hadn't fallen to my death, the individual might try to finish the job.

It didn't take long for me to realize my best course of action would be to wait it out. Trying to climb the steep hillside had better than a 95% chance of failure. Failure meant I'd be dead. I looked at the six grooves cut into the muddy slope. Two were from my hands, two were from my toes that had frantically tried to stop my slide. The other two evenly spaced shallow furrows told me how soft the mud was. They were made by my breasts. Patience, I told myself. Someone would come looking for me. Eventually!

The survey of my predicament showed me how lucky I had been. Three feet on either side of the slide marks and I now would be being fitted with wings. After giving thanks for my good luck, anger focused on whoever pushed me and replaced my feelings of good fortune. This gave me another reason to stay alive. I'd get even.

I laid my head to one side and waited. Any time you're forced to wait and have nothing to do, time lengthens. In my situation, it was stretching out to a mental breaking point. My reassurance was that I'd told Mark I'd be back in two hours. He'd start looking for me when I didn't return to camp.

I looked for something to preoccupy my time. Counting seconds, minutes, and hours was futile. I'd constantly lose track of the count, so I quickly abandoned the effort. My mind replaced counting with trying to determine who shoved me over the cliff's edge. That worked for a while. Who was it? Was it someone from our group? Was it some outside interloper whose presence I'd felt when I stared into the building minutes before being shoved? Migdahlia's words about her grandmother's warning that this place was haunted came to mind. Did I have a paranormal experience ... something I believed was the fabric of novelists, not reality? This conjecture led to more questions than answers. I abandoned it. I decided to follow the shadows made by trees on the ruins to assess time's passage. The creep was so imperceivably slow my frustration rose, not lowered. This ended when the overcast deepened, and the shadows disappeared. With the thickening clouds and their darkening, my anxiousness increased. Thought of clinging to the mud in a driving rainstorm was terrorizing.

I felt sure two hours had passed long ago. Three, possibly four, must have transpired. Still, no one showed, the clouds looked angrier, and fear clawed at me. If I could have reached a panic button, I'd have pushed it. Yes, the first peal of thunder put me in full panic mode. Winds increased. The eerie sound they made whistling through the trees intensified my apprehension. They almost made a human sound, as if someone was calling my name. Then I realized someone was!

"Chessie!" I screamed, "I'm on the cliff. Help me!" "Chessie!" I screamed louder, "I'm behind the buildings. I need help! I'm hanging on the cliff!" Reading's voice shouted, "We hear you. Yell so we can locate you."

"I'm here, I'm here, I'm here," I continued to scream. Three faces appeared on the ridge above me, Reading, Mark, and Sergeant Garret. I wasn't sure which one yelled, "Don't move!"

"Move? I can't move or the only direction I'll go is down! Get me a rope!"

I saw Garret disappear. Mark and Reading exchanged a few words, and Mark disappeared too. Reading called down to me, "Don't panic."

That made me angry, "Don't panic?! You get your ass down here and tell me that!"

"We told you to be careful back here," Reading

sounded like a parent rebuking his child.

"I was. Explain that to whoever pushed me down here."

"Somebody pushed you?" Reading screamed, "Who was it?"

"I don't know!" I started to cry and hated it. "Reading just get me out of here."

"I'll go see if I can help speed them up," Reading said.

I shrieked, "Hell no! Don't you dare leave me alone!"

Reading turned away from me. I heard him shout and they shouted back, but the words were too muffled to understand. Within a few minutes, Garret and Mark reappeared. Garret asked, "Do you think you can get this rope around you?"

I thought for a second. "Do I have to tie it?"

"No, it already has a loop on the end. You'll just have to slip into it," Mark shouted.

"I can get it over my head and under one arm. I'm not sure I want to risk letting loose of this little tree. It's the only thing keeping me from ..." I looked up at them imploringly. "Can you pull me out that way?"

The three talked briefly. Garret said, "Yes, we can do that. You'll have to be sure you keep your arm down at your side while we're pulling you up. I'm going to tie a slip knot in the rope, so the loop stays open, and you can get in. I'll throw the rope past you then pull it back even with your head and shoulders. Don't try to catch it on the way down! The slip knot will pull out, and the loop will pull tight as we haul you up."

I closed my eyes so I wouldn't be tempted to reach for the rope. It made a swishing noise as it went past me. In seconds, I felt the rope against my side and arm not holding the sapling. I watched the loop appear and stop at my shoulder. Reading and Mark were talking to me, but I wasn't listening. The only thing in my universe was getting that rope around me and getting off the cliff.

Deliberately and slowly I put my arm that didn't have a death grip on the sapling through the loop. After that, I used my free hand to pull the loop over my head. The men on top yelled, "Good," and I felt the slip knot open and the rope pull tight against my neck and underarm. One of them shouted, "Keep your arm down at your side no matter how much it hurts!" The rope was tight.

Mark said, "Chessie, when you let loose of the tree, grab the rope with that hand. We're going to pull you straight up half way then slide you off to one side. It gets more level and you can crawl up from there, so you don't get hurt any more than you have to. Understand?"

"Yes. Just do it."

The rope tried to crush my armpit and neck as I slid up the hill. They dragged me a lot easier than I thought hauling my body up the hill would be. Garret said, "Okay Chessie, we're going to reposition so we can pull you to a spot where it isn't so steep."

The three men kept tension on the rope as they moved

thirty feet to the side. I saw the shelf they were going to pull me on to ... its slope was 30° compared to the 70° to which I'd been plastered. Garret yelled, "Ready?"

"Go!" I replied.

The rope tightened again, and I was dragged another twenty feet to and over the lip of the shelf. Reading asked, "Can you get on your hands and knees and crawl? We'll control the rope so you'll be safe."

"I think so." My body protested, but I was able to get onto my hands and knees.

Mark cautioned me. "Move straight up the rope. The edge of the shelf is only a few feet to your left. You don't want to roll off of it."

"Okay." I began to crawl the remaining fifty feet to Garret, Mark, Reading and level ground. With each movement of my hands and knees, I felt exhilaration building. I was actually going to make it!

I was fifteen feet from them when I heard a metallic, "Plop."

Garret yelled, "Mine!"

I froze, waiting for the explosion and my death. It didn't come.

"It's a dud," Reading said. He watched the 'Bouncing Betty' bound down the hillside to the vertical cliff's edge then disappear.

"Oh, shit!" Mark exclaimed.

I quickly scrambled up the fifteen remaining feet to the

three men and collapsed beneath them. Physically and mentally, I was exhausted.

"Right here." I pointed to the spot where I had stood when I was shoved. The three men stared at the ground. Reading's trained detective eye read the mud quickly. "Someone has obliterated all the footprints. See how the area has been rubbed with a stick or something similar. Anyplace a track was made has been wiped out all the way back to the stairway and porch. The rest of the ground isn't disturbed."

"That's a dead end," Sergeant Garret said.

"Not really." Reading walked back to the rock stairs and porch retracing the steps I'd made hours before. He found my footprints in the thin layer of dirt covering the stone walkway to the stairs where I'd ascended the porch ... and none others. Reading said, "I think it tells us this. Someone thought we could identify their footprint and that tells us they are probably part of our group. Whoever pushed Chessie probably was hiding inside the building. That means that a person knows a lot more about this place than we do because I don't see any prints indicating they entered the building from here. They came *through* the building."

We stood silently as drops of rain started falling. The four of us all thought the same thing ... *we have a killer among us*.

Chapter 43
Outside Mess Tent at Base Camp

"Garret's off to tell Mug now. I'm sure he'll call Naleeva." Mark shrugged his shoulders. "Who can we trust?"

"My thinking is there are only three of us we can be sure about." Reading spoke softly to Mark and me. We stood a hundred feet away from the mess tent in the cleared area. We'd chosen the spot so no one could overhear our discussion. Mark nodded. I took a deep breath. I was still so shaken from my brush with death I wasn't mentally sharp. I trusted Reading to think for me for the moment.

"Surely, it's only one or a few in our group that's doing things to sabotage this expedition." Mark looked at both of us. "The problem is determining who?"

"I'm afraid it's more complicated than that. When you're in something like this, you have to consider every possibility. That means, however improbable; you have to assume anything is possible. What if there is someone, or even multiple people, in hiding around here we don't know about? What if they are working with someone from our group? Is one of our people solely responsible? Are there two or more working together?" Reading took a breath.

"Right now, we can't say for sure. All we can do is to

assess individuals we think are the least likely to be our enemy." Enemy! The word slapped me in the face. We had an enemy, probably among us, and that enemy was a determined one.

"What we can do is make some guesses about whom we can afford to place some trust in and whom we can't," Reading said. "Let's talk about our friends and put them in trustable and questionable groups."

"Okay," Mark said, "I'd say we can trust Naleeva. Why would she put us here if she didn't want us here?"

Reading nodded. "I'd put Sergeant Garret and all his Marines in the trustable group. He handpicked them from his local garrison force. They weren't brought in for this."

"What about Mug?" I asked.

Mark and Reading looked at each other. Mark said, "My best guess is we can trust him. He was selected by Naleeva. There's history there. If we trust her, I'd say we have to trust MacAphee." He shook his head. "As far as his people are concerned, I don't know. We need to know how they ended up with him. None of us know much about them, I guess they go into questionable until we find out more."

"That leaves our core people." Reading asked Mark, "What do you think about Eduardo? You've had more contact than anyone else."

Mark thought for several seconds before answering. "I think Eduardo is all right. He has the normal amount of resentment that you could experience if you have someone invading your space. That's why I'd say we can trust him.

If he were trying to do us in, wouldn't he be more likely to show resentment and hostility? He seems to actually like us."

I cast my vote. "I think we can trust him. He was as surprised as we were when we found those steel drums on the radar."

"How about Ida-Marie?" Reading asked.

"Personally, I don't like her." I was being honest. "That doesn't mean she's the one."

Mark shook his head. "Her lack of interest in keeping site discipline bothers me. It makes me wonder if she's a phony with some knowledge of archaeology. She has a better knowledge of martial arts than the old Spanish missions which is why she was supposedly sent with us. I think she goes on the suspicious list."

"Have either of you had much contact with Petro?" Mark asked us.

"I haven't spoken a hundred words to the man since we got to camp," I said.

"Sorry," Reading shrugged his shoulders, "I haven't had enough face time with the man to get that kind of read on him. He's damned smart and observant, I've seen enough to know that."

"What do you think?" Mark asked.

Reading remained silent for ten seconds. "If we don't

know about somebody I say we put them in the suspicious group."

Mark and I nodded.

"Besides Dr. Dean and Cleggenhiest that leaves Migdahlia and Miccolee. I don't think we have to worry about Don and Elroy. They would have gone down with the plane, know what I mean?" Reading paused. "Miccolee is in the tent so much I can't see her as a threat. Chessie, what do you think?"

"Most of the time I've been around her she's been asleep on the cot or had her nose stuck in a book." I snorted. "I guess we need to put her in the 'don't know' group, but my impression is if she was in a butt kicking contest with a grasshopper, I'd give two to one odds on the hopper."

We all looked at each other. Everyone liked the beautiful young woman, but she had the most knowledge of the site and, we guessed, the buildings. Migdahlia. She had to go on the suspect list.

I said the inevitable. "I hate this, but Migdahlia has to be a question. My gut tells me not, but ..."

Mark looked torn. "She has the knowledge, but why try to get this expedition in here? She was the driving force to set this up. I like her. It's hard to believe she'd try to kill you, Chessie. She seems to like you a lot."

"I like her, too." Reading took a deep breath. "Leave it up to me to find out more. We've developed the start of a relationship. I think I can find out one way or the other." He looked my way warning me to keep my mouth shut. "Until I do, she's on the suspect list."

Chapter 44
At the edge of the cliff, Little Berlin Site #5

"Mug, I'm sure. I was shoved hard enough. I remember my head snapping back some." His questions irked me, but I knew he had to ask them.

"You never saw who it was?" Mug asked.

"No. I was sliding face first with my nose in the mud. I was only interested in not going over the cliff." I shivered as I thought of clinging to the hillside. "By the time I looked back up here, they were gone."

Most everyone from our expedition was assembled at the place I'd been shoved. I wondered why. Everyone divided their time between staring at me and the steep slope leading to the sheer drop. Only Sergeant Garret and his Marines weren't there. They were guarding the camp and the road in.

Mug positioned himself in front of us like a choirmaster before a choir. He examined everyone's face as he spoke to us. "Chessie says she was pushed and I believe her." He paused again scrutinizing everyone. Later Reading told me he thought Mug had taken us there to gauge each individual's expression looking for a hint of guilt. Reading told me it was a waste of time. Professionals don't show guilt.

Mug continued, "That means either we have guests we don't know about or we have someone willing to commit murder among us. Until I figure out which is true, I don't want anybody going anywhere by themselves. I'm going to team everybody up. It's the 'buddy system.' You take care of each other. If you get up to take a leak in the middle of the night, your buddy goes with you. If you want to go into the woods to catch a butterfly, your buddy goes with you." He hesitated. His eyes became harsh. "If something happens to your buddy, I'm assuming you did it until I find out otherwise. Whenever you can, go in groups of four." He shook his head. "I know it's a pain in the ass, but I brought you all in here in one piece, and I'm getting you out of here in one piece."

"What about our work groups? Chances are our buddy won't always be in the same group." Mark was sure we'd be separated by sexes as a necessity.

Mug rubbed his forehead for a second and came up with a solution. "Here's what we'll do. Stay with your buddy until I form our groups at the mess tent each morning. Stay with your workgroup to the sites and back. Pick up your buddy after supper." He looked for objections, but there weren't any. "I'll split my group up later. Mark, you're with Eduardo. Don, you're with Petro. Elroy, you're with Reading. Miccolee you're with Ida-Marie." Mug looked at me. "Migdahlia you're with Chessie. I'll hook up with one of my people. For you folks, the buddy system starts now. Get back to camp, get a night's sleep, and be ready to get back to work tomorrow morning." As we connected with our partner, Mug added, "Be damned careful. The snakes and the mines are a hell-of-a-lot less dangerous than two-legged monsters."

Chapter 45
Little Berlin Campsite Latrine

The quiet that settled over Migdahlia and me as we made a night-time stroll from our tent to the latrine was uncomfortable. It was the first time since Mug divided us into teams we were completely alone. I tried not to show my suspicions, but my emotions are as hard to hide as my size "D's." Migdahlia became quiet after a few attempts at starting a conversation with me that ended with my guarded, three or four-word responses. I'm not known for my unwillingness to talk, so it was apparent the last six hours had created a problem, real or imagined between us.

She stopped, reached out, and grabbed my shirt. I spun around assuming a self-defense posture. Migdahlia said, "I know you are suspicious. Please, it wasn't me. I am as scared as you are."

I remained quiet for a few seconds. The only sound was the drone of the gasoline generator that furnished power to light our campsite until 10:00 PM. Migdahlia's features were obscured by shadows cast by standing with her back to the lights. I shuffled my feet so I could see the light strike her face. The young woman was smart; I could see she knew exactly what I was doing. "I'd like to believe that,' I said.

"What can I do to convince you? The three friends who came with me when I discovered this place are all dead!" There was anguish in her features. "You know about the two that were found here. My other friend was struck and killed by a truck. It was most mysterious. No autopsy was performed, though his parents requested one."

"They're dead, but you're alive." I took a deep breath and shook my head slowly. I extended my hand and stopped just short of her cheek. "Some people are good actors, very good actors. Right now, I can't be sure you aren't one of them. I can't afford to make that kind of mistake."

"That is fair. You must consider that I am in the same situation. Someone wants me as dead as they wanted to make you. They have tried. A 150-pound cylinder of chlorine gas was placed in my apartment, and the valve was opened. I was gone, but the gas nearly killed my neighbors on either side and below me. If I had been there, I would have surely died." The fear on her face looked real.

My brother was training me well. I asked, "What did the police say?"

"They said they found out who purchased the cylinder. It was an ex-boyfriend. But ... no one has seen him since. He has disappeared as if he is dead and buried." It was obvious that was what Migdahlia thought happened to him.

"Give me another suspect." I held up my index finger. "Just one will do. Of everybody here, you're the only one who knows their way around the site. No one can swear they saw you at the time when someone pushed me. You say you were at Site #2. There's no proof you were."

"I will tell you what I believe. There is someone here that is not of our party. I know there was someone when I was here before." Migdahlia put her hands together as if she was praying. "I know you won't believe this. My friend and I saw two men dressed in uniforms. German Wehrmacht uniforms. And ..." Migdahlia hesitated, having a hard time vocalizing the rest of her comment. "They walked through a wall. My grandmother said there are spirits here. I believe there are ghosts and I saw two." There was fear in her eyes I didn't believe she could fake. "Please!" she implored.

I stared at her for a few seconds. "I believe you saw something. Whether they were ghosts, well I'm not sure of that." I put my hands around hers and said, "I'll trust you until I can't." She looked relieved. And ... I hoped I wasn't making a big mistake.

Chapter 46
Little Berlin campsite, Field Forensics Tent

"Somebody needs to know this besides me." Dr. Donald Dean's face was far more serious than I was used to seeing. His normal smile had turned upside-down. In the tent with him were Mark, Reading, Mug, Sergeant Garret and me. "There will be six of us that will know what I believe happened here. Mark, Mug, and I agree that all of us aren't involved in what I believe ..." He didn't finish.

He motioned to a stack of the white plastic boxes the human remains were stored in. "Showing is easier than telling." Dr. Dean removed the top container and placed it on the examination table we were seated around. After unlocking and lifting the lid, he removed a pelvis from the box. Dean pointed at a round hole through it. "That is a hole made from a 50 caliber machine gun. Until I was sure, found enough slugs, looked at enough remains, I didn't want to believe what I was finding. Germans didn't use fifties. Those slugs were fired from a Browning air-cooled machine gun. That's an American weapon. I bet they were fired from the machine gun we found buried under the steel drums. The slugs were fired into the backs of two-thirds of the men's remains we've recovered." I could see the edge of the hole confirmed the Dr.'s theory regarding the bullets direction. "I'm sure these men came on a mission, did it, and were silenced ... forever."

Stunned silence filled the tent. After a full minute of quiet, Mug asked, "Are you sure?"

"There are forty-two sets of remains. Twenty-eight show evidence of being shot from the rear or nearly so. All of those shot in the back was shot with the fifty." He pointed to another pile of containers. "The ones in those stacks died in various ways you'd expect in combat. Most died from 7mm bullets, four from grenades or mines, one was killed with a knife."

Mug shook his head, "I can't believe that. Where are the German bodies? Maybe the Germans, or whoever they fought, over-powered these guys and executed them. Who would have done it if it was us, another group? That doesn't make sense, because you still have more people to silence."

"It does explain a lot of things, Mug," Reading said. "Think about it. The people that crashed the plane we were supposed to be on had to be from the States. Not finding this is a good reason to want us from coming here. What really bothers me is how intense the effort is to keep this quiet. I know about the history thing and all that, but everybody that was in government then is dead or close to it. It's like somebody that has a direct tie to the assassinations is orchestrating this whole thing."

"Where are the German bodies?" Mug repeated.

"We found one," Mark said. "We've only run GPR over a small portion of the land; they could be in a mass grave or scattered all over. It means we have to look until we find them or prove they aren't here. If we find a lot of bodies, then Don is probably correct."

"Why in the hell send us down here if they wanted to keep this a secret? I know Naleeva had all kinds of support in getting this project approved. I can't believe the government is behind this." Mug was adamant.

I looked at Mug and shook my head. "The whole government isn't after us, just a few assholes that have some reason that is dangerous for them if this is discovered."

"If what we suspect is true, we have to assume that whoever isn't going to be happy for us to come marching out of the jungle with all our information and proof. It means we have to be careful as hell. I don't see how they could make us disappear. Too many know about us being here. But ... they might try." Mark thought as he talked. "Don, you have to be sure all this is kept locked and protected." He straightened as though struck by electric. "Does Dr. Beltran know about this?"

"We've never talked about it, but I don't see how he couldn't have made the same deductions I've made. The man is smart," Dr. Dean said.

Mug growled, "This isn't something we can keep secret from the rest of the people here. They're going to find out if they haven't already. I'm getting everybody together tomorrow and tell them."

"Yes, it's better to tell everybody than for them to find out and think we were plotting against the rest." Mark shrugged his shoulders. "They have to participate in anything we do."

"What next?" Reading asked.

"I think we should try to find the bodies we think are here. If we do, it tells us a lot." Mark shook his head. "Finding them isn't going to be easy. This is a big area."

"I don't know about that." Sergeant Garret pointed toward the buildings. "If this place was assaulted, you can bet that whoever was defending it stayed inside or wasn't far away. My guess is we'll find the bodies close to the gun positions or in the complex. I wouldn't want to fight a trained mobile force in the open if I had digs like those buildings to hole up in."

"We start looking for them tomorrow. I'll clear it with Naleeva." Mug took a breath. "What a frigging mess."

I looked at Mug and shook my head. "No, Mug. A mess is something you sweep into a pan and throw in the garbage. My life isn't ready for that."

Chapter 47
Little Berlin, Site #4

Mug wasn't a happy camper. Holding a survey rod was a waste of his time, or so he maintained. He couldn't understand Mark and Eduardo's stubborn insistence on maintaining their archaeological procedures and standards. Site #4 was being enlarged on the side of the buildings away from the graveyard. It took time to check for mines and clear it. Mug understood that, but he couldn't cope with the delay the meticulous measuring and mapping caused. It was the second day since Dr. Dean told us his theory of how the bodies of the Marines got shot and that evidence buried. He growled, "This is a damned waste of time!"

"Patience my friend," Eduardo grinned as he spoke. He shouted information for me to enter in the site log book.

Patience was a virtue Mug lacked. "We should start running that radar machine right now, find what we are looking for, then go back and map this place afterward."

"Once you find what we are looking for do you think those who run this project would let us prepare properly? No, they would say, dig now." Eduardo put his hands on his hips.

"Just don't do what they say."

"Sure," I said, "And if Naleeva gives you a direct order to make us, you're going to disobey it?"

"Shit, let's just get this over." Mug took his frustration out on the rod, his knuckles turning white as he tried to strangle it.

Eduardo bent over and gazed into the theodolite eyepiece, "Okay, move—"

"Freeze what you're doing folks." Mark came striding from around the corner of a building. His face was grim. "I just came from where Garret and his crew are clearing booby traps and mines. We think we found what we're looking for."

"By the graveyard?" I asked. "No. Inside the buildings."

~ ~ ~ ~ ~

The corridor we were walking was blasted out of solid rock. It was wide enough to allow three of us to walk side-by-side on its downward sloping floor. A light from deep inside sent enough rays to let us get a deep twilight view of the passage as we traversed it. I could see a gray wall illuminated at the end where there was a 90° turn in the tunnel. We reached it at what I guessed was forty yards from the entrance. When we made the right turn, a few more yards of tunnel ended in a very large storage area. I saw Sergeant Garret, Corporal Cole and two other Marines were illuminated by electric lights. The power was furnished by a generator that chugged ominously in the far corner of a five-car garage-sized space. Garret's crew and the light system slipped from my notice as I stood in the entrance to the room.

Edward exclaimed, "Madre de Dios!"

Mug whistled and Reading, who'd joined us, said, "Oh, shit!" A ghastly site monopolized our complete attention.

The entire warehouse was filled with bodies, burned when they were left here. The bodies were arranged neatly in rows against one wall. Piles of charred materials that defied instant recognition filled the rest of the room. A few items could be identified ... part of a chair, charred gasoline cans, a mattress, what appeared to be an opened safe, and smashed plates. The rest was gray-black heaps of rubble.

Mark asked, "Did you get a count?"

Garret nodded. "Sixty-three here. Corporal Cole found five more in a side room down another passage. There may be more. We have another third of the complex to check before we're done." He pointed to some blackened objects piled in a corner. I recognized the distinct shape of Nazi helmets. Garret added. "Looks like it's time to bring Cleggenhiest here to see what he can tell us about the scraps that are left."

I walked to the bodies and knelt looking at the remains. Some scraps of cloth, boots, and other items on the bodies didn't completely incinerate. I wondered why until I realized how a confined area like the one we were in would run out of oxygen. In fact, I wondered how they got them to burn at all. I looked at Garret, and he anticipated my question. "Flame-thrower." As I scanned the remains, I was shocked. A third of the skulls belonged to women and children. The assault had been ruthless.

Mug said, "Everybody listen. We can't start work until Sergeant Garret rigs the generator outside and runs power chords in here. I don't want everybody dead from carbon monoxide poisoning."

We left the room and made our way back to the outside. Halfway back, Garret turned off the lights, plunging us in darkness. The sunlit entrance was truly the light at the end of the tunnel.

I noticed my safety-mate wasn't with the group. "Where's Migdahlia?"

"She went in, looked, got emotional, and asked to leave. She's outside somewhere," Mark answered.

"Where's Ida-Marie?" Eduardo asked.

Mug shook his head. "Don't know. When I got Miccolee from the tent, she wasn't there. I looked around some before I brought Dean, Beltran, and the rest over here. I guess she'll get an individual guided tour. Any volunteers?"

Chapter 48
Site # 5 and the women's tent
Little Berlin Camp area

Migdahlia was an emotional wreck as we walked the quarter mile from the buildings to the campsite. She plainly needed a tree to lean on, and Reading provided the trunk. When he offered his arm, she hugged it like a small child hugging a parent. Migdahlia stumbled along at Reading's side in a thought world that transported her to some spot whose location we could only guess.

I tried to imagine I'd just viewed the remains of the massacre of my family. Shivering, I understood her deep emotional reaction. Imagining was bad enough ... what must the actual experience be like to endure? Migdahlia cried softly but said nothing. Reading was wise enough to maintain the silence. The whole group walked at her pace, cognizant of the turmoil inside her.

Clouds blew in, and within minutes, a light drizzle mixed rain with our body's perspiration. It was cooling but was a harbinger of what was to come. Before we reached the campsite, the clouds were darkening and black storms were on the horizon. Lightning flashes captured our eyes and claps of thunder reached our ears. We were still more than a hundred yards from the camp opening when a blazing bolt struck so near the thunder was instantaneous, and the smell of ozone filled the air. Mug yelled, "Run for the Mess Tent!" It was an unnecessary command. Most of us were in a full sprint before the second word left his mouth.

We straggled into the tent in twos and threes, a gaggle of soaked geese. Water poured from our clothes, saturating the floors. Only Reading and Migdahlia continued at their slow pace, one who didn't care, one who refused to abandon someone in distress.

After Reading and Migdahlia entered the tent, Mug did a head count. Sergeant Garret and his people were still at Site #5 finding a way to illuminate the storage grotto without poisoning us all, so he began with his men and accounted for all of them. When he finished counting noses, everyone except for one person was accounted for, Ida-Marie. He was obviously concerned when he asked, "When was the last time anyone saw Ida-Marie?"

Everyone looked at each other with searching vacant stares. I spoke when it seemed no one else would. "I saw her at the latrine, after breakfast. Miccolee, you were with her. Where did you go next?"

"Oh, that far back? We walked to our tent to change shoes. She told me to go ahead to the mess tent. Last time I saw her, she was sitting on her cot." Miccolee smiled.

"You're supposed to stay together!" Mug was not happy.

"She said she'd be fine."

"When did you go back to the tent?" Mug asked. "Around noon. Dr. Dean and Dr. Beltran walked me over."

Miccolee smiled again, "See, Mug, I follow the rules."

"We have to find her quick." Mug peeked at the weather. It was raining hard, but the lightning had moved on. "Reading, you and I will check her tent and the area around it. Mark and Eduardo, you two check the latrine and that area. Don and Petro, will you two check the forensics tent?" All nodded agreement and promptly left to find our missing comrade.

$$\sim \sim \sim \sim \sim$$

Migdahlia, Miccolee, and I sat talking about the impossible conditions our personal hygiene was suffering, when first the sound of one, then rapidly, a second and a third pistol shot came from around the women's tent. I heard Reading's calm voice and Mug's excited one. Their voices came from inside our tent. The flap was pushed back; Reading appeared with a still writhing serpent in hand. He tossed it into the grass. Reading went back inside.

One of Mug's men asked, "Damn, do you think a snake bit that old gal?"

"Nah! It wouldn't have the nerve," another said.

"Could you tell what kind it was?"

"No, but it had a heavy body and bright colors. I'd guess one of those Crossed Pit Vipers."

The second man scratched his cheek before saying,

"You can bet it was poisonous or they wouldn't have shot it."

The first man repeated, "You think it bit her?"

"No. If it did the snake would die, not her." There were restrained half-laughs.

The questions everyone had were answered when Reading, Mug, and Ida-Marie exited the woman's tent and walked toward them. Other than being more disheveled than normal Ida-Marie looked fine.

$\sim\ \sim\ \sim\ \sim\ \sim$

"I don't remember a thing." Ida-Marie sat at the table while Mug grilled her.

"Let's go to the last thing you do remember."

Ida-Marie squeezed her eyes shut, trying to remember. "After Miccolee left, I laid back on the cot a few minutes. The bugs were biting so I got up to go to the mess tent and work. I remember I didn't feel well. When I leaned over to unzip the tent ... I ... I guess I passed out."

Dr. Dean and Dr. Beltran hovered around her like flies circling road-kill.

"Miccolee says you weren't in the tent when we came to get her. If you were passed out how did you get out of there?" Mug wasn't buying her story.

"I don't know. I was out until you shook me and woke me up."

Mug put his hands on his hips and looked skeptical.

Ida-Marie snarled, "I don't know, you son-of-a- bitch!"

Dr. Dean interrupted. "She's probably telling you the truth." He pointed to a red spot on the back of her neck. He asked, "The bug bit you on the neck?"

"Uh-huh."

"I'm guessing that bug was a hypodermic needle." Dr. Dean gently rubbed the dime-sized blemish. "Somebody put you out."

Mug asked, "Did you unzip the tent fly?"

"I don't remember."

"How did you get back into your cot?" he asked.

"I don't remember."

"Did you leave the tent unzipped?" Mug was insistent. "That viper could have bit you. Never ever leave your tent open."

"I don't know if I ever touched the zipper. How in the Hell can I know if I left it unzipped!" Ida-Marie's eyes had fire flickering in them.

Mug turned to Miccolee. "Ida-Marie was not in the tent when we came to get you?"

"No."

"You're sure?"

"Yes."

Mug's eyes went from one to the other. They finally settled on Ida-Marie. "Either you were sleepwalking, or you were out, or," he turned to stare at Miccolee, "You're lying. One of you has to be."

Both looked indignant, both puffed up like toads, both

looked like they had something to hide.

Chapter 49
Women's tent at
Little Berlin Camp area

"Reading said the snake was under your cot." I passed along what my brother told me.

"Shit happens." Ida-Marie's answer was glib, but her face showed fear.

"Ahhh, that could be a bit more than manure. Getting shot-up with some kind of drug and having a deadly poisonous snake in your tent at the same time is a big coincidence, don't you think?" I repeated Reading's conspiracy theory in my words.

"I don't believe someone put a knock-out drug in me." Ida-Marie was adamant. "Every time a bug bites me, I get a blotch like that. Everybody is becoming afraid of their shadows."

"How did the tent get open and you get back in your cot?" Migdahlia asked.

"I don't know. Probably, I unzipped it, felt bad and wandered back to my cot. I really can't say."

"Miccolee says you weren't in the tent when Mug came looking for the two of you." I looked at Miccolee, and she nodded.

Ida-Marie remained quiet for several seconds before

glaring at Miccolee and in an icy tone said, "Miccolee is a liar."

Miccolee didn't answer, she laughed.

Chapter 50
Inside the building storage area on Site #5

"Not again!" Mark moaned. The fragile lighting system that illuminated the cavern containing the burnt bodies and materials from the compound had failed once more. We were in complete darkness.

"Everybody stay where you are. I'll get Sergeant Garret to get the generator going." Mug was in the entrance to the huge room when the lights went out. He yelled loud enough to be heard in the U.S. "Hey, Garret, get the lights back on!"

There was a muffled assent, and within a few seconds, we had light. The length of the lightweight cables required to feed electricity from the generator outside, to the electric fixtures deep in the buildings, created such a large load that the circuit breakers frequently shut down the system.

I was on my knees separating, collecting, and documenting parts of a body and artifacts that we believed were connected to it. Elroy Cleggenhiest knelt next to me. He held part of a uniform in his hand that hadn't burned. We believed it had clothed the remains I was collecting. Cleggenhiest provided a running commentary on whatever object he examined.

"This uniform is from a member of the SS. This was

black. The stitching is all wrong for something that was made in the Reich." He turned the piece of cloth over in his hands. "That would be natural. Even ten years after the war, new clothing would be needed to replace worn-out pieces and uniforms that no longer fit."

"This guy was a member of the SS?" I asked. Cleggenhiest grinned. "He won't hurt you now." The skull in my hands was now more ominous.

Involuntarily, I extended it away from my body. I shivered, and Cleggenhiest laughed. He said, "I doubt this individual spent much time gassing people. Can you guess at how old he was?"

I looked at the dental work in the skull. There was little wear on the molars and little dental work. "I'd guess twenty-five to thirty."

"If this happened in 1958 or later as is supposed, let's see, if he was twenty-eight, he would have been fifteen at the war's end. That's seven years older than me at the same time. We probably experienced many of the same things. Went hungry. Saw death." Cleggenhiest's smile was one of knowing ... not with one touch of humor.

"You're eighty-one?" I was shocked. He didn't look or act it. My guess had been he was in his late sixties. Then the full import of his words sunk through my thick skull. "You were there!"

"Yes, *young* lady, I was there. No, my family members were not party members. Yes, for the most part, they supported Herr Hitler. No, fortunately, they weren't involved or even aware of the Holocaust until near the war's end. Yes, they suffered, but not like those who lived in Berlin. Should we have? Probably. We lived in the small city of Erfurt. Topf and Sons. A business there built the crematories for Auschwitz and such. My father was a tailor and made custom leather goods. Friends told him of the ovens in January of '45. The Americans came. They weren't angels, but they were nothing like the Russians. There were no mass rapes. When we found the Soviets would be our masters, we found a way to leave with the Americans. And ... here I am today. Does that answer your questions?"

I looked at him. He preempted all the questions he'd received his whole life. I nodded and said, "Yes, for the time being, but I won't promise that something might occur to me later."

I rolled the skull around in my hands. It was less sinister than it had been a moment ago. A horrible thought occurred to me. The man whose skull was in my hands was a person not much different from me but controlled by a totalitarian system that would not tolerate differences in political and social views. I could not help but shiver again, this time knowing the same thing was occurring in the U.S. as I held the man's remains.

There was no bullet hole in the skull as there were in many of the skeletons. I tagged a collection box and identified its contents as "Find – human remains – skeletal – male – some charring – designated," I looked at a log to take the next available identifying number, "39." I placed the skull inside and began the task of sorting the jumble in front of me. They were owed that.

Cleggenhiest examined the pitifully few bits of surviving clothing, buttons, wallets, hats, anything that would provide evidence for identifying who these people were. He was amazingly good at what he did. I began calling him, "Sherlock Cleggenhiest."

The huge task ahead of us was daunting, but it was a diversion that kept our minds from speculating, "*Just how bad does someone want to keep the secrets we were uncovering here?*"

Chapter 51
Outside the building storage area on Site #5

Migdahlia, Reading, and I sat chatting on a portion of the stone wall that enclosed the yard on the west side of the building complex. The conversation was morbid, but necessarily so, considering our tasks. The discussion included observations on the number and ages of children killed, the severe damage to the remains caused by explosive devices and machine guns, and the imbalance of males to females.

Shouts and excited calls for "Sergeant Garret," came from the rear of the complex. I recognized Corporal Cole's alto; her tone was as close to panic as possible for her.

Garret charged to the sounds, an M-16 clutched in one hand. I watched him leap up the stairs leading to one of many entrances toward the building's rear. I waited for shots, but none came.

"I wonder what's going on?" Migdahlia asked, her eyes focused on the spot where Garret disappeared. "Another snake maybe?" I guessed. When I swiveled my head to look at Reading, he was already off the stone wall and was trotting to join Garret. Mug raced around the building from the rear. Both entered at almost the same time.

Migdahlia and I stared at each other for several

seconds, before I asked, "Think we should go check out what's happening?"

"No!" She was frightened. *"El Fantasmas!"* Her hand quickly went to head and chest as she crossed herself.

"What's wrong?" I asked.

"Ghosts! That is where we saw them. That is where my grandmother warned us they would be." Migdahlia was shaking.

Three Marines raced to join their Sergeant. Each carried weapons that included rifles and a grenade launcher. They entered the house in a disciplined manner, reflecting their training. I noted that was something their officer forgot.

Migdahlia clutched her throat with both hands. Her terrified eyes reflected something she'd seen but hadn't shared with us. I split my attention between the entrance and my frightened friend.

There was silence. No shouts. No gunfire. No explosions. Even the wind stopped whistling through the tree leaves. The silence and stillness intensified the tension building in us. We waited for something to shatter the quiet, but nothing kept the grip of possible impending doom from tightening.

Finally, two of the Marines emerged from the entrance and quickly disappeared behind the building. Time slowed. What I was sure was a half-hour was actually less than ten minutes. Reading, Mug and Sergeant Garret finally stepped into the sunlight from inside the complex. When they reached the bottom of the stairs, they stopped to have what was obviously a serious discussion. Migdahlia crossed herself again.

When the conversation ended, Reading and Mug walked straight toward us. Their faces were serious, but I couldn't detect any degree of alarm in their features, posture or demeanor.

As they approached, I asked, "So, what's the emergency?"

Reading read the fear in my countenance. "Nothing earthshaking. At least, nothing we hadn't expected."

Mug's face told me he didn't agree, but he said nothing about what he'd just seen. "Excuse me. I have to find Mark, Eduardo and the rest." He nodded as he walked past.

Reading backed up to the stone wall and boosted his rear back on to it. Migdahlia and I waited for him to explain. When he didn't, I said, "Oh no, you're not getting away with that. What is going on?"

Reading's pupils alternated focusing on Migdahlia's fearful eyes and my angry ones. He took a breath, tilted his head to one side, and spoke. "We found evidence there are people here besides us. Three of Garret's men were searching rooms in a building we hadn't entered before. When they entered one of the rooms, they thought they saw some motion, but when they examined it with their flashlights, they didn't see anything, at first. They called for Corporal Cole to tell her what they saw or thought they saw. Cole is sharp. She spied a triangular piece of paper, just an inch or so. It was trapped under the wall." Reading paused and placed his hand on Migdahlia's shoulder. "I believe we can explain what happened to you when you were here before. From what you've told me, the Marines discovered the room where you saw the skeleton appear. Cole found she could pull the paper from under the wall. It turned out to be a candy bar wrapper, a very recent one. She systematically checked the wall rock by rock until she discovered a loose one. When she pushed it, a whole section of the wall rotated, just like something out of an Indiana Jones movie." Reading moved his hand away and concentrated on me.

"After playing with it for a while, she found that if you pressed the rock when it was in motion, the panel would stop while it was 90° into its rotation. That exposed a hidden room inside. When she went inside, she got a real surprise. There were four sleeping bags in there, a couple of cases of MREs, boxes of ammunition and some other cartons she didn't have time to look at. Cole said there was evidence that whoever was in there had scooped up what they could and fled while she and her men were in the next room. There was another hidden door in another wall and a trap door in the floor. The trap door goes to a tunnel that leads outside. The other hidden door goes into a room inside the building. Corporal Cole says it looks like it was used as a command center. They looked around it, but didn't go farther." He returned his attention to Migdahlia. "There were skeletons assembled and attached to the inside of both hidden doors. My guess is they were to scare anybody who discovered this place by accident."

I tried to digest what I'd just been told. It didn't sound good to me. "You said four? What good is it for us to pair up if there are four that could jump us if we're isolated? You said they had lots of ammo. You've seen what someone did here to keep this place a secret. Four people with plenty of fire-power could do us in pretty quickly. It sounds damned dangerous to me."

Reading nodded. "Mug is going to have to rethink what we're doing."

"I sure as shit hope he does his thinking fast. Real fast! You said nothing we hadn't expected? Bull shit!" I wasn't volunteering to become another skeleton that would be found later and placed in a specimen collection box.

Chapter 52
Little Berlin Mess Tent

Everyone was assembled inside the tent, with the exception of the Marines. Sergeant Garrett had posted his troops at key spots around the campsite. All agreed they were the most likely *not* to be part of a plot. Mug stood at the head of one of the tables, grim-faced, filled with anger that was barely buried behind features that were contorted to reflect calm. He didn't have to explain what we were gathered to discuss. Within a half-hour of the discovery, everyone in our expedition knew we weren't alone.

Mug started in the middle of what needed to be said. "I've requested that Naleeva send us additional protection personnel. Until we have adequate security, here are the new rules. No one leaves their tent without being armed. For anyone who doesn't feel comfortable using a gun, see me. I'll get you to the point you're a pro real fast. Go in groups of four or more...that's everywhere."

"What if we have to take a leak in the middle of the night?" Ida-Marie asked. "Do I have to wake up my whole tent? We won't get much sleep if we do."

Mug stared at her for several seconds before establishing a new rule. "It's back to the 1800s. We'll set up a slop jar of some type in your tent, ladies. One of my men will empty and clean it for you daily until we get reinforcements."

"What about us?" Dr. Beltran asked.

"You're better-fixed equipment wise than the ladies. If you need to take a leak, do it somewhere close to your tent where we don't walk."

"What if—"

Mug frowned. "Doc, you'll just have to wake up your tent. Tough shit."

Everyone laughed. The laughs were weak, but the tension was broken. Mug said, "That wasn't meant to be funny. It came out that way, so good."

Mark asked, "Has Naleeva told you how long it would take to get some additional security down here?"

Mug looked uncomfortable. "No."

Mark pressed, "What *did* she tell you?"

Mug remained silent for several seconds before explaining. "I haven't been able to contact Naleeva."

"Is the equipment down? Can't you use some of our cell phones or the Marine's radio gear to contact her?" Eduardo asked.

Mug looked up at the tent's ceiling as he said softly, "There's nothing wrong with our equipment. I've sent messages, but she hasn't answered."

"Oh, that's just great!" Mark was pissed. "We're out here, stranded in what amounts to the set for a horror movie and the people that put us here can't be found. Welcome to

Nightmare in Argentina, two." He slammed his hand down on a table. "What do we do until they decide to tell us we're expendable?"

"Sergeant Garret has contacted his commander in Paraguay and asked for more men. He tells me the request is going through channels. He expects to know something tomorrow." Mug looked like he was lying. I spotted it and asked, "Mug, what aren't you telling us?"

"There are some complications. The base at Mariscal Estigarribia is the little base that isn't there." Mug took a breath. "There's a minimal garrison that is more a maintenance group than an active force. There are a lot of touchy situations involving the stationing of US troops anywhere in South America, and there's history because of what happened with Stroessner. He was a brutal dictator, our ally, and the stench from that relationship is still floating around. Long story short, it isn't a simple matter of driving a platoon in here. Getting them into Argentina will be tough."

"What about Garret and his Marines? They're here," Dr. Dean asked.

"What Marines? Who is Jim Garret? Neither, you, me, nor anyone here has seen any such people. The agreement you signed guarantees that." Mug shook his head and finger reminding us of our situation.

"That puts us in one hell of a lot of danger." Mark wasn't happy.

"I don't think so. At least, not until we finish cleaning up this mess." Reading had been silently listening and formulating what he believed was happening. "My guess is that we are being observed more than threatened ... that's for right now. Things might change drastically when we're done and get ready to pull out of here.

Logically, why let us progress and do the things we're doing if they didn't want it done?"

Eduardo asked, "What about the attempt on your sister's life?"

"We could be dealing with more than one group that has different interests in what we're doing. Honestly, I'm not sure I have a clue." Reading looked around at all the people in the room. "The scariest part of all this is one or more of us sitting in this room might be involved."

"I agree with you, Reading." Mug nodded his head. "We're going to change how we work the sites. No more division into crews. We all work together. If there is a bad actor among us, having everyone watching him or them will make life very difficult.

I quickly looked around the room. Were there tell- tale signs of guilt on the faces or body language of any of our fellow expedition members? I didn't see any. Sighing, I realized there weren't any truly "bad actors" in our theater company.

Chapter 53
Site #5 Storage Room

"Those are the last three." The light from the electric bulbs behind Mark cast shadows on his face. The three he referred to were skulls left in the subterranean grotto where we'd spent our last eight days. Those skulls marked three intertwined jig-saw puzzles we had to solve. Mark's features were cloaked, so it was difficult to see what the five weeks, and in particular the last eight days, of intense stress, had done. My associate handled his years gracefully. At least he had until now.

A week passed since we discovered we had uninvited visitors at Little Berlin. Though we didn't find another trace of their existence, we feared their presence. Mark simply reflected the pressure and apprehension we all felt. The stacks of white plastic boxes were down to seventeen. The three skeletons we were standing over would take three more. Fourteen. That's the number of containers we had remaining to exhume the cemetery. There were twelve headstones.

I said, "Well, at least we don't have to haul in more specimen boxes. We should have two left over after we dig up Woodlawn. We shouldn't have to sort bones, and guess who belongs to whom when we open the graves."

Reading suddenly got up from where he was kneeling, walked in front of the plastic containers, and announced, "You don't have any of these left. If we're going to finish this job, you need at least twenty more remains boxes."

"Has this place gotten to you?" I asked.

"No, my common sense has." Reading got Mug and Mark's attention. They stood staring at Reading.

"I'll explain." Reading hunkered down in front of the boxes. "We've tried to get an answer out of Naleeva about increasing security for a week. All we get is an automated 'out of the office' email note or voice mail. Something's wrong up there. But, if I'm right, they want us to finish collecting all the evidence."

Mark finished Reading's thought, "They'll get us the additional containers, so we finish! Brilliant, Reading!"

"It will buy us a little more time." Reading looked at the four gathered around the remaining skeletons. Migdahlia was the other person. "Nobody but the five of us need to know the additional bodies we're going to find are bogus."

Mark said, "I'll run the radar over part of the graveyard we elected not to scan because there weren't stones there. It will make things look normal."

"That gives me an idea." Mug rubbed his forehead as he finished his thought. "If we get those additional containers, Naleeva is supposed to approve them. If she sees we're asking for them because we found more graves of potential Nazi's, she'll be here in no time." He nodded. "We'll find out what's going on quickly."

Migdahlia asked, "What about Eduardo? He'll be asking all sorts of questions. What about sharing what we're doing with him? I know how he is. If he feels left out, you can bet he'll be prying into everything he thinks we're doing."

Mug looked at Reading, Mark, and me, polling us. I said, "I trust him. I'd rather take that chance than have him snooping and talking to the others."

Reading said, "Sorry, I think we can probably trust him, but everybody we add is one more possible leak."

"I'm with you Reading," Mug agreed, "I guess it's up to you."

Mark closed his eyes. I could see him inventing different scenarios. "I agree with Chessie. I think we run a greater risk excluding him than making him part of what is going on. I do have a suggestion. Have Chessie be the one to share the confidence. He'd like to be her protector." He looked at me and raised his eyebrows. I frowned as he started and scowled deeply as he ended.

"Protector, not lover," Mark clarified.

I felt foolish and mumbled, "I had no idea." I nodded, "Okay, I'll talk to him."

~ ~ ~ ~ ~

Reading and I carried the three boxes of remains into the forensics tent for further examination. Drs. Beltran and

Dean were busy at work tables where they had laid out individual skeletons. They hardly noticed us as we placed the containers on the piles of boxes that were left to examine. As we started to leave, Dr. Beltran, said, "You people do excellent work. I've only found a few cases where you've missed sorting the bones correctly. When you have, the documentation you've done allows me to check with the other specimens to find the missing part."

"It's not our first rodeo," I said with a smile, "but thanks for the compliment."

"I would image you are good at everything you do. Are you?" Beltran's look was more leer than smile.

I started to make a smart-assed cut-down when I noticed Reading making a motion I took to mean ... "talk to him."

Getting and keeping a man's attention is never difficult for me. I arched my back some and stood on the opposite side of Beltran from where Reading and Dr. Dean were engaged in a secretive discussion. I was to be a distraction. So, I distracted.

Beltran's eyes kept flitting to my parts like they were magnetized. I tilted my head to one side and tried to look mischievous. "Oh, I am." I batted my eyelashes at him. "Why do you ask?"

Beltran wasn't prepared for my aggressive posturing. He stepped back, looked confused, but still had a problem ignoring my boobs. I decided to toy with him. "You thinking I might be good at ..." I spoke my last word in a gassy whisper ... "*sex.*"

He managed a smile. "Yes, that was precisely what was on my mind."

"I have all the tools." I did a slow lurid 360° turn.

"I can see that." Dr. Beltran was completely oblivious of anything around him. I'd heard a lot more clever comebacks than what Beltran mumbled, but thirty-eight "Ds" and a nice bubble butt do things to a man's concentration. Reading waved his hand and motioned he was ready to go.

I leaned over close to Beltran. "You may enjoy the view, but you may never touch." I lowered my voice more and whispered to him. "I am very, very, very good, but unfortunately ... I'm very, very, very sorry; I'm not for you." As I turned to join my brother, Dr. Beltran's whole body sagged. Correction, not every part did.

~ ~ ~ ~ ~

"What was that about?" I didn't mind being bait as long as it was for a good reason and I wasn't eaten.

"Dr. Dean had something important to tell me."

Reading looked around to see no one was within hearing. "Dean decided to see if he could get some DNA off of the sleeping bags. He was able to."

I interrupted, "That's good news. Why keep that a secret?"

"Because he caught Beltran stealing some of the samples. Luckily, Dean had already taken one complete set and put it away before Petro took the duplicates." Reading shook his head. "If that doesn't put a scarlet letter on the bastard ... He goes to the top of the, *don't trust list.*"

Chapter 54

The path from the campsite to Site #5

"Wait up." Mug was running to catch Reading, Mark, Migdahlia, and me as we walked to Site #5 and the graveyard. It was the next, and possibly the most important site at Little Berlin. Excavating or even investigating the mission site or the Guarani Indian site had slipped from the realm of possibilities on this trip. For me, that meant never. I'd made a decision. If asked, I wouldn't return. Mug inhaled two or three deep breaths as he fell in step.

"I'm out of shape," Mug managed between his tortured breathing.

I figured it was a good time to complain. Mug would have to listen and not talk. "Can't you do something about breakfast? There were more weevils than oats in the oatmeal this morning."

"I'll take it under advisement. I have something important to tell you. We got approval for immediate shipment of the additional remains containers. Naleeva didn't approve it, that pimple-faced Ford kid did. I also got a message that was supposed to come from Naleeva. The note didn't mention the request, and it asked how we were doing and when we'd finish. I can guarantee she didn't write it and I'm about as sure she's not gotten the messages

I've sent her."

"Mug, she may not know what's going on here." Reading stopped walking ... we were about to catch the rest of the expedition members. "When do you think your messages began being intercepted?"

"My best guess is when I reported that we had four people observing us." Mug took one last gulp of air before his breathing returned to normal. "I think I know a way to let her know there are problems here. Take a look." He handed Reading a piece of paper with a note scribbled on it. Reading read it to the rest of us:

Naleeva,

I intend to put your emergency plan X3S or X3A into action. Advise immediately.

Mug

Mark asked, "What are those emergency plans? I never heard of them."

"No one has. I made it up. There's a fifty-fifty chance Ford will panic because he doesn't know what those *plans* are and he'll give it to Naleeva. She'll know something's wrong as soon as she sees it. I bet she's down here within forty-eight." Mug was smug.

"Good thinking!" Mark patted Mug on the back.

Reading's face was clouded. "Did you send that thing?"

"No."

"Good. Think, they don't want Naleeva involved. That's why they're holding the info you're sending her. If you send that note now, it will trigger whatever they have planned. That's probably not good." Reading paused, thought for a few seconds then asked, "Do you know if Garret has heard anything about getting more Marines in here?"

"No, but I'll get with him right away." Mug took the note from Reading and started to rip it up.

"Hang on to that. It's a great idea, but not right now," Reading said.

Mug nodded, folded the paper, and slipped it into his pocket as he went to find Sergeant Garret. As he walked away, he said, "I'll let you know what Garret was able to do as soon as I do."

"What was that about?" Eduardo asked as he joined our group. He looked like he felt he was being left out of something. It was time for me to share our secret with him.

Chapter 55
At the Graveyard

Eduardo and I were assigned to run the GPR unit over ground that we were sure contained nothing of interest. We were the 'red herring' ... the excuse to stretch out the time at the site. My talk with Eduardo went very well. He instantly agreed to the need for secrecy and was a willing participant in our plans. While we pushed the radar over what was sure to be empty land, Mark, Migdahlia, Ida-Maria, and Reading did the tedious preparation to begin the graveyard excavation.

Sweat poured off Eduardo's brow. He stopped pushing the radar long enough to remove his bush hat and wipe his brow. It was hellishly hot, so I volunteered. "I'll take a turn following that thing around for a while. Take a rest."

"No, no, no. I should do this. The machine is too heavy for you." His words said no; his eyes said yes. I waved him away and began to push the GPR while he found a place to sit in the shade for a few moments.

I barely looked at the screen as I performed a function that could have been done on a stage. My efforts were strictly for show. I hoped whoever was watching us were being eaten alive by insects, dehydrating, and were bored to distraction.

"*Buzzzzzzzz.*" The alarm that rang when radar waves rebounded from a something solid beneath it caused me to check the screen. My eyes opened wide. Maybe our red herring would turn out to be a whale.

~ ~ ~ ~ ~

Mark and Eduardo crisscrossed the area. It was huge, definitely man-made, and buried a meter and a half beneath us. Mark measured the distance between the metal stakes marking the corners of our find. He yelled, and I wrote in the site log. "Measurement of side A, 404 centimeters." He stretched the tape again. "Side B is 396 centimeters." He watched while Eduardo made a slight adjustment to a stake marking one of the remaining corners.

Mark stretched the tapes twice more. "It is almost a perfect square," Mark said. He glanced at notes he'd written on a pad. "Side C measures 402 ... Side D 400."

"How far does it go down?" I asked

Eduardo answered, "At least 250 centimeters. That's as deep as my instruments can measure."

I asked, "What do you think it is?"

"I can tell you what it's not." Mark wound his tape measure back into its case. "There aren't any evidence pipes were ever to or from it. That means it isn't some sort of septic system or cistern. Those are the most likely candidates for something of that size and shape. It isn't a swimming pool. The structure of the earth tells me the ground was dug out all around it. Some kind of a tomb, maybe? It's less than a hundred meters from the graveyard."

"It might be some type of bomb shelter. That would be in keeping with the military nature of these ruins." Eduardo pointed to the complex of buildings. "But why build it with all the tunnels and rooms hollowed out under the complex that would serve as well? That does not make sense."

Reading shook his head. "We won't know until we dig it up. What do we do first, exhume the graves or tackle this?" He was wandering around the edges of the location of the mysterious object.

Mark and Eduardo glanced at each other and answered at the same time, "The graves."

Migdahlia turned away, a motion that Mark noticed. He said, "Migdahlia if you don't want to participate in what's coming next we all understand. You don't have to."

"No Dr. Card. That is why I came here. I will be okay."

"What's this?" Reading was kicking at the dirt twenty feet away from the rest of us. "It looks like some kind of metal plate. Might be a grave marker or a monument." He stood amongst a jumbled line of quarried rocks.

"Chessie, bring a camera." Mark was already on his knees looking at what Reading pointed to with the toe of his boot. I clicked images as Mark carefully exposed a part of a bronze plate. Eduardo recorded GPS coordinates and other information into his cell phone. Mark removed the dirt from around the artifact and cleaned it with a rag. Indeed, the item looked like it had been part of a marker of some sort. The plate was 3⁄4 of an inch thick. One edge was curved and ornately cast in the shape of vines and leaves.

Two surfaces looked like they had been made by a cutting torch. They formed a parallelogram. Deeply engraved in the brass were letters.

Eduardo broke the silence, "I believe I know what this was. Those stones formed a pillar, and a plaque was mounted on it."

"I think you're right," Mark said. He looked at me. "Do we have plenty of pictures and is this location documented?"

I answer, "I have shots from every way possible."

"As good as it can be done without setting up our survey equipment," Eduardo said.

"I'm harvesting this piece," Mark said and picked it up in his hand. He used the rag to clean the engraving. The wiping motion slowed then stopped. He looked up at us and said, "We'll have to do a survey on the area. It will be Little Berlin Site #6." Mark turned the bronze plate so we could read the lettering. The inscription was cut in two, but what remained was electrifying. Parts of two lines were decipherable. Part of the letter "E" followed by the bottom of a "V" was all that was left of the top line. Under it was a clearly visible portion of what had been the bottom line of the plaque. It read: *Nee Bra* ... with part of a "U" cut in two.

Reading said softly, "Braun. Nee Braun."

Mark looked at us; his eyes traveled to the bronze and back. "We're going to be here a while longer. I hope Garret can get us some help."

Reading took the slab of bronze from Mark's hand and examined it. He shook his head. "This looks legit." He handed it back to Mark and said, "I guess it's time for Mug to send that message to Naleeva.

Chapter 56
At the Graveyard

Whatever they were discussing wasn't going well. Mark, Reading, Mug, Eduardo, and Sergeant Garret were deeply involved in what was obviously a contentious discussion. There was much waving of arms, jaws thrust forward, storm-filled faces. They had isolated themselves on the stone porch that led to the main entrance of the building complex. Even at thirty yards, snatches of conversation drifted to me. Mostly, the words that reached my ears were curses, vehemently spoken.

I smarted a little. The five *men* were discussing something vital to all of our futures, possibly to our lives. Were my breasts a disqualifying factor for joining the summit? Then I thought for a second. The whole thing started with Mug, Mark, and Garret talking. Eduardo then Reading joined them. *Without an invitation.* The limitation was one I'd placed on myself. I remedied that by climbing the steps and asking, "What in the hell is going on? Watching you guys, it looks like World War III was just declared."

Mark nodded empathically. "We are just as screwed as if it had been." He looked at Mug then Garret. "You explain it to her, Sergeant."

Of the five men, he appeared to be the least angry. His features showed signs of embarrassment. Garret looked me in the eyes, but he was doing so with difficulty. Forming words weren't happening, so I tried to help. I asked, "Did they turn down your request for more men, Sergeant?"

"Yes, they did." The shadow of embarrassment faded, and pure anger replaced it. "My base commander was ordered to get my people and me out of here. I'm going to have to leave you here."

His words shocked me. The first thing I thought was I was going to end up being hauled out in a specimen box, as a skeleton, many years in the future. My second thought was no frigging way. "You bastards!" came out of my mouth before I could control it. I knew Garret was not leaving because he wanted to, he was being ordered out.

Reading was the only one that had gotten past the shock. He was looking for a solution. He asked Garret, "Did your base commander give you a time when you have to be out of here?"

Garret looked puzzled, then suddenly smiled. "No Reading, he didn't. My orders were to contact him when I'm able to get to the Parana. A boat will be sent across to pick us up. I have GPS coordinates to go to. But, *no* exact times were set."

Mug was following Reading's line of reasoning. "What about your weapons and ammo? No direct orders on that?"

Garret looked uncomfortable. "Mug you know my

limitations on that. When I go most of the weapons have to go with me. I can manage to leave some stuff. We'll work that out."

"If you can leave that M134 mini-gun and the ammo for it, I wouldn't need much else. A few M80's. A good supply of grenades for them."

"Shit, Mug!" Garret shook his head. "I'm too old to be busted. I'm planning on retiring in two years."

"What if you were to leave one or two of your group to guard the weapons you were forced to leave behind until other arrangements can be made to retrieve them," I suggested. "That happened when I was in the Corps. Our lieutenant got an atta-boy for it."

Garret's face lit up. "I can do that. I'll leave Corporal Cole and Private Duvall. They'll be under orders not to engage or allow the use of the weapons in any actions *unless* they're attacked." He looked at Mug. "I'll have to put Cole and Duvall under orders they are to do *nothing,* but guard weapons. It works that way. They have to be the little leprechauns that aren't here. Everything I don't need to walk out of here, I'll leave with you." Garret looked at each of us in turn. "That's the best I can do, and it's a hell of a lot more than the brass will like." He winked at me. "Chessie, you have a big beautiful brain to go with those big boobs of yours."

I extended my hand to his cheek and tapped it. "You've been slapped."

Everybody laughed.

"Okay. We have to get everyone together and figure out how to finish up this mess in a few days." Mug looked at us and asked, "Any suggestions before I get everyone into the mess tent?"

"What about those among us we feel can't be trusted? What do we do about them?" Eduardo asked.

"Good question. That's Petro and Ida-Marie as far as I can see." Mug raised his hands in a supplicating manner. "Any other candidates?"

"What about Migdahlia?" Reading asked. He looked straight at me.

Without any hesitation, I said, "She's one of us. I don't have any doubt." I turned to Mug. "You sure about your people?"

"Yep. I worked with all of those men a long time. I'll bet my life on any of them."

Reading cocked his head to one side. "You are."

Mug ignored Reading's comment and said, "So, I'll assign Dr. Beltran and Ida-Marie to something where they can't hurt us, and we all need to keep our plans away from them as much as we can."

"I'll set up ... oops, store the M134 up in the top of the tower," Garret said. "You can cover 270° from there, and the ninety you can't, is cliff. Nobody is coming up that."

"How do we get to it? I've never been up there," Mug said.

"You know the hidden room with skeletons attached to the doors? One of those exits has a short passage and stairs that lead to it. You have an unbeatable field-of-fire from up there. It's built from the same rock the rest of this place is made from, but hope they don't have anything heavy. You can kiss your ass goodbye if they have mortars or rocket launchers." Garret wasn't making us feel optimistic about surviving a full-fledged attack. Mug nodded grimly. "Any other ideas?"

"Yes," Reading said. "I've got some thoughts about that message you're going to send Naleeva. It might buy us more time."

"I'm all ears."

"It appears that whoever ... is waiting for us to get all the evidence collected before they make a move. If they know the last thing we do is see if Hitler is buried here, they're going to wait for that, don't you think?" Reading lifted his eyebrows as he smiled.

Mug smiled too. "I think!"

Chapter 57
Mess Tent

Mug was winding down his remarks. "So, that's it. We need to do all that I've spoken about as quickly as we can. I guess we have a week to do it in. We start this afternoon in the graveyard. Everybody's on the work schedule. Petro, you and Ida-Marie, will stay here at the camp and run the forensic tent. You'll have to log in what we find, take pictures, everything. I'll leave Terry and Bob from my crew to protect the camp and you two. Don, Elroy and Miccolee, sorry, we need you on site. The rest of my guys ... you're shovel engineers until we get everything dug up. You go back to M-16 duty when Garret and his people leave. Questions?"

"Are you sure you need me in the tent?" Dr. Beltran asked. He looked like he didn't want to be confined to the forensics area. "I can be of more use at the excavation. We can do the cataloging after the sun goes down."

Mug shook his head, "Sorry, Doc. Besides, we may have to string some lights and work after dark. There's only so much time, and we have to get everything done." Mug asked again. "Questions?"

The birds and monkeys chattering were the only noise.

"Okay, we got over five hours of light to work if the

rains miss us. The four I said stay here, everybody else, be at the graveyard in a half-hour." Mug started to leave, but Miccolee asked, "Are we going to work in the rain?"

"If there's enough light, yes. We'll have tarps over some of it. If not, we'll get wet."

She pressed the issue. "If it's lightning?"

Mug frowned. "Pray it doesn't hit you and be sure your insurance is paid up."

~ ~ ~ ~ ~

At the Graveyard

"We haven't got time for this!" Mug was mad. The first shovel of dirt hadn't been tossed, and he saw problems. We'd been at the graveyard less than twenty minutes. Mark and he were nose to nose. Mark held a tripod with a theodolite mounted on it. He was insistent that the site was to be properly located. Mug wanted one thing, to get what was in the ground out as quickly as possible.

"This is going to be done correctly, or it isn't going to be done at all." Mark and Mug looked like two dogs squaring for a fight...one a pit bull, the other a cocker spaniel. Enter the German Shepherd.

Reading interceded. "Look, guys, we're wasting time. Mug, we or someone else, may have to come back here if we can't get finished. It's got to be documented in a way that can be done." Mug frowned, Mark smiled. Reading continued, "Mark, we don't have to do what you normally would. We don't have time to plat the surrounding area and other potential sites. Just locate where we're going to dig." Mug smiled, Mark frowned.

"Okay," Mug said, "get on with it."

Mark nodded, "I promise I won't do anything that isn't absolutely necessary." He spoke to Reading. "Will you grab the survey rod? I'll tell you where to go."

Mug grunted and started to walk off. "Don't let him tell you to take that rod to hell, Reading." Mug was still a little steamed.

"Where are you going?" I asked.

"Down to the part of the graveyard you've already mapped and help Eduardo and Migdahlia dig up 'whosits' or 'whatsits'." Mug stomped off. He didn't like losing arguments even if he knew he was wrong. He was yelling at people when he was thirty yards from the other group. I wondered if his mother or father was an English Bulldog. He had the stubborn tenacity and intensity to never let go of something within his grasp. I chuckled to myself. He was built and looked like the breed. The backhoe's diesel engine cranked up, and I knew Mug was 'cracking the whip.'

I held the site log waiting for Mark to give me data to record. Every few seconds he'd give me something to enter. I was fully absorbed in keeping the book.

"Can I help?" The voice came from a foot or so away. It scared me so much I jumped and almost fell on the ground. Miccolee grabbed my shirt to keep me from falling. She said, "Sorry, I didn't realize I'd scare you."

"It's not your fault. I'm a little jumpy since I took the header over the hill." I didn't realize the girl was as big as she was until she stood next to me. She was a couple inches taller, and I had thought just the reverse. Miccolee was thin, but the muscles in her arms and legs were pronounced. She possessed a body that did not spend all its time at a desk as I had supposed.

"What are you doing?" she asked.

"I'm keeping the site log."

"What goes in there?

I was surprised she was interested. "Everything. It is

the definitive record of what, where, how, and when of all we find. It's our proof that authenticates everything we do at the site."

"Then the stuff I see Drs. Dean and Beltran work with on their computers are something different?" Miccolee held her hand out. "May I take a look?"

I handed the log book to her and said, "What you see on the computers is entered from these logs. They add their forensic information. They also print out a hard copy. Keeping a duplicate is important. From a scientific view, those observation records are what makes our expedition a legitimate endeavor. Without them," I tossed my hands in the air, "It's pretty much like we never came here."

"I guess this one is particularly important. Isn't the

whole reason for coming here to prove or disprove Hitler lived and died here?" Miccolee pointed to where Mark and Reading were surveying. "The possibility his burial vault is under this ground probably makes this the most important information you've ever recorded."

"How do you know about that?" The hair on the back of my neck stood up. That was something that hadn't been verbalized. It was a 'common sense' secret. I watched for anybody's actions that might indicate deceit.

There weren't any. Miccolee smiled as she answered, "Really Chessie. Anybody with an IQ larger than their hatband size knows why we were sent. I overheard Mug talking about a large concrete object buried here. You don't have to have Mr. Spock's intellect to work that one out."

I looked at her and nodded. "No one has said the words, but everyone knows the possibility exists." Everyone, including me, had drastically underestimated Miccolee. It was a mistake I wouldn't make again.

"These are very thorough. I can understand why they're important." She turned several pages reading our expedition's history while I watched.

When Mark called out some datum, I took the log from Miccolee's hands and said, "Sorry, back to work." "Hey! Mark, Reading, Chessie, Miccolee, we're getting ready to pull the first coffin out and open it. Come down here." Mug yelled.

I laid the log book down to join the others. We ran as one. Seeing what was in the first coffin was exciting if a little morbid. That was except for Miccolee. She picked up the log and began reading.

Chapter 58
In the graveyard, at the first opened grave.

Mug, Eduardo, Migdahlia, Elroy Cleggenhiest, and Dr. Dean were supervising the careful removal of the casket by four of Mug MacAphee's men. I had supposed that the secretive nature of the enclave and its isolation would have caused the deceased to be put into wooden coffins. Maybe I just watch too many old Western's on TV and assumed pine boxes were the standard for pioneer, remote living ... and dying. This was certainly not the case. It was ornate, made of some variety of metal, and had survived being buried for the sixty-six years very well. The headstone proclaimed its inhabitant, one Heinrich Von Schoenkopf, died May 22, 1952.

The backhoe grunted as it tugged on the spreader bar and lifting straps under the coffin. As the casket began its journey to the light of day, the men exhuming it responded to Mark and Eduardo's constant warnings with vile looks and muttering curses under their breath. When the straps were removed, and the backhoe chugged away, we gathered around the casket. Dr. Dean had the same sensitivity to the situation I did. He said, "If we don't look like a bunch of vultures gathered around an animal, waiting for it to die, I don't know what does."

Everyone exchanged glances, most varying from

uncomfortable to embarrassed. Not so, Mark and Eduardo. They quickly resumed their scientific roles and took steps to preserve as much archaeological integrity as they could.

Eduardo was in command. He said, "Migdahlia, be sure to enter everything I say in the log book. Write it exactly like I say."

"Can we help?" Mark asked.

"Yes. Mark, please help me to be sure we miss nothing. Chessie, will you take photos? Dr. Dean, will you run the video camera?"

We responded by picking up the cameras and Mark by moving to Eduardo's side.

There was no visible seal on the casket, but it was locked with a padlock. A heavy wire had been strung through matching holes in flanges in the coffin and its lid, then the wire was twisted. It insured the lid would remain a snug fit. Eduardo constantly described even the most minute details to a furiously writing Migdahlia. Mark occasionally added an observation. Neither took into account Migdahlia's ability to keep up with their constant harangue. She was forced to have them repeat items and request they slow down.

The time came to open the coffin. I snapped pictures as Eduardo used bolt cutters to remove the wire and the padlock. The lid wouldn't yield to lift it by hand. A pry bar and every ounce of one of Mug's biggest and strongest men were needed to free the lid and swing it up on its hinges. When the lid was fully opened, we all gathered at the front and stared inside.

Cleggenhiest took over the narrative. "Oberst – that's a colonel." He pointed to the skeleton in uniform. "He was in the 6th Panzer army. Three iron crosses! This was a brave man. That division saw service when France and Poland were captured and was in many major battles on the eastern front. Moscow. Kursk. Korsun-Cherkassy."

I didn't realize that the camera had become inactive in my hands.

"I thought SS wore black uniforms," Dr. Dean said.

"This man was not SS. He was Wehrmacht. He was once in mechanized maintenance. If I am correct, he commanded a tank unit in the 11th brigade at some time." Cleggenhiest pointed to various medals and ribbons on the gray blouse. "Fighting for as long as he did and being in as many terrible battles as this man was in, it is a miracle he survived them."

"Gentlemen," Mark saw my frown and quickly corrected, "and ladies, there can be no further doubt this was an enclave designed to house escaped Nazi survivors. This grave proves they were *here* for an extended time and participated in World War II. We need to be sure every detail is captured." His slight frown in my direction reminded me of my responsibility. I started snapping pictures in double time.

Eduardo, Mark, and Cleggenhiest continued to narrate

their observations while Migdahlia, Dr. Dean and I did our best to provide written and visual proof of what we had uncovered. It took an hour-and-a-half before everything observed was documented. Finally, Eduardo turned to Mark and said, "Do you agree we are done here?"

"Yes." Mark swung his hand out toward the remaining graves. "I know the number has increased from our first estimate. What is it up to now?"

Migdahlia turned back pages in the log book. She announced, "There are twenty-seven plus the possible three in Site #6."

"We don't have enough specimen boxes even with the twenty additional we're supposed to be receiving," Eduardo said as he mentally added.

"I have a problem with going forward with this," Mark set his jaw. "I have to draw a line between archaeology and grave robbing." He pointed to the casket. "This proves what we came here to find out. We have detailed it; the evidence is incontrovertible. Why disturb those that lie here? What will we learn?"

"The job was to come in here and bring out the evidence." Mug puffed up like a challenged rooster. "*All* the evidence."

"Evidence of what?" Mark was clearly agitated. "It seems to me we already have more evidence than a lot of people are going to like. What else is wanted from *here*?" He emphasized the last word. "There's evidence that

Nazi's did live *here*. We already have plenty of evidence that a bunch of people were killed *here*. Evidence, our government sent a group to kill everybody living *here*. Evidence that the first rule of assignation was followed *here*: Assassinate the assassins." He paused a couple seconds. "We've got gravestones over most of the coffins that tell us who is in them without having to dig them up. So we have a half-dozen that don't. I can justify digging them up, not the rest."

"*All* is part of our job. That's what we signed on for ... that's what we're going to do." Mug was incensed.

"You may be, but I'm not, and I'm sure most of my people feel the same way." Mark looked at each of us suspecting we'd support him. Everyone remained as silent as the graveyard we stood in.

His rebuttal came from an unexpected source. Reading. "You forget the most important reason we're here. We don't talk about it, but we all know we're in this jungle to see if Hitler is buried here. We won't know for sure unless we exhume *every* body. Mark, I know it's easy to forget about that with all we've seen and experienced." Reading paused then walked over, so he stood eyeball to eyeball with Mark. "That's what we're really here for and being that some people don't want us to find out if that's true or false so bad they've tried to kill us. I think we need finish what we've started."

Mark stared into Reading's eyes as he thought about

what my brother just said. He took a deep breath and placed his hand on Reading's shoulder. "I really hate to say this. I'm wrong. Let's get on with it."

"Will wonders never cease!" Mug turned to one of his men and yelled, "Get that backhoe to that next grave. Eduardo, you ready?"

"I'll be with you in a minute. I need to finish here. Go ahead and get everything ready to begin to dig."

Mug, his men, and the backhoe moved on to the closest grave.

"What are these?" Cleggenhiest was leaning over the coffin, pointing to something inside.

Mark, Migdahlia, Reading, Eduardo, and I all joined Cleggenhiest in staring at the items to which he pointed.

"Mementos," Eduardo identified what they must be. I saw a pipe, several books, written awards, and several pieces of correspondence. The letter on top was signed in a distinctive scrawl. The name, *Adolf Hitler*.

"What's it say?" Mark asked.

Cleggenhiest shook his head, "You should get an interpreter to translate this. It has been so long I might make a mistake."

"Where is Miccolee?" Eduardo asked.

I looked at Site #6. Miccolee was still there. She sat cross-legged on the ground, engrossed in reading my Site

Log.

Chapter 59
Mess Tent at Little Berlin

"Five in a day if there are no complications. There will be complications." Mark answered Mug's question. "That doesn't include the three at Site #6. I don't know what it will take for them. I don't even know if they're burial vaults or not. Figure two to four days there."

"Shit!" Mug was 'losing' Sergeant Garret and five of his men in three days. Garret's excuses had run out. He had firm orders to be off of Argentina soil by then. Cole and Duvall would stay only because Garret hadn't told his superior, he would let them 'guard the weapons he was forced to leave behind.' He wouldn't confess until he returned to Mariscal. Garret said his CO had sympathy for the situation. He thought he'd "be all right."

It got terribly quiet. The murmur of the generator and a few animal noises kept it from being completely silent. The tired expedition team sat slumped in their seats around the scraps of their suppers. Most were too exhausted to care about the conversation going on between Mark, Mug and Eduardo. Some had lost their battle with sleep. Elroy Cleggenhiest's gentle snore was just one more animal noise. I was struggling to keep from adding to the chorus.

In two-and-a-half days the crew had managed to dig and document nine caskets. They had never reached five in one day.

Mug ciphered out loud. "Twenty-seven less nine, that's eighteen, divided by five, that's damned near four days. And that doesn't include Site #6. Shit!" Mug repeated more harshly.

"If we don't get those additional specimen containers, we'll have to stop. You have to factor that in our thinking." Mark shook his head. "Have you heard from Naleeva?"

"Not her. I did hear from Ford. We were supposed to get the boxes today." Mug was seething inside and doing his best to control his less than controllable temper. "I sent the bastard a follow up before we ate."

"I only have seven containers left." Eduardo looked at Mark. "We might be able to double up some of the remains if we placed all of the skeletons and other items in a bag, sealed it and found a box that wasn't too full to put the bag into."

"If worse comes to worst." Mark looked at the tent's ceiling in disgust. "Yes, that will work. Some of the burnt ones...there wasn't much left of the bodies. If more boxes don't come in time, we'll use them."

"Naleeva hasn't answered the message you sent?" Eduardo asked.

"No, and I know why. It's been two days, and I was about to resend when Ford sent a note to me saying my letter to Naleeva was garbled in transmission and asked for it to be resent. I've done that. This time I marked it urgent and for her eyes only. It will be very hard not to give this one to her. I'll get an answer this time; I just hope it's actually from her."

The spring on the tent's screen door's "zing" told us that Reading, Garret, Dean, and Beltran had returned from the latrine. Dean tried some humor. "Before anyone asks, yes, everything came out all right." There was a polite titter, but the smart-assed reply he hoped would come, didn't.

"Figure out how to get us out of here?" Reading asked.

"Not hardly. Best I can figure we have eight to ten days to finish. It will take a couple of days to pack up everything and get it out of here. I don't know for sure if we have that much time left." Mug stretched his arms and legs, finishing with a big yawn. "Assuming the notes I've sent Naleeva got through, it should buy us the time we need. As long as Ford thinks we're not done, I don't expect company. I'm sure he's involved in the shit somehow."

Reading and the men who had returned from the latrine looked at each other. "You tell him, Reading," Dr. Dean said.

"You're forgetting we already have company. Yes, I can tell you they're still here. I saw three of them sneaking around the trucks and machinery we have stored near the latrine, so I snuck up on them. I got a decent look. I even shouldered my carbine figuring they were going to try to sabotage our stuff. They just walked around it once and disappeared. I can tell you this—one of them is a woman."

Mug looked dubious.

Reading smiled, "That is unless some guy decided to implant the biggest silicone sacks in his chest he could buy."

Mark suddenly became alert. "Was she tall?"

"Extra tall," Reading responded.

"The hair. Long or short? Blonde?" Mark asked.

"Couldn't tell."

"Damn it! I know who that could be." Mark slapped his hand on the table pulling me out of my twilight consciousness and awakening Cleggenhiest.

"Who is it, Mark?" Mug asked. Mark shook his head and didn't answer. "Well, who do you think it might be?" Mug insisted.

Mark took several breaths, fidgeted for a while. He finally decided to answer. "Someone we don't want here. She works for the CIA, kills people for a living, and she's damned good at it."

"Sounds like you know her pretty damned well," I said. My eyes turned greener. I just couldn't help it even though our relationship had cooled to a sometime thing.

Reading said, "Talking about killing people isn't something someone does. That's especially true of professionals. How did you come by the knowledge?"

Mark looked at me and frowned, but it looked like an apology. "She talks in her sleep."

Chapter 60
At the Graveyard

"They're gone." Mug looked forlorn. "Garret said they had to be at the rendezvous point on the Parana tonight at 300 hours. It's a twelve-hour walk. He's given his people three hours slack. I've got to have at least four people at the campsite guarding that. I've talked to Cole and Duvall. They'll cover us here as best they can, but I have to have at least one guy as security ... in case."

"What you're telling me is I'm down to three that can help," Mark knew it was coming but the lack of labor would lessen their already slow pace. "I'll have a backhoe operator and two guys to help him."

"That's the best I can do. If we get some kind of probing or unfriendly activity, I'll have to jerk the three you have left. Our second priority is to help you. Our first is to keep you alive."

Eduardo shook his head in reaction to Mugs statement. "If that happens we will have to move Petro and Ida-Marie to here. We have to have the labor."

With the exception of two of Mug's men, Dr. Beltran and Ida-Marie, what was left of the expedition stood in a tight knot near the twentieth grave scheduled for opening. Looks varied from resignation to disgust. The task ahead had just become more taxing on every remaining person at Little Berlin.

"What happens if a couple choppers full of mercenaries drop in to visit us? Do you have a plan, Mug?" Mark asked.

"Yes. We're going to go to ground just like the folks that built this place did. I just hope we have better luck. I've got guys at the camp moving all our reserves of ammunition and most weapons into the building complex. I told them to haul enough water and rations over there to last five days. If they have a big enough force to keep us in there longer than that, we're toast. The camp will be okay for a few days. It will take a while for our creeping around friends to figure out the Marines have left. By then we'll have what we need, transferred."

Mark asked, "Why do you think we'll have better luck than our friends in the white boxes did?"

Mug grinned, "We know there's a possibility of an assault. We'll be ready for it; they weren't. And, we have one hell of an equalizer in the tower. That M-134 is like having three 50 caliber machine guns covering all the ground around the complex. Cole and Duvall are our insurance. There are three approaches that offer defilade from the position. I'm going to repair those Teller mines and put them where they'll do the most good. Anybody that tries using those approaches will need more than Humpty- Dumpty's army just to pick up their pieces."

"It is what it is." Mark shrugged his shoulders. "Mug,

get your guys on the backhoe and start digging up the next one."

I watched as everyone went about their tasks ... tasks that were now routine. We all knew things were coming to an end. The question: What would that end be?

Chapter 61
Mess Tent

"I think there's something we need to do that we haven't thought about before." Reading tapped his fork on the side of his aluminum mess plate.

Mug, Migdahlia, Eduardo, Mark, and I sat around him. All of us looked in his direction with dejected resignation. When Reading used those words, everyone present knew what he was about to say needed to be done and it would add to our already crushing workload.

The rain's loud drumming beat its tropical deluge concert on the tent. It was the only other noise. Night had long since fallen and chased us from our work at Sites #5 and #6. Most of our crew had forced down their meal, staggered to their tents, and dropped into their cots. Every tired body at Little Berlin was close to exhaustion. No one would welcome another task to do.

Mug tilted his head to one side, blinked, and pulled his head down like a turtle retreating into its shell. "So, what is it?"

"If we have any unwanted visitors, they'll be looking for the evidence we've accumulated to confiscate it. If we don't have evidence, what we've done here ends up as an elaborate urban legend." Reading let our minds catch up to his. "Part of what we found needs to stay in camp, so they believe they're getting what they came for. We leave them volume, but the least important items. What's critical, we hide. We need enough specimen containers and documentation to prove what we've found. If we disperse it around and they don't find it *all* ... that's a get out of jail free card."

"Aren't you forgetting about our shadows?" I asked. "How are we going to keep them from finding what we hide and telling anybody who shows, right where to go?"

"We can't guarantee it, but we can make it real hard." Reading shrugged his shoulders. "I've thought of several pros and cons. Everything from taking it with us inside the old compound to burying it. I think just hiding it and camouflaging is our best bet."

"Why not take it into the buildings?" Mark asked.

Reading lifted his eyebrows. "If they know we have it in the complex with us, that doesn't leave them an alternative. They'd have to kill us to get it. That's the reason we need to leave most of it, so they think they've recovered what we've found."

"We need to start doing this right away?" Mug asked.

"No. Not until we're a day from completing Site #6." Reading placed his hands behind his head and leaned back in his chair. "They aren't going to disturb us until we've done the dirty work for them."

"What's next?" Mark asked.

"You and Eduardo select what we need to hide to be sure we have the evidence we need to prove the Nazi's were here and there were two massacres on these sites, you leave the rest up to me. I'll hide the stuff and I'll set us up some insurance contracts that will be hard to break!"

Chapter 62
Site #6

"I hit something," the backhoe operator yelled. He waited for Mug, Mark and the rest to gather around the pit and issue instructions.

Eduardo and I scrambled around the pile of dirt we were sifting through screens. We joined Mark and Mug who stared into what we all assumed was another grave. One of Mug's men asked, "Same process as the others?"

Mug nodded as he and another man grabbed shovels, climbed into the hole, and probed for the edges of the buried object. Soon a trench marked the surmised coffin's location and the backhoe operator carefully scooped as much earth from above it as could be done safely. The area inside the trench was larger by at least twenty-five percent than any of the caskets exhumed prior to this one. Mark and Eduardo supervised removal of four feet of soil all around the trench to provide working room. To our surprise, what the removal of earth disclosed were rock walls that formed a rectangle and a huge steel plate serving as a cover. Mark assessed what we'd found correctly, "It's a burial vault for the coffin." This was special treatment, and we anticipated a special find. Within forty-five minutes we were ready to go to work.

We removed the last earth from the vault's top with

trowels and brushes. What it disclosed was a three-eighth inch plate with three heavy pieces of angle iron welded to its top to keep the earth's weight from crushing it inward. I was the one whose brush strokes uncovered something spectacular. My whisking exposed weld beads on the plate at one end. They formed the numbers, "1962," and the letters, "EHB." As they became visible, my mind and mouth functioned simultaneously, "1962, EHB, that has to be Eva Hitler-Braun!"

My words instilled fresh hope in tired bodies, and the pace of work increased dramatically. Within another ten minutes, the steel plate was chained to the backhoe and lifted away. Inside the stone, the vault was a very large, structurally rugged casket. A four-foot long representation of the Virgin Mary was embossed in the lid. The vault had done its job; the coffin was in excellent condition. Both side handrails were still serviceable and soon lifting straps were in place, and the casket was removed. We gathered around it as the backhoe moved away. Anticipation was sky high.

~ ~ ~ ~ ~

The only noise was the last tortuous screech of the casket's hinges as they stopped in the fully open position. Our team's collective sigh sounded like air rushing from a ruptured balloon. I fingered the site log page waiting to record Mark or Eduardo's fateful words.

Mark closed his eyes and pronounced what we all saw.

"Let the site log show that the casket was removed from the vault as cited in the location as recorded in the previous entry and was opened at," he looked at his watch, "10:24 AM. Upon examination of the open casket, we found it was empty." Mark looked inside once more, hoping, but knowing what he wouldn't see. He shook his head while he spoke, "Stains on the interior fabric suggest there was a corpse housed in the coffin at one time, and it was removed." He paused and bent over so he could see the discoloration better. "There are some hairs inside which I'll remove and place in a specimen bag." I handed him a plastic 'baggie,' and he picked up the hairs with his surgically gloved hand then shoved them in. "I'll also remove several samples of the stained fabric for further study and possible DNA identification."

Mug shook his head as he stared at the vacant space. He straightened up and cursed loudly, "Horse shit!" Mug expressed all our disappointment and anger in those two words.

Mark looked crestfallen. "That leaves one to go." There wasn't much enthusiasm in his voice.

"Yes, one to go. Let's hope it is not a replay of this," Eduardo said. Both he and Mark began removing pieces of material from the casket. Both Dr. Dean and Dr. Beltran hovered around them making suggestions on how to select samples with the best chance of collecting DNA as they "surgically" removed swathes of cloth and padding.

Cleggenhiest's disappointment was visible. Ida-Marie stood next to him looking bored. I didn't see Miccolee, but that didn't surprise me. She proved squeamish when witnessing the first few openings and stayed a fair distance away on those that followed. This time she'd disappeared completely.

I looked for Migdahlia and Reading to see their reactions. Migdahlia sat on the edge of the pit her legs dangling inside. She vainly fought tears that rolled quietly down her cheeks. Reading...Reading was nowhere to be seen.

Chapter 63
Site #6

"This thing is huge," Mug said.

"It should be 400 centimeters square," Eduardo remembered the measurements from his ground-penetrating radar readings.

The backhoe grumbled as it removed more soil from whatever it covered. Mark instructed Mugs men to remove an area that would provide six feet of clearance on each side. That meant the backfill pile would be huge. The overburden had to be checked for specimens. Three groups of us worked the screens, searching for artifacts, but we weren't finding anything of consequence.

The backhoe grunted as it deposited another load from the dipper bucket. I watched while the clods of earth slid down the sides of the ever-heightening pile. I shook my head. Patience is required when excavating a site, but we were finding so little, particularly items from the period of time Little Berlin was active. Two pieces of pottery and a stone hand ax was our team's sum total. I was bored and disgusted, so I was happy when Eduardo called me. "Chessie, will you keep the site log? We should be close to making some recordings."

When I reached the edge of the pit which was nearing

the large entity in its middle, I saw that Mark had already found one corner of the structure. He smiled when he saw me. "You ready?"

I held the site log out so he could see it.

"Good. Write this down. First exposure of the item shows it to be made of rock and similar in construction to the previous discovery. Therefore, it must be treated as though we have uncovered another burial vault. There is one major deviation. There is no metal plate to form a roof on this structure. It appears the top of this structure is made of concrete."

"It's huge for burying one body," I observed.

Mark looked at the structure he was uncovering. He nodded. "There is a possibility. This may have been designed to serve as a last chance hiding place." Mark swung his focus onto the group gathered around the pit. When he saw who he was looking for, he asked, "Hey, Eduardo, would you get one of the ground penetrating radar units and check the area around this pit for something I might have missed. Look for what might have been a hidden entrance. There might have been electric wires, air vents, or water lines to this thing. Honestly, I wasn't zeroed in on something that small given the timeline."

Eduardo nodded, said, "Right away," and trotted off to find a GPR unit.

"Four hundred centimeters," I did the quick calculation in my head, "thirty-nine inches to a hundred, multiply that by four and divide by twelve ... that's thirteen feet square. That's way too big to be logical for a burial vault." I thought about what it could be. It was in the wrong location to be a septic tank or a cistern for a number of reasons. "How far down does it extend?" I asked.

"No idea," Mark mumbled. He picked up a post- hole digger and removed dirt next to the rocks until he could go deeper. Mark said, "Deeper than this digger. I'm betting a minimum of the height of a man standing. Seven feet, maybe more. Dr. Dean, Mug, will you give me a hand removing dirt on this one side so we can see more? I don't want to use the backhoe until Eduardo finishes."

Soon the three men were filling buckets of dirt and handing them to Mug's men who carried them to the piles of backfill earth. Within a half hour, the excavation next to the rock structure was six feet deep. Mark was correct—the depth was going to be as tall, or taller, than a standing man.

"Oh! I think I found something." Eduardo peered at the radar unit's screen. He carefully moved the unit back and forth over an area ten feet square. "Come look."

Mark scrambled from the pit and hurried to Eduardo. I met him there, site log in hand to record what had been found. All three of us stared at the screen. It disclosed something entirely different from what we had expected. The earth's structure clearly indicated it had been disturbed from its natural state. We stared at the screen that showed a buried rectangle ... probably identical in size to the burial vault that had housed the empty casket. However, this rectangle had nothing buried inside it. The radar disclosed only earth. Mark made a running commentary as Eduardo manipulated the radar. I recorded his words, including his conclusion: "It appears that this was a burial vault. What or who was interred here was most likely removed. We will, time permitting, have to excavate to make a further determination."

"Hey guys, take a look at this," Dr. Dean said from deep inside the pit. We left Eduardo to his radar explorations and returned to see what the professor and Mug had discovered. Mug and Dean had concentrated on finding how deep the wall extended into the earth. They'd removed three more feet from the pit, then used the post-hole digger to find the depth. Dean pointed to a spot on the digger's handles close to the top. "This thing is close to being a perfect cube. That means thirteen feet high, but that's not what I wanted to show you." Dr. Dean set the digger aside and motioned to Mug. He said, "Go ahead." Mug reached deep into the hole and wiggled a stone in the wall until he removed it. I saw the frown form on Mark's face until Dr. Dean said, "Behind that stone is solid concrete. My bet is something, or someone has been placed in there and then the whole thing filled with concrete."

Everybody stood in stunned silence. We knew who we believed was inside that solid block. Dean verbalized our thoughts. "We know who we believe is in there. Maybe Eva was placed in with him. I'm guessing that's who was in the empty coffin. We know it, but we're not going to be able to prove it. We don't have the tools or time to break into the damned thing. We're screwed." He looked at Mark, then Eduardo who had wandered over, and finally Mug. "So ... what's next?"

I waited for Reading to express an opinion. He didn't. Reading wasn't where I could see him. The last time I could remember him being around the excavations was an hour or two earlier. Before I could worry about him, Mug shouted, "Everybody! Pick up your stuff and head to the mess tent. What's next is a good question. We need to find the answer."

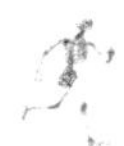

Chapter 64
The Mess Tent that evening

"Not until I can get Naleeva," Mug said.

"How are you going to do that? Everything you've sent has obviously been intercepted. If you send a message that actually tells her what we found, we're likely to have a bunch of black helicopters in this clearing in a few hours," Mark said. He tapped the table with his fingers. "I say we finish the job, then get out of here. We haven't done what we were sent to do."

Mug starred at Mark for several seconds making up his mind as he did so. He finally spoke. "I like the 'get out of here', not the 'finish the job' part. We don't know there *is* a job to finish. We have a solid cube of concrete, and we can only guess what's in it. It's too big to remove and transport with the equipment we have. Trying to carve our way into that block takes tools and time we don't have. The probability we'd damage or destroy what's inside with what we've got to work with is 90%. Where does that leave us? We fold the tents starting tomorrow, take what we've found, and get out of here as quickly as we can. I want to be gone before whoever wants what happened here to remain secret can react. That's my decision. That's final."

"How in the hell can you do that?" Mark's face was as

red as I'd ever seen it. If he had an anger gage, it would have been bending the needle over at full. "We've done so much. Why abandon what we've come here to do right when we're at the threshold of finding the answers?"

"Because Naleeva's last orders to me were ... 'if you have to choose between the project and the lives of the expedition members, you choose the lives.' So, that's what I'm doing. I'm sure you can come back here *if you really want to*. Besides, didn't you want to pull out a week ago?"

"You know damned well we won't be able to get within a thousand miles of here again." Mark got up from the table where we were sitting and stormed out of the screen door. As he left, Reading entered.

"What's wrong with Mark? He looks like someone took his Teddy Bear away." Reading pulled a chair out and swung a long leg over it, so he was perched in the seat in the opposite direction the design called for.

"I just told him we're going home." Mug didn't wait for an answer. "Where in the hell have you been? I haven't seen you since we started excavating the last site."

"You really want to know? I did what I said I would. I spotted our four shadows fully absorbed in what you were doing at Site #6, so I came back to camp, took the boxes we discussed, and hid them. I don't think anyone will find them. Our insurance is paid up, so to speak." Reading surveyed who was at the table. Everyone except Elroy Cleggenhiest, Miccolee, and Mark were seated around him. "Where's Miccolee and Elroy?" he asked.

"Elroy headed back to his tent fifteen minutes ago. Miccolee ... in her tent, I guess. She disappears when we cracked those caskets. Doesn't have the stomach for it. She took off long before she thought we were going to open the vault."

"What did you find? Did you get to the coffin?" Reading asked.

"We found a frigging block of concrete thirteen feet on a side. Solid concrete. And that's the way we'll be leaving it. You think that's wrong?" Mug was challenging the whole table, not just Reading.

Everybody remained silent. Reading grinned, "Mug, I was ready to pull out of here a week ago. We're a hell of a lot better leaving here with what we got and not waiting for something we're pretty sure that's going to happen." He yawned. "It means all the cloak and dagger I did today was for nothing, but ... that's fine."

"It won't be for nothing until we have the stuff on the trucks and the trucks are on the road out of here."

Chapter 65
In our tents, middle of the night, Camp Little Berlin

"Wake up!" I felt someone shaking my shoulder. I tried to disregard them, but they wouldn't go away. The shaking became more violent, "Wake up you asshole!" The voice was familiar. I opened my eyes. Corporal Cole's face was a couple feet above mine, her features illuminated by faint light from a lantern inside the tent.

"Why are you here?" I asked.

"Get your big ass out of that cot! Mug wants everybody into the buildings over at Site #5 in fifteen minutes." It was the first time I'd seen Cole since she had been assigned to the tower and perpetual guard duty. "Meet your brother at the mess tent. He'll see you three get there."

I sat up, slapping my face to chase sleep away. "What's happening?" I mumbled, hoping for, but not expecting, an answer.

"Sarge Garrett radioed that we're going to have company here soon. There's a bunch of choppers getting ready to head this way." Before I could ask anything else, she was gone, the tent flaps wriggling in the gentle night breeze.

Migdahlia was rapidly dressing. Ida-Marie, already

dressed, was kneeling beside Miccolee's cot and going through Miccolee's personal effects stashed under it.

Miccolee was already gone, or I assumed so. Her clothes were missing, and she wasn't in the tent.

I practically jumped into my still damp cargo pants and shirt I'd worn earlier. I was pulling my socks and boots on when Migdahlia asked, "Can I help you?"

She was standing in front of me, completely dressed, her duffel bag slung over her shoulder. I nodded, "Thanks. Stuff anything you see under my cot into my bag." In a flash, Migdahlia was on her knees busily packing as I finished dressing.

"Oh, yes!" Ida-Marie was doing the opposite of Migdahlia. She was tearing things out of Miccolee's bag. Ida-Marie held an object up for us to see. It took a few seconds for me to recognize what it was. "Is that a cell phone case?"

"Yes! Now you know who you shouldn't have trusted, and it wasn't me!" Ida-Marie sounded vindicated.

I asked, "When's the last time either of you saw her?"

"She was in her cot when I came in and went to sleep," Migdahlia said.

"Corporal Cole told me she was gone when she came into the tent to wake us. She took some of her stuff with her and left enough clothes and junk to make us think she isn't a plant." Ida-Marie sneered, "I hope a Fer-de- Lance bites the bitch."

"Oh, I hope nothing bad happens to her." Migdahlia was unwilling to conclude there was a traitor among us.

I wasn't. "She's CIA. The letters tell the story. If a snake bites her, the snake will die."

Chapter 66
Inside the buildings at Site #5

The trot, for that's what it was, from the mess tent to the building complex was uneventful but terrifying none-the-less. Reading led the way with a flashlight. Migdahlia, Ida-Marie, and I followed behind like ducklings following their mother. The jungle night noise was multiplied by the knowledge that if Reading disturbed a snake or a lurking predator, we were more likely going to be its victim.

Branches slapped at us as we ran, each tap causing us to jerk, utter an alarm, and deepen our fears. The flashlight's beam gave birth to all manner of ghastly distorted shapes and shadows. I heard gasps accompanying mine coming from my running mates. The minutes it took to reach the forbidding silhouette of the Nazi complex seemed more like an hour.

Corporal Cole waited for us at the entrance that led to where the hidden room was located. Reading asked, "Any sign of them?"

"No." Cole's night vision apparatus made her look like a member of the Borg from the Star Trek TV series. Elroy Cleggenhiest and Dr. Beltran stood beside her.

"MacAphee said you are to wait with the NCs until he tells you to get them inside, or, if you see the choppers arrive, do it on your own. Come back here and wait for him or me to get you." She started to walk away.

"Where are you headed?" Reading wanted to be able to find her if things went wrong. That's the way he thinks.

"The tower. Duval can't handle the M-134 without help. We don't want to have to hold off a sizeable force with these pea shooters." Cole held up the M-16 assault rifle she carried. The woman disappeared into the dark.

We all stood just inside the tunnel leading to the bowels of the complex. In a few minutes, Migdahlia asked, "What are NCs?"

"Non-combatants." Reading and I answered simultaneously.

"Who are they?" Migdahlia asked.

It was evident that Mug had discussed what he wanted to happen with Reading. It pissed me off. I could handle a weapon very well. "You think I can't protect myself," I growled. I'd match my Marine training with anyone.

"Oh, Sis, don't light off your panties. You and Ida-Marie are going to be the protection for Migdahlia, Elroy and Petro." Reading spoke to Migdahlia, "You three are the NCs. It will take too long to train you to handle a rifle well enough to hit anything." His silhouette turned toward Ida- Marie and me. "You two will be stationed outside the doors at the secret room. There are two M-16s and boxes of loaded magazines waiting for you. Our food, reserve weapons and ammo are inside the room where Migdahlia,

Elroy, and Petro will be.”

“What about Mark, Dr. Dean, and Eduardo? They don’t know anything about weapons handling.” I didn’t mind being the protection for the NCs, but I didn’t like being posted in the claustrophobic depths of the tunnels.

“Actually, it turns out Eduardo and Donald both were in service and can shoot. Dr. Dean says he’s a good shot with an M-80 grenade launcher.” Reading pointed up to the tower perched on top of the complex. “Mark volunteered to handle ammunition for the mini-gun.” I couldn’t see his face, but I knew Reading was grinning. “Sorry, you’re stuck.”

“Why can’t I—” My comments were interrupted with the sound of shots being fired back at the campsite. The sound of our ATV’s engine starting with its customary backfire told us someone was headed our way. The question was who?

“Stay inside here until I come back. I need to see who is on the four-wheeler.” Reading asked me, “Do you have your automatic?”

“It’s in my bag.”

“Get it out and have it ready.” Reading crouched over and disappeared into the blackness leading to the gate. I removed my 9mm from my duffel bag, inserted a loaded clip, worked the action to chamber a bullet, put the safety on and waited.

I could hear the ATV engine noise getting close. No

shots were fired. Good, I thought. The engine shut off where I guessed the gate was located. Even better, Reading would have shot his forty-five if the person was unfriendly.

Reading called back to us, "Everything's okay. Mug and I are on our way." Within a few minutes, Mug and Reading walked out of the darkness.

As they stopped in front of me, I asked, "What were the shots?"

"Our shadow friends have come out of the woods and have taken possession of our camp. I was going to get a few more things I thought we needed out of the supply dump. When I started to cross the clearing, they opened fire."

"You're lucky," I said.

"No. If they wanted to hit me, I'd be fit for buzzard meat right now." Mug took a breath. "The fire pattern they laid down was aimed so there was no chance of hitting me. They wanted me out of there, so I obliged them." He hesitated a few seconds then added, "There were five sets of muzzle flashes. We don't have to worry or guess about where Miccolee got off to."

Reading said, "Seems to me that's good news and bad news. Good news is, you're alive. They'd have killed you if they were sure they were going to end up doing that to us. The bad news is, Miccolee knows what we've been doing, and that's going to make things a bunch easier for them."

"Are we going to go get them before the others arrive?" It was Mark's familiar voice coming from the dark as he came close enough to see.

"You're a little old to be getting excited about old John Wayne movies. Hell no! We are going to set here, hope like hell they leave us alone, get their business done and get out of here, so we can follow." Mug rested the grenade launcher he carried on his shoulder. "Hope and pray they don't decide we have something that they have to have." He rubbed his finger across his neck in a slitting motion. "There aren't enough star shells to keep the approaches lit up. We have five. I'll save those until we're damned sure they're moving against us."

"If they get close?" Mark asked.

"Kill them before they kill us." Reading said, "Now what?"

Mug handed the grenade launcher to Reading and then the backpack full of grenades.

"Go out to the stone emplacement that covers the approach to the gate. I'll send Wolf and Stevenson out to you with assault rifles and plenty of rounds. Strain your eyes until they pop out of your skull. We wait."

Mug tapped Mark's shoulder then motioned for Mark to come with him. They started off, Reading toward the gate ... Mug and Mark toward the tower.

Mug stopped abruptly and told Mark to wait for him. He walked back to me and extended both hands. He said,

"Take these flashlights. You'll need them." Mug leaned close, so his mouth was only inches from my ear. He whispered, "I regret not having the chance to ask you to share a sheet with me. You're one hell of a woman." His brushed my cheek as he left.

I stood silently as he disappeared into the night. I wasn't offended. It was Mug's way of complimenting me and warning me things could go badly.

Chapter 67
Site #5

None of the group Ida-Marie and I were in charge of wanted to spend more time in the rock and concrete vault than necessary. The secret room forced them into tomb-like incarceration. There was no harm in letting them alone for a short period. If the hiding place could be entered quickly, we could wait until the last second to bury ourselves. I walked down the long tunnel through the room where we'd found the burned remains of the complex's inhabitants. Through that room, I entered a side tunnel that connected to the main entrance and the wall where the hidden door provided clandestine access to our hiding place. I operated the lever I'd discovered embedded in the rock. Since the door rotated and closed in one motion, I used a flashlight to keep it from closing. That would allow Migdahlia and the rest quick access if something happened to me. The last thought was even more disquieting.

I returned, explained what I did, and the five of us waited in undisturbed silence. Questions like, "Do you really think they'll come?" "What do you think they'll do to us?" "Do you think we should try to escape before they get here and kill us?" — Though wide time spans elapsed between each comment, none of those helped our morale. I'd had enough. After Ida-Marie asked if we thought those coming to kill us would rape us before our murder, I told everybody, "Shut up. Just shut the hell up! Talking about this doesn't help. If you want to talk about how good a steak will taste when we get home, fine! Otherwise, keep your mouths shut."

They did. It did little to reduce the tension. Ominous sounds of jungle cats screaming, rustling noises of animals moving in the trees near us, and at times the most frightening condition, absolute silence, was crushing to our psyches. Time refused to progress and seemed to even move backward. I wondered how long it had been since Corporal Cole rousted me from my cot. After my emotional tirade, I didn't dare ask.

"Look there!" Ida-Marie pointed toward the Little Berlin Campsite. A strange red glow arose from behind the trees and underbrush that blocked our view of the camp.

"Flares. They're marking the landing zone for the helicopters," Petro said.

Within seconds the faint, thump, thump, thump, thump of rotor blades became audible. Lots of rotor blades. As the noise increased, our heart-beats increased with the thumps. Elroy eased outside the tunnel entrance and began counting the unlighted low black blotches flitting across moonlit clouds. "One ... two ... three ... four ... five ... six ... seven. Three of them are really big ones."

Before they landed, bright landing lights shone down on the ground where they intended to land. Only one stayed aloft. "A lookout," I analyzed aloud. One by one they dropped from the sky, the exception being the one that circled the camp in broad circles. The engines quieted one by one. I heard Mug yell, "Movement in the woods! Chessie, get your people inside!"

I yelled, "Follow me." My mates raced behind me to the 90° turn, through the large room, into the adjoining hall and to the flashlight that held the door ajar. I pushed against the door, holding it open for my friends to enter. They rushed inside. As Migdahlia entered, I gave her one of my flashlights and said, "Good luck." The weak light from the flashlight disclosed she tried to smile and nodded as she stepped through the entrance. Only Ida-Marie remained outside. "Go ahead," I prompted.

Ida-Marie bent over and picked up the flashlight, took one of the M-16s and a few magazines. She straightened up and stared at me. Her eyes were wild and flashing even in the low light. "I'm not going to go outside the other door and wait alone. I can't do that! I'll stay in the room with them." She took one step inside before saying, "Chessie, you should come into the room with us, too."

"Just go!" I pushed her inside and let the door slam closed.

I was alone ... totally and completely alone, to face whatever was to occur.

Chapter 68
Site #5

Waiting isn't pleasant, at least, not for me. That's particularly true when there is something hanging over my head. I remember waiting for a number of potentially life-altering events. Results of job interviews. Cut lists to see if I made high school basketball and softball teams. Orders from my sergeant in a fire-fight. Waiting to see if Rooster Cocker would kill me when I discovered where he murdered his victims. I had one to add. Waiting in the bowels of the old stone fortress ranks with being hunted by Rooster, the worst waiting experience I'd experienced previously. Waiting is hell!

I backed up until my rear touched the wall opposite the secret door to the hidden room. The quarried stones ground into my flesh, and my head bumped the wall causing me to swear. My words sounded hollow in the dank subterranean tunnels. I swung the flashlight beam around my surroundings. Stark and barren, the tunnel provided no place to hide. It was close to a hundred feet long. It opened into the large room that had housed the burnt bodies of the massacred victims. The rectangular tube went off in the other direction. It appeared to end in another hall. I'd never been further into the confines of the complex than where I stood.

We had no concrete knowledge of intentions of the force that had just landed in our camp. We surmised they were "enemies." There was no proof that they wanted to destroy us and what we'd done. What we did know was where the group had taken off from and what had happened a half-century ago. The human remains in specimen boxes we'd collected were a result of what we all envisioned as a similar adventure. Knowing we'd been under observation, our connection to our sponsor in government had been intercepted, and a very large force had come to do something we didn't have control over, made me conclude they hadn't come to invite us to a picnic.

Mug's instructions to me had been to stay hidden where I was until he came to get me and the rest. I looked at my surroundings. Stay hidden? Where? Only a cockroach could find grooves large enough in the stone walls to vanish from view. Ida-Marie's suggestion that I join the rest inside the secret room sounded prudent and me a fool for disregarding it. Turning my flashlight off would only work if our visitors weren't equipped with night- vision equipment. "Fat chance of that," I said to the empty hallway.

I decided I should find someplace to retreat, if necessary. I picked up the remaining M-16 and the half dozen magazines, stuffing them in my cargo pants. There weren't any potential hiding places in the area I was familiar with, so I walked cautiously down the tunnel, away from the room that had housed the burnt victims ... into what, I had no idea.

After I walked two dozen paces, I could see my guess was correct. The tunnel I was in terminated into another tunnel that looked identical with one exception. The floor I stood on was concrete. The floor I was approaching was made of the same stones the walls were constructed. When I reached the crossing tunnel and stepped into it, I stopped and used my flashlight to see what my chances were of finding an escape route. What the beam disclosed wasn't heartening. To my right, only a few yards away was a heavy steel door with a series of padlocks and interlocking latches that would take special tooling or explosives to dislodge. I immediately turned my attention in the opposite direction. The tunnel was 150 feet long and it didn't end in another door. The ceiling sloped downward. Stairs or a ramp! I ran to see which.

The stairs descended what I guessed was forty or more feet. That was more than four stories! Halfway down a landing provided a resting point. I descended the stairs as quickly as I could. When I reached the bottom, the flashlight disclosed another tunnel. This one was short and ended in a wall, but this wall had a window in it. That meant possible escape. I ran to it and peered outside. What I saw crushed me. If I wished to commit suicide, I had a way to do it. The dim moonlight disclosed that the window was built in the side of the cliff I'd almost been pushed over. The 90° drop ended a hundred feet below with the river and large boulders acting as a mat.

After my disappointment subsided, I tried to find some logical solution. The tunnel I was in had no doors or connecting passages that I saw, except the one which was near the junction of the two tunnels. That was strange. Why even build this part of the tunnel? For a window that overlooked space? It would be useless as a defensive position, for no one would attack from that direction. There was no way to escape from there short of repelling the cliff. It was unthinkable to believe the tunnel was built to provide a vista of the gorge below. Germans were pragmatic, practical people. They wouldn't have constructed something so elaborate without a useful purpose. As far as I could tell, the tunnel I was in was like the one where the hidden room could be accessed from. Just like that hall?! I realized the answer to my question. There were probably one or more hidden access doors along its length. I decided to focus on finding them *if* they existed.

It was logical that one of the exits would be in the area where I stood. Why build it otherwise. And, it didn't take long for me to find something to explore. A large steel ring was mounted to one of the stones on the floor. I gathered my strength, expecting that a device un-operated for a half-century would strongly resist efforts to move it. To my surprise, it lifted easily. Beneath the rock was a lever and mechanism that was attached to a winch. When I pulled on the lever, a noise came from the wall on the opposite side of the tunnel. It was another hidden door. I opened it and looked inside. The corridor was entirely different. It was only wide enough and tall enough to allow one person to use at a time. When I shone my flashlight into the darkness, I heard a whirring sound followed by a cloud of flying objects that exploded in my face. Bats! That told me the passage connected to the outside. Most of the loathsome beasts quickly found the window and the night air filled with insects. Bat dinner!

My thoughts returned to the door in front of me. The ease with which I'd been able open this escape hatch meant it had been operated recently, undoubtedly by our adversaries. That was sobering. They could have been observing more closely than we ever imagined. It also offered an explanation of how someone could have snuck up behind me and shoved me toward the cliff seemingly appearing from 'nowhere.' I pushed the door closed, removed one of the M-16 magazines from my pocket and used it as a wedge to hopefully keep the door from opening from the other side. That would make my rear secure and still provide me a possible way out if it came to that.

Further examination of the short section of tunnel yielded zero. I climbed the stairs to the landing. I looked at the walls on either side. Something was wrong, but what wasn't registering. I concentrated on them and the floor.

There were no steel rings on the landing. The construction was the same; rock and mortar. There were handrails on one of the walls. Handrail! There were no handrails on one of the walls next to the stairs. I immediately started to examine the area around the rail carefully. Within seconds, I discovered its secret. On one end, a pole and hole latch was hidden behind the railing. I removed the pin from the mating clevis, pulled on the handrail, and most of the wall swung out toward me. My flashlight beam illuminated something that temporarily made me forget the precarious situation in which we were involved.

Behind the panel, there was a small room. I guessed it was fifteen feet wide and thirty deep. There were wooden boxes stacked in a random fashion. Most appeared to have been open. A desk and a couple of chairs were a few paces inside. The lamp sitting on the desktop and papers scattered about its surface gave me the feeling I saw a scene that hadn't been touched since the day the complex was assaulted a half-century ago. There were several framed photographs and paintings hung on the walls and propped against boxes. That was all interesting, but it wasn't what sucked the breath from my lungs. There was a huge safe against one wall. The door was wide open.

It was filled with documents and gold bars.

Chapter 69
Site #5, 'Gold Room.'

The open safe door drew me like a magnet draws steel. The thought that someone might be slinking down the tunnels, looking to kill me, slipped from my mind's prime focus. History was before me and the chance for our group to rewrite it. And, most importantly, to prove our narrative was true.

Remembering the profuse use of mines to protect the compound, I was very cautious as I approached the open safe door. Something so critical *could* be booby- trapped. I checked the floor for pressure plates, for switches on the door, and anything that could be connected to an electrical or mechanical detonator. Nothing was suspicious. I moved to a foot of the steel giant and shone my flashlight inside. Large stacks of envelopes, files cases, loose documents, and twenty-seven gold bars, I counted them ... filled over half of the space inside.

My hand had a mind of its own. It had one of the gold bars clutched in its fingers before I made the conscious decision to fondle the treasure. My mind said that was not why we were here. It reprimanded my sweaty palm, and reluctantly the hand eased the gold bar back into the place from where it had been lifted. I blew on a couple stacks of documents sending a cloud of choking dust into the dank room's air. They were printed on stationary with an eagle perched on a circle containing a swastika. To me, that meant these were most likely official Nazi documents. I picked up the top three or four from one of the stacks and tried reading them.

I mumbled, "Duh, they're all in German." It took a second for me to realize that Miccolee was no longer 'one of us.' Suddenly, the reason we'd been assigned the talents of an interpreter was evident. It also told me that those folks involved in sponsoring this trip knew a lot more about what we were likely to uncover than we did. I returned them to the stack of papers.

I picked up a framed picture from a stack of four or five. Blowing on the glass covering the photo only removed a portion of the accumulation of dust. I used my shirt tail to remove the rest. A severe-looking middle-aged man scowled up at me. The man's clothes and obvious age of the yellowing photo paper prompted me to guess the photo had been made in the early 1900s. A tarnished metal nameplate identified the scowling gentleman as "Alois." I set it aside and cleaned the second picture in the stack. The nameplate on this one stated "Klara." I brushed the dust from the glass. My effort revealed a matron of forty, whose features shouted she had endured and suffered more than her share. The smile was forced in that unhappy face.

I picked up the third frame. It was ornate and the

woman whose likeness it bore dressed in more modern clothes. "Looks like the fifties," I said to myself as I used my tee to clean the glass and name-plate. This woman's features had a genuine smile, she was blonde, and had soft, friendly eyes. I read the short name ... "Eva." I knew I was looking at Hitler's family photos. I took a step away from the safe.

Slowly, very slowly, I circled the room with the beam from my flashlight. I stopped on every item that was left from a past that was undoubtedly evil, but historically significant and steeped with melancholy just the same.

When the ray reached the desk, I held it on what had once been rich polished wood. I tried to visualize one of the two men who was, and is, the embodiment of evil. I could visualize him, seated there, lost in a dream world. His schemes to recapture his power were as dead as the millions he slaughtered. How fitting and torturous for a man with such an ego and thirst for power, to languish in a jungle surrounded by rot, just like the rot his dreams had become. For such a man, this type of existence was far worse than death in a noose or at a wall.

The sudden chattering of machine gun fire and explosions jarred me from the historical fairyland to where I'd traveled. The real world knocked. I wouldn't have long to find out what was going to happen. Impetuously, I grabbed a handful of documents and one envelope stuffed with papers, twisted them into a tight roll and stuffed them in my cargo pants' largest pocket. Without further thought, I stuffed one of the gold bars into another pocket. It was heavy and awkward. I knew I might have to toss it later, but ...

I sprinted out of the room and up the flight of stairs, deciding I would come back to close the door later. I didn't stop running until I reached the last tunnel and the opening to the outside. Star shells turned the night skies into bright phosphorus white light. There was lots of firing, but not much hitting close to where I stood and stared. Things were reaching a climax. I knew it wouldn't be a good one. I just hoped to survive it.

Chapter 70
Site #5

The fire I heard all around me was suppressing in nature. I could tell it was aimless, designed to keep us immobile rather than to search us out and kill us. My question was, *why*?

Star shells light up the surroundings effectively. However, the effect they produce bathes everything in color robbing white light, and casts eerie shadows. It brought back unpleasant thoughts of my time in Afghanistan.

That experience taught me a lot. The fire I was hearing was all incoming. Mug was maintaining excellent fire control. That meant he didn't see any movement threatening us. That was a good thing, I thought. When the last star shell went out, inky blackness took its place. The firing ceased at the same time the light disappeared. It took me a couple of minutes for my eyes to adjust to the absence of light. Absolute silence replaced the bedlam of automatic and small weapons fire. I figured that Mug had denied them targets to shoot at by not returning any fire.

The question was how they would respond. It remained silent. Were they content to keep us pinned in place or were they stealthily advancing on us? I reached for my cell phone and realized I'd left it under my pillow back in the tent. My watch was stowed in my duffel bag in the room where Migdahlia and the rest hid. Not being able to keep track of time would lengthen it exponentially. I strained my eyes and ears for a movement or a sound that would betray an advancing enemy. They saw and heard nothing.

Suddenly, another series of star shells exploded above the complex. Within seconds, small weapons fire zipped high overhead. It was intense, but aimed so high I couldn't hear any bullets tearing through the underbrush. That was weird! I had an excellent view of the yard from the entrance I stood in. The stone fence was brightly illuminated as were the three gun emplacements, the gate, and the portion of the jungle I could see on the other side of the fence. Once again, not one shot came from our positions. The firing lessened, but a steady stream of shots came from fewer guns until the star shells burned out. The silent black night returned.

I cursed. They, whoever 'they' were, were playing a cat and mouse game with us. After my eyes readapted to the dark, I eased a few steps out of the entrance and looked around. Afterward, I wished I hadn't. Dark shadows surrounded tunnel openings. Any one of them could house advancing enemies, and I wouldn't see anyone until they were right on top of me. I stepped back inside the tunnel with that sobering thought in mind. No doubt. If a number of them rushed the tunnel at once, I would be toast. I summoned up my mindset from service days...I'd see how many I could take with me before I fell.

Several more minutes passed, as black and quiet as before. Then the star shells brought the return of the firing. It was clear they would repeat this pattern, *but why*?

Each successive flurry of shooting held me captive at the entrance. Time periods varied...sometimes the star shell illumination and firing would last for what seemed forever. Sometimes it would be over in a minute. The same was true of the periods of silence and inky darkness. I quit counting the alternating periods when I reached twelve. Were they trying to keep us from sleeping? They would have had to do a small portion of the demonstration of firepower they displayed to do that. Logically, were they using it to infiltrate the area close to the complex? That didn't make sense. Why illuminate everything so brightly? That would increase the problem of moving forward. It focused attention on the direction of our campsite where all the fire was coming from. It focused *all our attention* in one direction. The firing commenced again.

"Oh shit!" I pulled my flashlight from my pocket and directed the beam into the tunnel. As I ran to the place I should have been standing guard, I realized that we'd been witnessing a diversion. I just I hoped I hadn't screwed up too badly.

Chapter 71
Site #5, In the tunnels under the complex.

"Think, Chessie, think!" I shouted at myself as I ran down the tunnel toward the door to the secret room. I'd left my post. It wasn't an officer berating me; I was doing enough of that. My words sunk in. If I wanted to stay alive, I'd better think ... right now. I stopped so quickly I lurched forward, nearly falling on my face.

Think. Process what you'll do next. You don't want them to know you're coming. Turn off the flashlight and be as silent as the inside of a coffin. The instant black my surroundings became clutched at my throat, making it difficult to breathe. Bedlam from guns firing behind me made it difficult to discern noises being generated close.

Think. Process what you'll do when you face them. A lot depended on how many. I locked and loaded my M-16. The sound was like the roar of a lion in my mind. If anyone was in the tunnels, they surely heard it. I mentally said, "Damn." I reached down and felt for an old friend, the Kabar combat knife my father gave me years ago. I'd always carried it as an ornament. Now my life could depend on it and on the lessons my father had taught me about its use.

Think. Confronted by a group, do I stand or retreat? I could answer that ... stand. There was no place to hide, and

I wasn't able to dodge or out-run bullets in the confined space. I had little doubt they would have night vision. It put me at a huge disadvantage. Having my flashlight lit was an even greater risk. What could I do? Think!

I'd need to stay in contact with the wall to my left side. That side and route had no breaks that would force me to turn on my light to orient myself. Being against the wall would give me a degree of decreased visibility unless the invaders had thermal image detection as well as night vision. If they did, I was toast city. People tend to look out at eye level, so I decided to duck walk, crawl if necessary, to be more difficult to detect. If I stopped and listened for any noise every few yards, I had a chance of knowing where they were before they discovered me.

I moved to the wall by side-stepping until my extended left hand touched it. As it came in contact with the rough stone, the firing outside the tunnel ceased and, if possible, the darkness became more intense. My knees complained as I squatted down in the position to duck-walk along the wall. After listening for several seconds to absolute quiet, I took a dozen waddling steps further into the tunnel. I stopped, listened, and repeated my actions.

By the time I reached the 90° turn, my knees, calves, and thighs were in revolt. I compromised with them by crawling on all fours until my knees put up such a fuss I gave them a few moments rest.

This extended period of time tested my hearing. That

test made me wonder if I was hearing something or my mind was fabricating a higher fear factor than I already was suffering from. At first, I thought I heard a rhythmic clinking as if someone was using a sledgehammer to beat on something. It stopped before I could be sure. Next, I fancied hearing something being dragged over the stones that formed the floor. It was so faint I determined the "*sssssssssssssssss*" sound I heard was in my mind. That was until I started thinking about what could have caused the noise. A snake? Maybe a big Fer-da-Lance? That was chilling! Getting bit in the ankle or leg was horrible enough, but the thought of being struck in the face or torso made my whole body quiver. When I started again, I alternated between the duck-walk and crouching over deeply from the waist with my knees flexed. I kept my left shoulder in contact with the wall and hoped for the best.

I knew I'd reached the huge room that had held the burned human remains and trashed compound materials we'd so carefully reclaimed. The smooth concrete floor announced where I was. I would have to cross a hundred feet or so before I reached the next tunnel, the one with the hidden door that led to the secret room, the one that led to the final tunnel...steel door...stairway ...safe room...back exit...where I expected to confront my enemies. Automatically, my feet moved to my next stop without thinking of starting or stopping. This time when I stopped and listened, I heard the faint, unintelligible murmur for a few seconds, and then went silent. I saw no humans. My heart beat increased like the engine in a runaway truck.

Before I resumed my stealthy approach, I removed the safety on my M-16. The crouch position was my best way to keep my weapon at the ready. Things were coming to a climax. I knew I'd probably come face-to-face with my adversaries in the next few minutes. Translated, that meant I might only have another few minutes to live.

Chapter 72
Site #5, In the tunnels under the complex

My feet felt the rocks that signaled I'd reached the tunnel on the other side of the storage room. That meant I was less than a hundred feet from the entrance to the secret room. What should I do when I reached it? If it was open or ajar, I decided I'd take a chance and call out to Migdahlia and the rest. If it was closed? By-pass the door and continue to the end of the hall where I believed I'd seen light, heard voices, and noise.

I decided the lower the profile, the better. Lying next to the wall, I belly crawled forward, keeping my M-16 in a ready firing position. I stopped halfway to the hidden door. I heard voices ahead, but saw no light. Straining to hear, I couldn't mak— one was a female. I recognized her voice, but couldn't put the name to its owner.

Suddenly, light shone from an unseen source in the cross-tunnel ahead. It illuminated the rocks around me so slightly I believed I'd be invisible unless someone got lucky when they glanced in my direction. I reached forward to crawl closer when my hand touched something soft. I froze as I felt it move. My eyes clamped shut, and I expected to feel fangs puncturing me in my most vulnerable spot ... my face.

The softness moved away from my fingers. Slowly I opened my eyes. A tarantula, the size of a glove, skittered off in front of me. I took a breath so deep it sounded like a foghorn marking my position in the dark. I hope ... prayed no one heard it.

Nothing happened. I resumed my crawl toward the light, the tunnel, and to the hidden door. Within fifteen feet I reached the edge of the secret panel. The crack under the door was black, and the door was securely closed. I hoped my colleagues were safe inside. I listened for several seconds. Faint, scuffing sounds drifted to me—the metallic clanks of steel striking steel— the sounds of someone moving materials.

Should I advance or stay still? Staying still was discretion as I decided the hell with valor. Within seconds my choice was vindicated. One by one, four people walked past the opening each heavily loaded with boxes and bags they carried. Night-vision apparatus on their heads made them look like aliens. They came from the side of the hall where the huge steel door was located. I moved another twenty feet forward and stopped. The closer I got to the opening and the light, the more danger I would put myself in.

"You get everything?" I heard a man say.

"Yes, everything important." It was the woman's voice I recognized, but couldn't place. She asked, "You have the C-4?"

"Oh yes! You want me to seal the entrance, no problem. You want me to flatten this whole place? I can probably do that if you give me a couple of hours to place my stuff in the right spots." The male voice sounded confident.

"You enjoy your work too much," the woman replied. "Put just enough to collapse the tunnel we're in and no more. And, do it quick. We have to be off the ground in two hours."

A voice yelled from the illuminated tunnel, "Hey you guys, stop bull-shitting and help me get this stuff down these stairs and outside."

"Okay." It was the woman again. "Terry, go ahead and plant the explosive. Just be sure it doesn't go off until we're back in the choppers and off the ground."

"I'll set it to go off in three hours."

It became quiet. Time began to slow again. I remained frozen, waiting for something to happen. After a couple of minutes that seemed like hours, metallic noises came from where the big metal door was located. It wasn't long after that a big man carrying an electric lantern crossed in front of the opening. Midway he stopped, turned and faced my direction, and held the lantern up. My heart did a flip. I recognized the face. It was Stan Hansen the FBI agent I'd first met at a meeting in the States. I waited for him to see me and give an alarm. He didn't. Hansen turned away and yelled, "No one in the access tunnel," as he walked toward the stairwell. The light faded with each step the man took after he disappeared from sight.

The muffled sound of voices came from the barely lit opening to the crossing tunnel. I decided to move forward half the distance to the opening. Moving as silently as I could, the only noise I made was a gentle scuffing sound of my clothes against the stones. It was time to freeze, listen, and wait.

Occasionally, I half-heard voices and some words when the individuals spoke to others a distance from them. The glow from the lantern was so faint it was more the suggestion of light rather than illumination. Then the woman said, "That it?" The answer chilled me. "Yes, Alexa." I now knew who the female was ... Alexa Lind, the CIA agent who Mark told us, 'killing people, is her business.'

Alexa wasn't happy. She barked, "Damn it, no names."

"There's no one alive to hear it. Lighten up." I wasn't sure, but I believed that voice belonged to Hansen. He added, "Let's get out." As he uttered the last word, the light went off and the inky darkness returned. I thought I heard some shuffling and footsteps, but couldn't be sure. What I did know was that within a couple minutes absolute silence reigned.

I remained frozen in place. True, they probably were gone, but I decided to stay put to be sure of that. They could come back because they missed something or could be setting a trap for anyone, like me, who had been spying on them. Dying because I wasn't patient enough to wait another ten minutes would be stupid. I began counting to myself. "One Mississippi ... Two Mississippi ..." until I reached 600 then I considered it safe to crawl forward.

I reached the opening to the cross tunnel. My curiosity nagged at me to turn on my flashlight and shine it toward the steel door, but prudence told me, "no." Carefully, I peeked around the corner of the tunnel toward the stairs. I couldn't see a thing, but black. That was good and bad. They were probably gone, but there was no way I could be sure.

Keeping my rifle in front of me, I maneuvered around the corner, keeping my body in contact with the wall as I slowly inched forward. Five feet. Ten feet. Fifteen feet. Nothing. I reached forward with my hand that was farthest from wall to resume crawling and put it into something wet and cool. I held my hand a few inches in front of my face, but I could barely make out its outline. I gathered myself and moved forward another foot, then extended my hand forward and away from the wall. Just before it was as far away from me as I could reach, my hand touched something solid, but soft. What I touched didn't move.

I pulled myself a little farther forward and moved my hand, exploring with my fingers. In one direction my sense of touch told me I was in contact with skin. Letting my fingers travel in the opposite direction, the skin entered cloth. Another couple of inches my senses found something they touched all the time, hair. I pulled my hand back in horror. It was a body, but whose.

Was it one of the people I was supposed to guard? The desire to turn on and shine my flashlight on whoever lay next to me was intense. I fought it, but the morbid question forced me to reach back and let my fingers explore. I touched the flesh; my fingers found the hair, it was long, as they moved they sensed they were in contact with someone's chin...someone's neck ... someone's chest ... and, some woman's breasts.

My heart sank, I knew the liquid I touched was blood, but whose? Migdahlia or Ida-Marie's?

Chapter 73

Site #5, In the tunnels under the complex.

What next? The shock of finding what I supposed was one of my friend's bodies left me reeling mentally. Tears dampened my face, though I fought their coming. My expressive nature took command, and though subdued I muttered, "Shit!" in a gassy expletive. The question remained, what next? I sat up, my back pressing against the wall and my M-16 pointing out toward a possible invisible enemy in the tunnel.

Think, Chessie, think. My next actions would go a long way to determine if I lived. I had to get up and move about and find out what my friends' fate was. Our attackers had night vision; that was now a fact. I had no advantage in keeping my flashlight off. At least, I'd be able to see them before they were on top of me. I elected to count to 600 again before resuming the search for my friends.

"Five-hundred, ninety-nine Mississippi ... 600." I scooted my back up the wall until I was in a standing position, took a deep breath, and turned on my flashlight. After sweeping it in both directions to see whether I had company, I shined its beam at the floor in front of me.

"Oh, no," I said. My light disclosed that Ida-Marie was the victim. She lay in a puddle of her own blood. Her assault rifle was still clutched in her hands, her eyes open, and the expression on her face was frozen surprise, not terror. Her throat had been cut all the way across.

I shuddered at the sight and shuddered again when I looked at my hands. My hands, my arm, and part of my shirt were soaked with her blood. It was blood I knew I'd never ever be able to cleanse. I languished in guilt for a few seconds before realizing I could do nothing to help Ida- Marie, but I might be able to help the others and myself.

The first place I checked was the stairs. Looking down at the landing, I saw the door to the room containing the safe was closed. Fear accompanied each step down to the landing. From there, I could see the door was still open to the narrow escape passage. My flashlight beam found the mechanism that opened and closed it. The levers were bent, and one wire was broken. It lay on the floor. I wondered if they took much from the safe, but finding out would wait until later.

Next, I decided to look inside the steel door, see what was there and determine if it was possible to disable the explosives. The stair and floor rocks wanted to trip me as I climbed the steps and ran down the tunnel. The door was closed, but not padlocked as when I'd seen it a few hours ago. I grabbed the handle and pulled the eight-foot square piece of steel open just enough to peer inside. Instantly, I was relieved that I hadn't jerked the door open. My eyes traced a cord attached to the inside of the door to the pin of a hand grenade. Being sure to maintain plenty of slack in the cord, I aimed my light inside. When the beam settled on what was in there, I had another shock. There were steel canisters and pieces of equipment I didn't recognize. What I did know was the symbol for radiation danger painted on several of them.

In bright yellow letters, the following German phrases were stenciled on two of the metal containers: *"Die Beachtung! Das Eigentum – Dr. Ronald Richter!"* I decided this might be important, so I repeated the phrases over and over and over, trying to commit them to memory.

The door swung open almost pulling the cord tight. Frantically, I pushed the door closed. A simple lift latch dropped into place. "Good," I said to myself. I could come back later and see about disabling the bomb. For now, I needed to find Migdahlia and the rest.

I spun away from the huge steel door, took two or three steps to get into the intersecting tunnel, and raced to the secret panel. The beam of my flashlight disclosed the exposed lever to operate the mechanism. Leaning my rifle against the wall, I clutched the steel, and as I pulled, I prayed my friends were still alive. The door rotated halfway and stopped. I didn't think why it didn't operate as before. I was too anxious to learn the fate of my friends.

I wouldn't learn about them until later. Frantically, I swept the flashlight beam around the room. Everyone was gone! Their bags were still there, but that was all. I circled the room again with my light. I saw nothing but bare walls, bare floor, bare ceiling except the pile of our baggage in one corner.

The door slowly started to close. Was someone after me? I turned off my flashlight at the same time I stuck my leg in its path to keep the door from shutting. My knife left its scabbard without my being conscious that I'd grabbed it. I waited for an attack and sighed with relief when nothing happened. Straining my ears, I listened for a sound betraying an attacker. It remained tomb-quiet.

After a minute, I was sure the only attack I was suffering from was my nerves. Pushing the door open, I leaned over to pick up my M-16. That action probably saved my life. I was jarred forward as I felt something swish over my back. As I twisted around to confront my attacker, a tall shadow towered above me. I felt a knife slice downward into my back beneath my right shoulder. "You'd have died cleaner if you'd gone over the cliff when I pushed you." Alexa withdrew the knife and prepared for the killing blow. I smashed the palm of my hand at where I knew her night vision goggles were and I got lucky. The equipment was shoved into her eyes and caused her to reset herself.

I heard my DI back on Paris Island screaming, "Partin, stay inside when your attacker makes a wide arc! Block with your arm!" I tried to do both as I pushed my body close to hers. Our blows were simultaneous. She drove her knife in my back on my left side. My Kabar entered the flesh of her abdomen, cutting edge up, and I ripped it upward with its thrust ending under her left ribcage. I knew I might die. I also knew she would too. I heard the gurgling sounds she made and her last breath leave her.

Intertwined, we both slumped to the ground. There were footsteps. I was fighting to stay conscious, but not winning that battle. A light shined in my eyes, and I looked up into it. I asked, "Who the hell are you?" And, I said what I felt. "I'm hurt, and it's damned painful."

I heard, but never saw, Reading say, "Hang in there, it's me, Sis."

"Reading?" I tried to reach up to grab him, but my arm wouldn't move. There was something I should, no, *had* to tell him. I was having trouble remembering what. Oh yes, I remembered. "Don't open the steel door in the next tunnel. Just open it enough to cut the string."

"What are you talking about?" Mug's face came into view over mine. "What string?"

Mug was dumb, or so I thought in my foggy world. "You know. Boom! The string goes to a grenade, and it is in with a big-assed bomb."

Mug yelled, "Stay away from that door!"

He was getting smarter. The world went warm, carefree, and black.

Chapter 74
On a tractor trail leaving Little Berlin

"Damn it! Don't drop her in the creek!" Mug's voice boomed and woke me up from wherever I'd been. I squinted as bright sunlight attacked my pupils. It was the third time I'd regained consciousness since my fight in the tunnel. I tried to raise my hand to shield my eyes from the sun. Mistake! I hurt from my waist to my shoulders.

"She's awake." I recognized one of Mug's men's voice.

A familiar voice said, "Don't try to move."

"Migdahlia?" I asked.

"Yes, Chessie. I'm here. What can I do for you? You want some water?"

My body was jostled around, and I realized I was being carried on a stretcher. This time the pain wasn't self-inflicted. I turned my head to the side to get the sun out of my eyes. That hurt, too. What I saw surprised me. Dr. Beltran and three of Mug's soldiers manned the four corners of my cot. They were wading through calf deep water. Migdahlia waded beside me. I tried looking up, but the sun forced my head back to the side. Another series of pains told me to stay still. They persisted, so I wouldn't forget. "Water would be good," I suggested. I wasn't awake enough to know if I was thirsty, but it sounded like the right thing to say.

Migdahlia said, "Is it okay, Dr. Beltran?"

"Yes. Just give her a very little at a time. I don't want her coughing and tearing a wound."

Migdahlia held her canteen to my lips and let me have a few small sips. I nodded, and she took it away.

Mug's familiar voice kept issuing instructions. "Bud and Reading, take over for Petro and Sammy when we get her up on the road. We'll take ten before we head out."

The men struggled up the side of a red clay bank. It wasn't that steep, but the foliage was close to impenetrable. When they reached the "road," it turned out to be the tractor trail we had driven in on to get to Little Berlin. They set me down. The stretcher had built-in supports that kept me from lying on the dirt tracks.

I was becoming cogent enough to begin to have questions. Mug smiled down at me and asked, "Sleeping beauty. You okay?"

"No! Somebody ran over me with a plow." I laughed a little, and the pain returned. "Don't make me laugh. It hurts."

"You aren't far wrong." Reading stood next to Migdahlia. "That old gal did a good job slicing you. You did a better job on her."

"She dead?" I asked.

He nodded.

"I knew it. What about Ida-Marie? When I found her—" I didn't finish for Reading was nodding. Things were returning. "What about Cleggenhiest ... I know Migdahlia and Dr. Beltran are okay."

"He's fine. He's walking with Eduardo and Dr. Dean." Reading said, "Everybody made it with the exception of Ida-Marie. Two of Mug's guys got minor wounds, that's it."

"Why are we walking?" I asked.

"Don't you remember waking up outside the tunnel?"

"No." I kind of did but wanted Reading's description.

"Our visitors completely destroyed everything in our campsite. You got real excited when you saw all the flames before you passed out. They put thermite on all the vehicle engines and shot up all the tires. What they didn't carry off, they burned. When they left, there was nothing but white ash where our tents, equipment, everything was. How much they took with them of what we found, we don't know. They found all but two of the boxes I hid. We figure Miccolee was following me when I hid them. Eduardo and Dean are carrying them out. We're walking out with our clothes and what we had hidden in the compound."

"Oh! You got my duffel bag didn't you?" I flinched, and pain reminded me to stay still.

"Yes, the only thing we were able to salvage was the big wagon we had at Site #5. Everything we could save is on it. Your duffel bag is there.”

“Be sure my makeup case is in it.”

“That’s kind of inconsequential isn’t it?” Reading looked at me as if I had reverted to being a Twinkie.

“Just be sure it’s in there. I have something in it that may be more valuable to us than the whole Cover-Girl plant.”

“What about the CIA woman I—” Reading shushed me.

“We’ll talk about that later.” Reading looked at Migdahlia, nodded, and she winked.

Migdahlia asked, “Don’t you have to pee, Chessie? I’ll help you after Reading and I stand you up. The men will give you privacy.”

I nodded and went along with whatever was happening. “If you say so.”

Migdahlia looked at the men, and they walked down the road fifty feet.

When they were out of hearing, she said, “Don’t say anything about stabbing that woman. Only Reading, Mug, Dr. Beltran, Cleggenhiest and I know what happened.”

“How do you explain her corpse?”

“We didn’t. Reading and Mug threw her body out the tunnel window into the river below. They said it would be so mangled no one will be able to prove anything. That is if the caiman leaves anything to find. Naleeva says we shouldn’t say anything about what happened to anyone until she gets here. Mug finally got word to her through Sergeant Garret."

"How long will that be?" I asked.

"She told Mug she'd be here with Garret and a rescue party by tomorrow afternoon." Migdahlia leaned close to my ear. She whispered, "Where did you get the gold bar and the papers?"

"Oh, that's right you probably didn't know about the room I found with the safe and Hitler's personal stuff in it." I blinked.

Migdahlia's eyes opened wide. "No. Really?"

"Yes." "Did you see what is in those papers?" she asked.

"No. I just grabbed as many as I could, rolled them up, and stuck them into the biggest pocket I have." I looked at Migdahlia. "Are they important?"

"They're the most important thing we found on the whole trip. When we stop for the night, I'm sure we will all talk about them."

"Come on, Migdahlia, you're acting like I found a silver bullet."

She was confused for a few seconds then understood. "You mean like you would use to kill vampires? Yes, you did. You found a whole ammunition dump of them!"

Chapter 75

Hotel Casa del Corazon, in Encarnación, Paraguay

I remember Naleeva's first words to us when she slid out of the truck Sergeant Garret drove. "I am so sorry all this has happened. I can't believe the people behind this took such measures."

I have an even stronger memory of Mug's reply, "When you see what we have with us, you'll understand completely." After I saw the documents I took from the safe, by sheer dumb luck, Mug was a master of understatement.

Despite pressure received from some sectors of the government, Naleeva refused to rush us back to the US. She used my injuries as a reason not to travel immediately. She lost her battle to keep us sequestered in Argentina in a hotel in Posados. Naleeva told us she knew officials in the Argentine Government were alarmed and furious because of an Argentinian citizen's death, Ida-Marie. Our government, or at least some portions of it, didn't want us held or questioned by the Argentine authorities. What had started as a joint venture, ended with the two governments as opponents.

The nighttime assault created a huge stir in the San Ignacio province. It was reported as an outer-space, alien invasion ... the beginning of a war with either Paraguay, Brazil, or Great Britain ... a government attack on political dissidents...and finally what it was, the US interfering with Argentinian affairs. We were spirited out of the country within hours of meeting Naleeva and two days before Buenos Aires could mount a military expedition to inspect Little Berlin. Our excavations had left a large number of destroyed American-made equipment, ashes by the ton, and an obviously disturbed landscape.

Mug had been successful in defusing the explosives in the tunnel, so Ida-Marie's body was discovered. We knew all that because Naleeva told us. She also told us that Migdahlia, Eduardo, and Dr. Beltran's presence with us was causing a major conflict. At any minute, we might lose their company.

Naleeva and our Argentinian expedition members concurred we needed to agree on an honest, united narrative on what had occurred. For that reason, I was putting on makeup for the first time in many weeks to attend a supposed meeting Naleeva had scheduled in a hotel conference room as a 'red herring.' Secretly she directed us to meet in her room instead. She was concerned about bugs.

Though there was nothing wrong with my legs, I was confined to a wheelchair. The medical personnel were concerned about one of my deep wounds opening and becoming infected. Restricting my movements helped reduce that possibility. More importantly, it gave Naleeva more credence to arguments for keeping us from falling into the control of those who didn't wish us well, before she could counter what they might be planning.

Hearing a knock on my hotel room door. I rolled from the bathroom to find who it was. I asked, "Who's there?"

"It's me, Sis. Migdahlia's with me." He hesitated then regurgitated the 'passwords' Mug insisted we use to be sure all was okay. "Escaping Skeletons. You about ready to go? We'll roll you down when you say so."

"It will be another few minutes." I pulled down on the door handle and opened the door enough to allow them in. "Come in and sit."

"Do you need any help?" Migdahlia asked.

"I don't think so. I've gotten pretty good using one hand for everything." The deep wound in my left side forced the doctors to keep my left arm immobile. "I'll yell if I need help."

"Can I push you back to the bathroom?" It was apparent Migdahlia wanted to talk about something.

"Sure."

She wheeled me into the bathroom while Reading picked up a magazine on beauty tips I'm sure he didn't need. I muttered some mangled Shakespeare, "Methinks something is afoot."

When we reached the mirror and my makeup, I asked, "What's up? I've lived with my brother long enough to know he's part of it."

Migdahlia looked shocked. After the few seconds it took for her to regain her composure, she nodded. "Yes, this is something that Reading and I have talked about. He said you might be able to help me. If you would talk to Dr. Card about helping me to come to the US and work with the two of you at your university, I would owe you my life forever."

It was my turn to be shocked. "Why, Migdahlia? That really surprises me."

"There are many reasons. After what has happened, it will be hard for me to have people feel comfortable having me work with them here. I have visited America several times, and I love it. I know I would be happy there, particularly if I can stay in my field of interest. Archaeology is very important to me."

I looked at her and shook my head. She was breathtakingly beautiful. I could see Reading's interest. I said, "Migdalia, Reading is a confirmed bachelor. You need to know that. He gets kind of serious now and again, but he isn't likely to cross the bridge. You understand?"

She nodded. "I understand that completely. Love does not always mean marriage."

I looked at her. I could see she was completely serious. "Okay, I can understand. But, you were mentioning what might happen in Argentina. What about what you just witnessed?"

"No government is perfect. Yours has faults, but your country is so much better than the rest. I will happily take what risks it offers."

I looked at her. I could see nothing but sincerity. "You and Reading?"

She blushed a little but stood up straight and proud. "Yes!"

"I missed that." I nodded, "I'll talk to Mark."

Migdahlia started to hug me, so I quickly reminded her, "Not hard!"

"Never hard. I am now your sister."

I believed her.

Chapter 76

9 AM, Hotel Casa del Corazon, in Naleeva's room

"Is that everyone?" Naleeva counted heads. "Mark and Eduardo are at the conference room to make sure our little secret is kept as long as possible." Naleeva had converted her hotel room into a meeting facility. She sat next to Mug behind the table that normally served as a desk. The three-foot by five-foot surface was covered with containers and briefcases. All that we'd salvaged from our expedition was in them. The table was positioned parallel to her bed with enough space between the two to allow the mattress to serve as bench seating. Migdahlia and I were positioned across from Naleeva and Mug. Migdahlia was seated at the foot of the bed, and I was in my wheelchair next to her. Dr. Dean and Dr. Beltran were on her right. Reading was separated by three containers from being next to Mug. Elroy Cleggenhiest sat at Naleeva's right. He nervously fumbled with a battered journal. "Nine, when they get here, a whole baseball team and their coach," she pronounced hoping to relieve some tension. She looked at Mug questioningly.

"I think we're clear of bugs. I checked and double checked with the equipment I could scrounge." He shrugged his shoulders. "They have some very sophisticated shit. We still need to be as careful as we can."

Naleeva nodded. "Does everybody understand? We don't want to make it easy for anybody who is listening. Nod if you understand." She dropped her chin.

We all responded like a group of monkeys emulating their leader. Everybody chuckled. The door opened, and the surprised faces of Mark and Eduardo entered the room. Mark looked down at his fly and grinned. "It isn't me."

"We were just discussing our need to be discreet when we have our discussion. The walls might have ears. Hopefully, not. I insisted that the room the hotel originally had me assigned in be changed at the last second. We've done what we can, but it's prudent to discuss things carefully." Naleeva searched for something in front of her, found it, and waited for Eduardo and Mark to be seated in the two remaining chairs. When they were settled, she held up a paperclip. She said, "None of us are to say the word for this!" She waved the clip in the air. "I have written a paragraph I want you all to read. Try to remember what's in it as we have our discussion." Naleeva handed us each a sheet of paper. I read mine.

Much of the information you have uncovered is related to a US government secret program that was put into operation after WW II. The name of that operation was Paperclip. Paperclip was the name that was given to a program used to gather as many German scientists and research people as could be found and remove them from

Germany before the Russians could get their hands on them. It is clear what you have discovered has a bearing on how that program was carried out. Some Nazis were given the opportunity to escape in return for their aid in finding and arranging for technical people to be delivered into US hands. Up to now, it hasn't been known how high and who these Nazis were. Now we know at least part of this information.

Everyone in the room looked at each other as the importance of what we had done crept into their consciousness. When all eyes were off of Naleeva's note, she continued, "The materials you found are what I believe attempts to rectify and cover-up a huge diplomatic blunder." She looked at us, sure we all knew the gravity of our situation. "We are in a difficult position. We possess secrets that could do great damage to both our countries. Those same secrets should be known to the world. There is the collision between the two truths. We must decide to do something or nothing. We must decide it as one for the protection of all of us. We also have to provide for our safety. What we know is dangerous to some. You've seen the lengths they'll go to protect the secrets we've discovered. If there is anyone who does not believe what I've just said, leave the room now. You and your defense are on your own."

No one stirred.

"We are agreed?" Naleeva nodded. Everyone dipped their heads, signaling their agreement.

"We will talk as low as we can." Naleeva motioned to Mug. "Check the hall. We're at its end so it will be difficult for them, but we should make it even more so."

Mug went to the door, checked the peephole, opened the door normally, looked down the hall, then closed it and returned to the table.

"Well?" Naleeva asked.

"I didn't see a soul." Reading said, "Consider." He pointed to the ceiling and to the floor.

Naleeva nodded. "We will do a lot of show and tell." She pulled one of the briefcases in front of her and opened it. "This is the atomic bomb," she said barely above a whisper. "This is thanks to Chessie." I had no idea what she was talking about other than it was something in the papers I had swiped from the safe. She loudly asked, "How many of you speak German? Raise your hands." Only Migdahlia, Dr. Dean, Dr. Beltran, and Cleggenhiest had their hands up.

"Mr. Cleggenhist, will you read them."

He said, "Yes."

"Good, I'm glad. That means everyone, will know everything." Naleeva spoke softly, just above a whisper. She reached into the suitcase and removed a half-inch thick stack of old papers. "These all have to do with this." Naleeva held up the paperclip. "Most are to or from." She held her hands in front of her using fingers and thumb tips to form the letter "A" then moved her fingertips apart while keeping her thumbs touching to form an "H."

Everyone's eyes opened a bit wider.

"I see you all understand. Elroy will be interpreter. He also has something to help him." Naleeva scribbled something in very large letters on a piece of blank paper. When she held it up for us to read, it said, "CODE BOOK." Naleeva looked at Cleggenhiest and reinstructed him. "You know what not to say."

Cleggenhiest took a letter that Naleeva handed to him and held it in shaking fingers. His face showed the stress he was under. Obviously, he and Naleeva had reviewed everything in advance.

Cleggenhiest used his hands to form an A. He said, "To that person." He took a deep breath. "I am sorry about ..." he hesitated as he substituted a title for a name ... "your wife's bad health. I will do all I can to have a doctor we can trust visit her. Heinrich has said he will arrange to find a very good one. A trip to Buenos Aires is out of the question, however. The Wiesenthal people have their tentacles everywhere. You must understand, that under the terms of," Naleeva held up the paperclip as Elroy hesitated, "we have little power over what we do. You must remember we are protected by a powerful few. Even Peron cannot help you if you go too far. If those protecting us are exposed to their enemies, we are all sure to be destroyed.

We do the best for you we can. You have our love and allegiance, but there is little more we can do than we have already done. You must know that if we are exposed, your destruction is sure within days, not weeks." Cleggenhiest looked up from the letter. "The rest is about their families. It is signed, Ludolf von Alvensleben."

"Read this one next," Naleeva handed Elroy another letter.

Cleggenhiest made the sign for A then began, "I read your letter and tried to keep in mind the greatness you once had. You were a force like the world has seen only a few times. And, I must remind you, those times are past. You must know by now that you will never obtain anything close to power like you once had. You speak of Richter and his work on the bomb. That is but a dream. If it was of use, the Americans would have already acquired him. They control everything the Soviets don't. You asked me two good questions, and I will give you good answers. Why do they allow me to exist? They allow me to exist because I can do things for them. Many things, they do not wish to do themselves. You asked if I believed that the Americans knew you still lived. Some few *know* you do. They leave you live as long as you are not a problem. If you are the slightest one, you are dead. Ask yourself this. Why do I, Schnieder, von Braun, Muller, and the rest still live? It is because we are useful to them. Now ask, what use can they make of you? Just one, the silent confirmation of your death. I do not know, but I believe Heinrich has convinced them that it would be best if the world believed your suicide was real. It would show a great deal of incompetence on their part and would put pressure on the church if their part is known. Resolve to be satisfied with living. Find a puppy to replace Blondi. Enjoy training it. See that it is what is left for you. You could be with Goebbels, Goering and the rest. You also asked about pressuring Heinrich to help you. It is the last thing you should attempt. Yes, of all of us, he has the most power. As the one who went to the Americans and proposed," Naleeva held up the paperclip, "and helped make it happen, he is in the best position of us all. However, it is also true he has, by far, the most to lose. He will put an ax to your neck if he believes you are a threat to him. Heinrich is loyal to you, but he is more loyal to Heinrich. Take the advice I have given you, for there is no other path except for your destruction. Think of today's dinner and be happy." Cleggenhiest chin rose. "It is signed ... Barbie."

Mark shook his head and said aloud, "Klaus Barbie."

Naleeva held her index finger to her mouth. Mark nodded and mouthed, "I'm sorry."

Naleeva motioned for Cleggenhiest to read the next note she handed him.

He nodded and started to read. "You must not write to Heinrich directly. Things are in turmoil here. Truman has shut down the OSS, and he does not like Donovan. A man named MacGruder has control now. He seems sympathetic, but it is too soon to tell. We do not know if he is fully informed about us. Remember Muller is the one that protects us. Do not risk his relations with the Americans. You endanger us all, and you endanger yourself the most. Channel everything through Rauff or Baby-boy. They can send notes to friends in Washington who can code and relay them to him. Repeat, please do not try to contact him directly again!" Elroy shook his head, "Alten G. I don't know who that is."

I whispered, "What's the OSS?"

"Office of Strategic Services," Mug answered in the same whispered tones. "Long story short, it was the CIA before there was one. Specialized in spying and espionage. Wild Bill Donovan was the General who ran it. He was a real loose cannon."

I nodded and kept my mouth shut because Naleeva was frowning. She handed Cleggenhiest an envelope and nodded.

Elroy carefully removed a folded letter from inside. When he opened it, there were two pages. He looked at Naleeva, and she nodded her approval. Cleggenhiest flexed his shoulders, sighed, and prepared to read.

"This letter is more recent than the others ... it is dated April 18th, 1960." Cleggenhiest turned the two pages over examining them. "And, it is much longer." Elroy took a couple of deep breaths and resumed reading. "Adolf,

Before I venture into the more serious subjects you have asked about, I will wish you a happy birthday. When you actually receive this letter, I cannot guess other than it will be months after I sit and write this to you. Seventy-one years! I join you in the seventies in just ten days. Who would have dreamed that both of us would have survived so long, Mein Führer? The dark days in 1945 made me believe I would not live to celebrate the 1946 New Year. But, here I am, living a life I would not have chosen, but one that I am satisfied to live. I am sure you miss Eva as I miss Anna, who I was parted from so long ago. My wife here is much different from Sophie, who I was glad to be rid. She is tall and has provided strong Aryan children."

Cleggenhiest took a sip of water, shook his head without smiling and continued. "I received your letter and was happy and aggrieved at what you had to say. I was glad you understand I cannot correspond with you because of the great danger to us both. That danger leads me to warn you that to act upon the items you propose doing would be suicide for you and lead to my exposure, trial, and in all probability, execution. Anything you do that would end in the discovery you survived the war and are alive would create such a disaster that the remainder of your life would be measured in days and weeks, not years, not even months. You must understand, those who brought me and the rest here did so at great risk. Elaborate fabrications have been made. Complete stories of investigations were created. They were designed to protect our secrets. If these great lies were exposed, many of the most powerful men in America would be destroyed. They will not allow this to happen, nor will I."

"The Weisthal barbarians pursue us all. They have chased you from the lake home and any semblance of an open life. You are exiled in the jungles. Life there is not as pleasant as you would prefer, but it is life. Coming here is impossible. Be satisfied with what you have it for it is all that is available for you."

"You know of my commitment to my duties. I was always steadfast in my duties to Germany, though my mind and heart was not always a mirror of what National Socialism decreed. I did my duty. I will do my duty today for those I now owe my allegiance. They have done what they promised and more. My son is in their security services, just as I was in yours, and my father before me served the Bavarian people. My son is in a position to help protect us all. I will not allow him to be compromised. Make not the slightest attempt to leave where you are, or face disaster."

"You will not hear from me again. It is too dangerous. I considered not replying, but I could not fail to tell you of the sure consequences of your plans. I have warned you. This is the last that you will ever hear from me. Live long, but in silence." Cleggenhiest looked up from the letter. "It is signed Heinrich. And, something else has been written on the letter by he who received it. Do you wish me to read that also, Naleeva?"

"Yes, go ahead."

"*Shieskopf*! I will see him hang on one of his own meat hooks!" Elroy looked up, grimaced, then added, "That is the way Heinrich Muller executed many of the Wehrmacht officers that tried to assassinate Hitler in July 1944." Cleggenhiest reached in the envelope and removed the photo of a grim-faced Gestapo Officer. He held the five by seven-inch photo so that all could see the image and said, "Traitor, has been written on the back of this in very bold letters."

We all stared at the evil green-blue eyes glaring at us from the picture. Suddenly, Naleeva's face changed dramatically. She said, "I did not see it the first time I saw this photo, but now I do. The genetic markers in that face are as good as a wanted poster. It explains who cannot allow us to tell our story and who has the power to do all that we've seen occur. He has changed the name's spelling, but ..." Naleeva didn't finish her sentence. There was a strong knock on the door.

Chapter 77

Hotel Casa del Corazon, in Naleeva's room

"Who's there?" Naleeva asked. She held her hand up at the same time indicating we should stay silent.

A familiar voice filtered through the wooden panel. "Sergeant Garret."

Naleeva looked at Reading who smiled and nodded his head. "Everything's set."

"I'll be sure they're alone," Mug said as he left the table and walked to the door. He squinted through the peephole and said. "It's them. Everything looks to be okay."

"Let them in as soon as I finish here." Naleeva took all the documents from in front of Elroy and quickly returned them to the briefcase in front of her and locked it. She gave the keys to Reading, then nodded to Mug.

Mug unlocked the door and swung it open.

"Madam, Assistant Secretary, I'm the official escort for materials specified as needing safe transport as requested by the Department of State. I have been detached by my commanding officer for such service." The salty old Marine fought a grin but was losing. Corporal Cole and four privates accompanied him.

"Thank you, Sergeant Garrett. What provisions have been made for the materials security?" Naleeva was speaking louder than needed. The plan was obvious, the question, would it be effective?

"We will be in constant visual contact with the materials. There will be a minimum of twelve armed personnel to act as guards up to the time the materials are loaded onto a plane, and they are to be loaded under your orders." Garrett spoke a little louder than necessary. I hoped that whoever might be listening didn't pick up on that.

When I surveyed the other faces in the room, I found that what was happening in front of them wasn't as obvious as I thought. Wide eyes and shocked faces were worn by everyone except Naleeva, Reading, Mug and, I surmised, myself. Maybe things weren't as transparent as I assumed.

Naleeva nodded to Garrett. "Very good, Sergeant. I want to add something to your assignment. Do not allow anyone to *change* your orders. There may be attempts to do that, to keep these materials from reaching safety in the US, do you understand?"

"Yes, ma'am. We will retain custody, if necessary by force."

Mark was alarmed, "What's happening here? That's all that's left to prove what we uncovered and what occurred at Little Berlin!" He shook his head in disbelief. "You're sending everything with *him*?"

"Let me assure you all, this is our one best method of getting these items home." Naleeva asked Garret, "Do you have the containers I requested and the seals?"

"Yes, ma'am."

"Please bring the containers and seals in, and then have your personnel stand guard in the hall. Your protection orders are now in effect." Naleeva motioned for Mug to stand aside as Corporal Cole and three other Marines wheeled in the containers that barely made it through the door.

Garrett told Cole, "Post three at the door and three at the elevator. Deny all access to the hall." Cole and the others left, closing the door behind them.

"This will go straight to Mariscal?" Naleeva asked.

Garrett nodded, "It will convoy in with no stops. We're carrying enough gas to get there. Once we arrive at Mariscal, it will go into the warehouse space and be under guard constantly. My platoon has the honor." He added, "Corporal Cole and I have been assigned to fly on the aircraft to its destination in the states, wherever that may be."

Naleeva nodded and faced the rest of us. "Okay here is what is going to happen. We will place all material, I do mean all, in these two containers. After it's in, we will place seals over the hatches, and each of us will sign them. If anyone disturbs what's inside, we'll know. We will fly in three separate planes that I've arranged. We will leave after the cargo plane carrying the evidence of what we've discovered takes off. The three craft I've arranged for are faster and will arrive before the cargo plane lands. That means we can meet it." She pointed to the specimen boxes, Dr. Beltran's computer, boxes of records, briefcases that held everything we'd salvaged from our expedition. The rest was either burned and scattered in the Argentine jungle or had been spirited off to some secret location. She said, "Load them. Put half in one and half in the other."

I fingered the dog-tags hanging around my neck. From my days in service I decided to wear mine on a chain around my neck. Between those two I'd placed the one I'd taken from the mass burial and hid from the others. In plain sight is often the last place that's examined. I decided not to let them know of its existence.

After all the material had been loaded, Naleeva put her index finger to her lips asking for quiet. While we watched, Reading signed four of the tape seals and climbed into one of the containers. He contorted his body to get into the small space. I looked inside and saw Reading pick up a submachine gun. He grinned and put it down. Reading saw me staring at him. He pointed to a box of rations and a camp toilet and put his thumb and finger together to flash the "okay" symbol.

Naleeva held her finger to her lips again, rolled out two of the seals, signed both across their width and motioned for us to do the same. Despite some confused looks, we all followed her lead.

Garrett handed Reading the two seals we'd just

finished signing, whispered, "Good luck," and closed the door.

Naleeva sealed the hatches with the remaining special six-inch wide tape. She told us, "I want each of you to sign the seal. Be sure your name crosses the hatch jam." We formed a line and dutifully scribbled our names on the tape, again.

"Take them away, Sergeant," Naleeva instructed. Garrett opened the hotel room door, called for the three outside and wheeled them down the hall. I watched as they disappeared inside the elevator. The thought suddenly struck me. I might never see my brother again.

Chapter 78

Argana International Airport

Things were happening so fast it was mind- boggling. Naleeva had things organized to the last detail. She'd given us an hour to pack all our belongings and meet in the hotel lobby. Waiting for us were a group of five old Continental and Cadillac town cars and limos. They looked like cars used in the funeral scenes in the *Godfather* movie. Their drivers were in character and could have been used as extras in that film. Mug loaded his men into the first and last vehicles in line. They were our protection. I heard the metallic clicks of weapons as they locked and loaded after they were inside. Naleeva separated us into three groups. Eduardo, Dr. Dean, and Migdahlia were packed in one car, Naleeva, Mug, Dr. Beltran, and Cleggenhiest another, and Dr. Beltran, Mark and I were steered into the third car. My wheelchair filled part of the rear seat. At the last second, a big man wearing a hoodie ran from the hotel and climbed in the car's front seat.

Mark asked, "Who are you?"

The big young man turned around in the seat and faced us from under his hood. I'd never seen him before. He said, "Reading," with a wide grin. Naleeva didn't miss a trick.

When we were all in our vehicles, consular flags were

attached to the three cars that had provisions for them before our hasty departure. The rush was to move so quickly that our enemies couldn't react fast enough to stop us. It was a high-speed trip. All the roads were paved. We left the hotel at 11:30 in bright sunlight. It took fourteen hours to make the trip through the slightly rolling lands between Asunción and Encarnación, then over the level marshes where the Ruta Transchaco led. Gas and one very quick meal were all we stopped for. We sat in an office deep inside the airport/US clandestine military base. I'd rushed to the restrooms on our arrival. When I returned to the office where we were sequestered, Reading was sitting with Naleeva, Mug, Eduardo, and Mark engaged in a serious conversation. I let them know I was joining them. "The restrooms are clean." They all looked at me. Seeing Reading removed my fears for his safety. Reading winked and mouthed the word, "later." He'd emerged from his cocoon, his trip in the container to the base, where he'd performed some secret plan. His returned presence made me feel secure.

Naleeva nodded. "It's getting close to time. Everybody gather around." She waited for the rest of our group to join us. When they were all within a few feet of her, she told us what to expect. "Okay, I know you're tired, and you've been pushed terribly, but I fear I'm going to push you harder and wear you completely out. Sergeant Garrett and Corporal Cole have already flown out. They will be stopping at MacDill, then flying to Patrick at the Cape. Eduardo, Petro, Migdahlia, those are Air Force bases in Florida. I didn't want the material we are bringing home anywhere near Washington. We will be on charter flights that will leave in less than half an hour and fly directly to Vero Beach's airport. If all goes right, we'll be in Patrick before they are. Try to get some sleep on the plane. They and we will have to stop to refuel. I arranged to get some food on each plane. I have no idea what it will be. Everybody stays with the group you rode up with. How long before we board, Mug?"

"Twelve minutes."

Naleeva shrugged her shoulders and said, "I said as quick as we could get off. That is quick!" She looked at me. "Can you function out of the wheelchair?"

I lied. "Sure. I'll be fine if I don't have to participate in a wrestling match."

$\sim \sim \sim \sim \sim$

Mark, Reading, and I stood on the airport tarmac waiting for a minibus to transport us across the field to a hanger where the airplanes waited. A couple of Oxycodone pills made the discomfort from my wounds go away, but standing wasn't comfortable. We were the last group to be transferred to our waiting jet. It was the first time I had a chance to ask Reading what plan he'd been able to convince Naleeva to accept.

"Well? How did you do it?" I asked.

Mark nodded his head, "Me too."

"How much did you figure out?" Reading asked.

"You were going to get to the base, here, and remove the material and send it back some other way. You'd reseal the containers and send them home under guard. Past that ..." I shrugged my shoulders. That hurt.

"Right on. I'll add what you don't know. When I got here, I found some empty white plastic artifact containers like we used, got a couple of empty boxes, a laptop I stole from one of the Paraguay freight offices, and a couple of briefcases. I filled them with newspapers and trash, put everything into the containers, and then resealed them. Hey, what do you do when it absolutely, positively has to get there? I sent out stuff FedEx. I broke it up into three separate packages. One went to Sheriff McGill, one to Jim Andrews at the University, and one to Lisa." He looked at Mark, "You remember my TV anchor friend?"

"Yes."

Reading nodded, "I sent them all instructions not to open the packages unless I didn't come back or something happened to me. Those three all will know what to do to create maximum damage. I put instructions on the inside telling them all that happened ... and that if they opened the packages, and I came home all right, it would put us *all* in a world of hurt."

"You think they'll follow your instructions?" Mark asked.

Reading flexed his shoulders one time. "All but Lisa. She probably will, but you can't be sure about reporters."

I asked, "What's our exit strategy? Or, is one possible? That's the question that bugs me. Seeing what happened at Little Berlin doesn't make us a good life- insurance risk."

"We have to be sure we retain possession of as much of the evidence as we can. It won't be easy to do that, but we'll find a way. We have to be sure all of us think as a unit. They'll pick us off one-by-one if we don't." Reading looked at both of us, waiting for us to say something. We remained quiet. "The hard part is keeping all of us together." Reading's face became grim. "We have to keep a balance in the way we use our knowledge and evidence. It has to remain a weapon that we can use to defend us, not used to right moral mistakes or benefit any of us. The temptation for one person to break those two conditions is going to be great."

"I don't see any of us selling out the others to those rectal apertures." I looked at Reading and Mark who were looking at each other.

Mark volunteered, "Do I think one of us will throw the rest under the bus for a bag full of money? That's not likely, but not impossible. It depends on the size of the bag. What I'm most concerned about is somebody deciding they can get famous and write a book, rewrite the Holocaust, something like that. I know Eduardo wants to do a paper on some of the archaeological issues we learned. He says he knows he can't ... problem is, things change."

"What bothers me most is having one of our group compromised in some manner. The people protecting the secrets we know obviously have enough power to dig up something that embarrasses or threatens one person enough to compromise all the rest of us. We have to divide up the evidence we have so it is equally threatening to our enemies and also that no two of us know where the rest is hidden." Reading stopped talking and pointed to the car ferrying us to our aircraft. It was racing across the taxiways at full speed. Reading said, "Something's up!"

The car pulled up next to us, and the driver shouted, "Get in, get in! There are five military truck-loads of Paraguayan officials and soldiers on their way here to stop all of you." As he spoke the Gulfstream jet carrying Eduardo, Dr. Dean, and Migdahlia roared as it raced down the runway to get airborne. As we piled into the car, he spoke, "We have less than fifteen minutes to have you out of Paraguayan airspace.

Chapter 79

**Inside a hangar at Patrick Air Force Base,
Cocoa, Florida**

The air inside the building was crackling with as much electricity as the storm clouds hanging above were generating. Just getting all of us to witness the arrival of the materials sent in a mammoth C-130 had been an ordeal. Our main interest was ensuring all of us were assembled and safe. We knew that the group of thirty plus FBI, CIA, and undisclosed others standing a hundred feet from us were waiting for something that was bogus. They didn't. Their anticipation was comical if one neglected to think of their reaction when they learned the two containers were filled with what amounted to garbage.

The sight of trucks with yellow and red flashing lights racing down the runway after us as our jet lifted from the Mariscal base burned in my mind as if it had happened ten minutes before. Mark, Reading, and my Gulfstream was the last to take off. Naleeva told us she'd planned it that way because the local authorities would have a hard time inventing issues to keep us grounded. It would be easy to find an excuse to take the Argentinians in our group into some form of confinement. They were off first. Mug had a few pages in his file that a government could find questionable if they wished to look for "problems." Their plane was off the ground and headed for Brazilian airspace as ours taxied to the end of the runway.

Reading saw the flashing lights streaming through gates in the tall chain-link fencing. He yelled to the pilot, who shortened his preflight check-list. Slamming the throttle forward, he was able to keep ahead of the vehicles trying to get in front of the plane stopping our escape. We were in the air, and the flight crew ignored both requests and orders to return to the airfield. Safe, we thought. That was until fighters started to appear off of our wings. Two French manufactured Mirage 2000s escorted us on either wing. The Brazilian planes kept a safe distance, but the fact they were there and escorted us to the Columbia border wasn't any comfort. After we refueled in Bogota and were on our way across the Caribbean, F-18's took their place. The Air Force escort evidently was to see we landed where we were supposed to and not at some clandestine location. They never threatened us and were more like shadows than substance, choosing to stay away from us, appearing and disappearing enough to let us know we were under observation.

When we touched down at Vero, we saw two groups of cars and people waiting. One was the welcoming group Naleeva had arranged to meet us. The other consisted of agents for the FBI and CIA that now stood on the far side of the hanger. Within an hour, we were on our way to

Patrick Air Force Base. Naleeva had to face the hostile tribes with little support. She saw that we were safe, then she became engaged in a non-stop series of heated and volatile conversations. The heat intensified when the C-130 landed, and the two containers were rolled down the ramp from the rear of its fuselage. As I looked across the hanger, she was still arguing with our tormentors.

As I watched, two big men wearing jackets with huge "FBI" letters printed on them approached. When they got within ten feet one man said, "All of you that were in Argentina, come over to the containers." All of us, Naleeva, Sergeant Garrett, Corporal Cole, and at least forty folks I had to assume were related to the government agencies followed them to the containers.

A hard-eyed man with graying hair stood in front of Naleeva. My thought was I'd seldom seen two more unhappy faces. Mug echoed what I observed, "Man, those two look like the *Titanic* just sank again!"

"They sure don't look like they got what they wanted for Christmas," I confirmed.

Naleeva forced a smile and said, "All my people, we are getting ready to open the seals on the containers. I'd like your help in confirming everything we put in them at Mariscal is still inside. If you see anything that's missing, please point it out immediately. Any questions?"

It was hard for me to suppress a grin. Naleeva was able to keep a straight face when she knew nothing of value was in the containers. I guessed she made the suggestion to further confuse the situation and gain us a day or two more to hide our discoveries. I glanced at the rest of the members of the group. All were stone-faced showing no reaction to her words. My guess was that everyone had become so used to weird being normal, nothing surprised them.

Naleeva walked over to one of the containers and placed her hand on the seal. She hesitated. "Sergeant Garrett, were you with these containers for the entire trip?"

Garrett squared his shoulders. "No ma'am. When we landed at Trinidad to refuel we were forced to leave the plane while fueling was taking place. They said it was safety rules. We were in visual contact with the plane while we were outside of it."

"How long were you away from the containers?"

"Twenty minutes, ma'am."

"That sounds fine, Sergeant." Naleeva put a hand on the seal and tried pulling it loose. It wouldn't budge. She asked, "Anyone have a knife?"

"You can use mine." Corporal Cole stepped forward and offered Naleeva a knife.

Naleeva looked at the weapon and said, "Will you cut the seal so we can open the container? That thing is too big for me."

Cole nodded and quickly ran the sharp blade down the length of the seal. Before Naleeva could open the container door, the man she'd been talking to moved between her and the container. He announced in an officious voice, "I have to inform you that all materials in these two containers are to be impounded and quarantined until we can determine what the materials are and if there are any potentially harmful items. You didn't file the normal paperwork for these shipments."

Naleeva bristled for show. "You're not customs."

"No, but we have them here with us." The man pointed to three clerkish looking men mixed in the gaggle of CIA and FBI types. He waited for Naleeva to make a strong objection. When she didn't, a glimmer of recognition settled over his face.

Reading stood beside me and saw what I noticed. He bent over until his lips were inches from my ear. He whispered, "I think Naleeva's friend just caught his first whiff of the genus *Rattus*."

Naleeva recognized she'd made an error and tried to rectify it. "Where are you going to hold this material? I don't want you to open the containers unless we're there."

Too late. The man knew something was wrong. He looked at Naleeva but didn't say a word. "Get Hansen up here," he growled.

Steve Hansen, the FBI agent, appeared in a few seconds. He looked at us like we were a pile of rotten vegetables. He addressed the man, "Yes sir?"

"Look inside that container and tell me if you recognize anything in there."

Hansen immediately hunkered down and stared at the inside of the containers. "Chief Morris, the white containers look like the ones that were used to store remains that this group found. I can't say whether the briefcases and boxes were there or not."

"A Section Chief. They do consider this important," Reading whispered to me.

"Get one out here. I want to look inside." The man now identified as Chief Morris was beginning to get a red face.

"One of the white containers." Morris was becoming more agitated by the second.

"Those are locked, and I don't have the keys with me," Naleeva warned.

Morris didn't say a word as Hansen reached into the container and removed one of the white plastic boxes. "Give me a wrecking bar," he croaked as Hansen laid the box at his feet. A surly looking woman wearing an FBI jacket raced to his side with a small crowbar. He glared at Naleeva as he went down on one knee and inserted the bar's blade under the box lid. As he pried the lid lock open, his eyes fastened of Naleeva. "This is unnecessary, but I'll do it anyway." The door opened with a '*pop.*'

We all stared down to see what was in the box. The CIA and FBI types hoped to see what we'd kept out of their hands when they, or their operatives, raided our camp. Naleeva's people all wanted to see what Reading had substituted for the human remains. In the one just popped open, Reading had substituted two pieces of a two by four, an old hammer, and a half dozen empty oil bottles.

Morris glared at Naleeva and said, "You aren't going to think this is funny when ..." He cut off his statement too late.

Naleeva jumped on it. "You threatening me, Section Chief Morris? Is the FBI challenging the State Department's authority and ability to conduct its business that relates to foreign affairs?" It was clear Naleeva was using lawyer speak for recorders she was sure were in use. "What is your interest in our business?"

Morris' face showed his seething anger inside. He wanted to explode but knew the possible consequences. "You aren't doing yourself any favors. This is a complicated mess. I'm not here because—" he didn't finish his statement again. He and Naleeva locked eyes. I was fascinated by what I saw. It wasn't hostility. It certainly wasn't fear. What I detected was resignation. Resignation that both were trapped in a situation that lacked any kind of sane resolution. That recognition, that there was no good answer to the problem each faced, punctured the pressure balloon. Stress flowed into the hanger, diluting it and allowing all to take breaths in a less labored atmosphere.

Morris rose to his feet. He looked at Steve Hanson and said, "No use opening the rest, you won't find anything we're looking for, right Ms. Ettiene?"

"You are correct," Naleeva answered.

"I was sent here to do a job," Morris said.

Naleeva didn't give him time to elaborate. "What was that, to seize the evidence of what we found? What would you do with that evidence? Destroy it?" She pointed at him and all those who accompanied him. "If that's what you're here for, you have to understand that *we are evidence too*. What do you intend to do with us?" Naleeva's words had an immediate impact on the agents and personnel wearing FBI and CIA shirts and jackets. Their faces were shocked and confused.

One woman spoke in a suspicious and half angry voice, "This is supposed to be about smuggling! Destroy evidence? What's going on!?"

"Shall we tell them what's going on?" Naleeva asked.

Morris just stared back at her. After thirty seconds, he made a decision. "Nothing more can be accomplished here. Hansen, McNeal, Cantor, Schultz...you stay here. The rest of you go back to the assembly point in the airport office building." He looked at Naleeva, "I'll have to ask you and your people to accompany me to a place we can discuss this and reach an agreement."

"Do we have a choice?" Naleeva asked.

"I'm afraid you don't." A man wearing a tie and suit walked up to Morris and Naleeva. "My name is Smith Smith. Yes, my parents had a strange sense of humor. Believe it or not, it has some advantages. I work for the

CIA. Jim Morris and I are both assigned to this operation so two of my people and I will be with you. We both are doing our job. I'm sure you understand."

"I understand. Do you understand I had a job and I did it? My superiors wanted me to find out the truth. I did that." Naleeva exuded self-righteousness.

Smith's faint smile was an insight into his character. He nodded and said, "If your superiors had known the truth, they never would have sent you."

Chapter 80
**Patrick Air Force Base,
Cocoa, Florida**

The walk to the conference room was a long hike from where the cars parked to the office complex. Even inside, it was hot, and my stomach began to protest all the exertion. Though I honestly thought I could handle being on my feet, the distance made me long for a wheelchair. I had to stop to rest.

"What's wrong with her?" Morris asked.

"Chessie has some serious wounds." Naleeva pointed to my back and side. "She has lots of stitches in both places. We had a wheelchair for her, but we had to abandon it. Think you might come up with one?"

One of Morris' people said, "They'll have them in the medical center. I know where it is. Want me to get one?"

Before I could say I'd be okay after few minutes rest, Naleeva said, "She definitely needs one. I'll stay here with her while your man gets the wheelchair. He can bring us to where we're meeting."

I started to protest, "I'll be—"

Naleeva stopped me. "No, she won't. Get the chair." Something in her eyes told me to keep my mouth shut.

Morris looked skeptical. "You aren't going to try

skipping out on me are you?"

"Skip? Run? Look at her. She can hardly walk," Naleeva sounded outraged at the thought. I tried my best to look fragile.

Smith said, "It's okay Jim, where would they run to if they could?"

Chief Morris sent his man to get a wheelchair. Morris and the rest left Naleeva and me to wait, while they continued to the conference room.

$$\sim \sim \sim \sim \sim$$

When everybody was out of hearing, Naleeva

looked at me and said, "Chessie, you don't admit to any contact with Alexa Lind in the complex tunnel. Don't say anything to contradict the story I'll tell. Try to look surprised if they mention anything about her death. I have thought of a way to handle this that will work for them and us."

I looked at Naleeva questioningly, thought for a few seconds then I asked, "She attacked me. What I did to her was self-defense. I don't understand."

"You did what you had to do. You're not guilty of anything. I want to be sure that they *don't have a reason to try to make you guilty*." Naleeva looked at me sadly and shook her head. "I must apologize to you and the rest. If I knew to what degree we were going to poke a hornet's nest, I might have changed my boss's mind. Not mine. I believe there is a need to know the truth of such things.

Yet, in this case, it isn't clear this is something everyone must be aware."

I leaned against the hall wall and looked at her. Anger boiled inside of me, and I knew my face would show it. I waited for her to say something to calm me, but she didn't. I stewed and finally exploded. "That's it? Bull shit! You damn near get all of us killed. And, that still might happen. You're sorry? I'd say that's right! What I hear you saying is everything we learned, everything we went through was for zero. Nothing. Nada. You're going to lift the rug and sweep everything under it. Why, so some degenerate son or daughter of a Nazi war criminal isn't embarrassed?"

Naleeva remained silent. I'm not sure whether she was giving me a chance to vent more or formulating a reply. Long after the fact, I believe she was doing both. She answered with troubled eyes. "I'm sad about what happened to you and to Ida-Marie and to all the rest. I do not feel guilty. I didn't push you over the cliff, attack you in the tunnel ... Forces I was unaware of did these things. There was no way for me to suspect that such extreme reactions would occur. Once things were in motion, I couldn't do more to protect all of you even if I had known how high the danger was." She hesitated, nodded, and continued, "If you ask me if I would ask you to do this again, I couldn't give you a simple, 'no.' If I knew what I believe to be the truth, now, when I formed the expedition, I would not have sent you. However, with one exception, that being I would go with you, I still would do it—"

The 'whoosh' of the entrance door closer informed us my wheelchair and its FBI errand boy was within fifty feet. Naleeva said, "Later."

Chapter 81
**Patrick Air Force Base,
Cocoa, Florida**

I didn't like the look of our situation when Naleeva wheeled me into where we were going to meet. By the time we reached the room, my friends were all seated at tables, chatting to each other. Their body language and expressions weren't happy ones. Our antagonists had greatly reduced in numbers. Section-chief Jim Morris was still present as was Steve Hansen. Three others wearing FBI lettered shirts sat with them. A lone CIA agent stood near the door, undoubtedly to observe and report all that occurred. All eyes fastened on us when we entered the room.

Morris rose and approached us. He looked at me and asked, "Are you comfortable?"

I answered, "Yes."

"You probably should have one of our medical people look at your wounds to be sure everything is healing correctly," Morris said.

Naleeva answered, "She's fine. Our medical people are familiar with her injuries. They'll continue to care for her."

"I didn't ask you." Morris glared at Naleeva, and she glared back.

"What she said," I answered in such a way to be sure to message the FBI there wasn't going to be *any* divide and conquer. He extended his glare to me. I wanted to shoot him a bird, did but didn't have the nerve to hold it up to his face. It remained, resting on my knee, where either he didn't see it or chose to ignore my derision.

He cleared his throat and started over. "Ms. Ettiene, you know how sensitive this whole affair has become. The subject of your group's activities is explosive enough, but on top of that we have the military activity to explain and the kidnapping of three Argentinian citizens," Morris saw steam building in Naleeva's boiler. He quickly moved to alleviate the pressure, "I understand much of these circumstances weren't of your making, but we have to be sure that we handle them diplomatically. I sympathize with your position, fully."

Government speak. I shook my head in disgust, and I'm sure I was frowning. Naleeva showed no emotion and asked, "I'm sure you're going to tell me where your agency *wants* to go from here. So?"

"That depends. My boss, your boss, some other interested individuals will meet with us and discuss the resolution. We want to be careful to get this right the first time." Morris was trying to make things as positive as he could. As he finished his words, Mug and Mark joined us. They weren't happy.

"Has he told you?" Mug asked Naleeva.

Naleeva looked at Morris, and said, "He's getting to it. Mug, what do you say when you hear flim-flam."

"He's greasing the shaft."

Naleeva smiled. "That's it. So, Chief Morris, what do my people know I don't?"

Morris was mad. I could understand his displeasure. Naleeva was tweaking his tail pretty hard. His face was red, and the veins on his temples were pulsing. "So, here's what you don't know. The big wigs are on the way here from Washington and who knows where else. They're going to decide how big a jam you and your people are in. Until they do, your people stay in this room. You'll be with Smith and me. Your people will be taken care of. I've got cots and food arranged."

"I'd prefer to be here," Naleeva said stiffly.

"Suit yourself. If we need you for some reason, don't doubt this. We'll come to drag your butt where we need it." Morris turned on his heel and rejoined his agents.

Chapter 82
Patrick Air Force Base,
Cocoa, Florida

After two days of working Sudoku puzzles, playing poker, and sleeping, our hosts came and took Naleeva with them. All of us knew, but didn't discuss the fact, that our fate was being determined, and we'd learn it soon.

None of us contemplated a disastrous future. Too many knew of our expedition and its association with the Federal Government. All types of "visualized solutions" were put forward, mostly for comic relief. Some had a smidgeon of truth or hope in them. They varied from exorbitant dreams of bags of cash to being conscripted into service and sent to some vacation location like the Aleutian Islands. There were jokes and laughs, but always with a nervous edge. After Naleeva left us, the jokes disappeared. The tension was palpable. I'm sure my comrades were contemplating what would change. We agreed our lives were likely to change, if in no other way than the way we viewed our government.

My previous experience with Uncle Sam had alerted me that an iceberg existed, but it didn't alert me to the size, power, and potential for evil included in the mechanisms of the state. The last two months drove the power of Goliath home. This monster was perfectly capable of destroying David and would do so without hesitation. I'd always seen the government as the elected officials supported by the administrative sections. I was learning it just wasn't that way. Where was the real seat of power? I wasn't sure anymore. What happened when Naleeva left, reinforced my thoughts that the "government" had evolved into an organization more interested in control than service.

We had chaperones prior to Naleeva's departure. Their numbers and the observation we were subjected to intensified after she left. If we went to a restroom, one of our *Duenas*, controllers in Spanish, would drift behind us. When a few of us would gather for a conversation, they'd manage to find a reason to be close and eavesdrop. I don't know if they thought we would hatch some plot with our leader gone. None of us were fans of *Mission Impossible* movies. Trying to escape never entered my mind, and I'm sure not in others of our group.

I was happy Migdahlia was with me. My wounds, though improving, remained painful, and my ability to do some simple activities like picking up something from the floor or parts of my dressing ritual were highly restricted. Migdahlia was so much a part of surviving my incarceration, we truly did become sisters. Without her I'd have been stuck with one of the female agents. My perception was they would have preferred to rip out my stitches rather than help me. I'd probably had better luck with the males.

Naleeva was gone for more than a day when Morris entered our community cell and informed us, "You're going to be in a meeting in forty-five minutes. Do what you need to be ready. You could be there for a long while. Hit the john, whatever." He left us looking at each other.

Mug said, "Looks like shit hits the fan time."

Mark added, "Yes, I keep seeing Charlton Heston standing in front of the burning bush in *The Ten Commandments*. I know how he felt."

"Who's Charlton Heston," Migdahlia asked.

We all laughed. I said, "The generation gap in action."

Reading sat silent and brooding. As always, he was trying to think ahead to anticipate what might happen. From his serious, almost tortured expression, he believed what would transpire in the next few hours could shape our lives.

~ ~ ~ ~ ~

Naleeva's face shocked me when we were ushered into a plush meeting room, the antithesis of the Spartan- stark room we'd been held in for seventy-two hours. She looked worn-out and dispirited. Naleeva managed a faint smile when we made eye contact. My eyes asked a question, and hers replied. She maintained contact and her smile deepened. She mouthed words which I took as "Its okay." I knew we were about to find out if that was true.

Chapter 83
Patrick Air Force Base,
Cocoa, Florida

The instant Migdahlia wheeled me into the executive conference room; I felt I'd been ushered into an area teeming with poisonous snakes. The feeling was so intense, my skin crawled with the sensation. I had expected eight, maybe ten people from agencies to be in the meeting. The room was packed with the venomous creatures. Twenty-two, I counted heads. I'd only seen a few of them before. Section Chief Morris was there, Steve Hansen, and one FBI lady that had been in the hanger. A number of "suits" flanked both sides. The CIA man with two last names, Smith Smith was there along with one of the ladies who'd been one of our chaperones for the past three days. They had some officious looking company I guessed were part of their group. Naleeva had two people on either side of her that I guessed were from the State Department. Their expressions varied from exasperation to embarrassment. At the head of the huge conference table, six older men were seated that had the self-important air of "big dogs." I guessed right on that. As soon as our expedition was seated, one of them took control.

"First, I will apologize to you all for the inconvenience

you've suffered. I can assure you that it was necessary given the sensitivity of what has transpired since you landed in Argentina." I watched his features; they were friendly, not threatening. They were going to try honey first. The man was short, small-framed, with gray coiffured hair. His smile was broad, but his eyes had a weasel's glint in them. He spoke like a man with lots of experience giving speeches. "This whole thing was most unfortunate. If all of us were aware of the danger you would face, and may I add, the information you would discover, I can assure you ... you would not have been allowed to be placed in that position."

Mark started to either make a statement or ask a question, but the man held his hand up, shook his head, and said, "You'll have a chance to speak later. I'll finish *first*." His heavy emphasis on the last word meant, *keep your mouths shut until I finish.*

The man looked at us individually, glancing at an open file folder on the table. I believe he was trying to assess us as he spoke and reacted to his words. The file probably had pictures of us or other ways of identifying every member of the expedition.

After a few seconds, he continued. "There are reasons some things are kept as secrets. Some reasons are to protect someone or thing because of the good that comes from it. Some secrets are to prevent great harm that can be done if they were to be revealed. And, some secrets are kept because errors are sometimes made, and there is no way to correct them. What you, as a group, have stumbled upon, has elements of all three of those reasons. In truth, many of us weren't aware of some portion of the secrets until you discovered them. Again, there are valid reasons to maintain secrecy. And this is one of them."

He smiled at Naleeva, who didn't react to his overture. He said, "I'd like to have Ms. Ettiene y Marcos talk with you a few minutes." I thought, orchestrated, carefully orchestrated.

Naleeva stood and looked at us, "Please keep an open mind as I speak. I want you to know I had a suspicion of only a small fraction of what we found. If I had known the danger that existed, I would not have placed you in the precarious position you were or in the complicated situation we all find ourselves today. When I approached the supervisory structure in the State Department, neither I nor anyone there were aware of the true nature of what we would find. While I don't agree with everything we'll discuss today, I do agree with the crucial need to keep what we've discovered between ourselves." She half-crumpled into the chair rather than sat. I perceived she was challenged, but not defeated.

"You have all signed a non-disclosure agreement. Is there anyone who claims they haven't? Raise your hand." No hands rose. "Good. I want to caution you about the severity of the problem you would have if you decided to disregard it. It ... would ... ruin ... you. Maybe you think a great book deal or satisfying a political motive would be worth contemplating ignoring that piece of paper. Let me assure you, living in a foreign country, even visiting a plastic surgeon would not protect you." The speaker's smile had disappeared. "Don't test our resolve."

His smile returned. "I'm sure all of you will keep the agreement as though your life depended on it. All we need from you is a few items, past keeping your word, you've already given in writing. Once those things are done, you can go about your life as if those things that *happened* in Argentina, never *happened*. No recriminations. No interference in your lives. Here is what we need: First, a statement from each of you that you can't, with certainty, identify those outlaw forces that attacked your camp and destroyed everything in it. Second, the surrender of all personal records, photos, or any other information you may have gathered while on your trip. Third, the surrender of all items you have taken from the site either as part of the group or individually. Everything, to the smallest item. As soon as we have them in our possession, you will be free to go...after you all are paid the amounts promised before you left on the trip. Now, do you have questions?"

I thought, carrot and stick and looked around at my comrades. No one looked happy. No one looked relieved. No one looked like they believed one word of what they'd been told.

Eduardo was angry. He said, "What right do you have to hold me here or include me in this deal you are offering? I'm a citizen of Argentina, not the USA."

The man looked down at the files in front of him. "Dr. Rialto, is that correct?"

Eduardo answered, "Yes!"

"Dr. Rialto, I can assure you that we have conferred with your government in Buenos Aires a great deal. Both our governments are in complete agreement in this matter. Dr. Rialto, you will be free to go home, as you are Dr. Beltran," the man pointed at Petro then at Migdalia, "and of course, you are Miss Macias. All of you will be offered similar terms there. You can accept them here and be done with it, or return home. I cannot promise your people will be as generous as ours. If you wished to stay here, in the US, it could be arranged for people of your education and stature in your fields. I don't know how your government views the results of what you've done individually based on each of your personal involvement." The man gave them time to let the veiled threat sink in before continuing. "I'd suggest each of you consider the best course of action for yourself. Now, may we begin?"

No one from our group showed any reaction.

"Let's not be difficult." The man's smile increased as if to convince us of his good will. It didn't work.

"Who in the hell are you? Who do you work for and what's your title?" Mark demanded.

The man didn't look at his files to know who Mark was. "Dr. Card, you can call me Bob Jones, I am a counsel for the Department of Justice. You really don't need to know more than that. What you do need to know is that I've been given the power to see this affair to a conclusion. I will do that. I don't hold any ill will toward anyone in this room...at this time. You are all innocent victims, and I'll treat you that way." The last part of his sentence was unspoken, but clear *unless you don't cooperate.*

"You really expect we will be morally bankrupt enough to not share with the world what we've discovered?" Mark's face was red, his voice high.

"What do you think that is?" The man who called himself Jones asked. He didn't seem to be upset by Mark's accusation.

"You spared one of the evilest men the world has ever seen. You hid him. And, when your secret was about to be discovered, you eliminated him, and then you followed the first rule of assassination, you assassinated the assassins. Only, these men were doing what they were told or commanded to do. Was what the government got from Operation Paperclip worth the principles that were compromised to achieve it?" Mark's eyes flashed with anger.

Jones smiled didn't waver. "You have some facts right, most wrong and, yes, what we gained was worth the compromise many times over."

Most everyone looked shocked including me. Not Mug and Reading. I wondered what they knew I didn't.

Mark recovered first. "Okay, what do we have wrong? That Hitler didn't commit suicide in 1945. That Nazi's were sheltered and allowed to escape? That operation paperclip was set up to do just that? That a group of Marines was sent to annihilate those living in the compound and in turn, they were assassinated?"

The man cocked his head to one side. He conferred with one of the six men accompanying him then nodded a couple of times as though he'd come to a decision. He cleared his throat. "I suppose that the circumstances you have been placed in means we owe you *some* explanation. I'll address what I can. Will what I say satisfy you? I doubt that. But, it is as much as I'm willing to explain."

"Were you right about Hitler escaping? That is what the expedition you undertook was to prove or disprove. The US government was not involved in aiding his escape ... *if* in fact, he did. The question is whether there were individuals in our government that took actions they believed were in the best interest of the country that the rest of our government only knew part or nothing about. I can tell you *that happened*. In May 1945, Germany was defeated, but we were still in a brutal war with the Japanese. There were German scientists, armament experts, and government officials who had knowledge many believed could shorten the war. Thousands were dying every week in the Pacific. Some of the people whose knowledge could end that war were Nazis. The problem our military and wartime officials had, that we forget, is the frame history put them in. The Soviets controlled Berlin and the area around it where many of these people were hiding or escaping from. Roosevelt had just died, no one knew how Truman would handle the job, and it was apparent relations with the Russians and Stalin were going down in flames. A lot of insiders like Bill Davidson, head of the OSS, agreed with Churchill that we could be in a war with the USSR in the near future. Davidson did what he thought was best. He had to find these scientists and alive, quick! There was a way to do it, but not a clean one. Some high ranking Nazis in the Gestapo and the SS kept track of where these critical minds were. They traded their ability to pinpoint the locations for their inclusion in Paperclip, the operation designed to gather up the people with information we could use and get them to the US and South America. In turn, they were able to help many of their friends and associates to flee, including some of the highest positioned men in the Nazi government. You all probably know of Werner von Braun's contribution to the space program. He was the key to its success. That alone would justify it, at least partially. But, let me ask you this. Is it a coincidence that our nuclear program advanced so fast in the months immediately after Germany's surrender?"

That possibility shocked me. The faces of my companions showed the same surprise when the logic of the possibility shattered their belief in what they thought was an unchallengeable truth.

Jones smiled, "We often forget that the necessity of the moment makes for decisions and associations we would not countenance at less volatile times. Were these all good decisions? No, some were terrible. When the full impact of these actions became wider know, many officials lost their jobs, the Nazis who were sheltered were often relocated and put on their own, but many found ways to be useful to governments, both ours and others. Few were able to fashion lives and become absorbed in the fabric of society. As these secrets slowly became known, they became a threat to both those who had been sheltered, and those who sheltered them. People in positions of power took action to," the man looked as though he had something vile in his mouth, "eliminate the problem. Sometimes, an identity was leaked, a person was moved to a different location, and in some cases there were assassinations. Often these assassinations were done in secrecy to shield others. What you uncovered was something done so skillfully that no one was aware of what happened in those jungles with the exception of the few who masterminded the operation. Those people are dead. The official reports and details of what happened to the Marines who perished there are stored half a world away. Until you found your evidence, only a few knew this ever happened. They elected to keep the secret because of the discredit that would come to the country and those who ordered what happened in the jungle. I have to ask all of you, even if you weren't legally bound to never speak of what you've learned. Would you want to be the one who would cause great turmoil in the world with no possible betterment? Not one concentration camp victim will come back to life, none of their relatives will see justice done for the perpetrators of these ills, those who took these actions are long since dead, the people that committed these deeds won't be punished for them, unmasking these events can do no good and can do much harm."

Everyone remained silent when the man finished. Each had his thoughts, but none expressed them. Most looked resigned to accepting what we'd been offered. I listened to the man, and there was logic to what he said I found hard to refute.

Jones took our silence for capitulation. He asked, "Who wants to start off. I have a prepared statement that you didn't recognize the force that destroyed your camp, for signature. Tell me where any items you have taken from the site are located. I'll have an agent pick them up." His smile returned. "You get paid, and as long as you honor your non-disclosure agreement, you live your life without any interference from us."

"Let me save you a lot of time, Mr. Jones." Reading

spoke as he rose from his chair. "I'll sign your agreement about not knowing who destroyed the camp. Since you don't say anything about the group that was spying on us as being involved in the destruction, and I don't know whether the four did or did not participate, I can honestly sign it. I know who they were." Reading looked at FBI agent Steve Hanson. "You got a great tan." He walked over to Jones who he towered over by at least eight inches. "As far as the rest of this group turning over material to you from our expedition ... they can't. You see, I took the responsibility of seeing that material was safe, and in places, no one, not even I can get to. The only way that material is turned in is if something happens to any of us. If it is, the people holding the materials, the bones, bullets, records, a computer you people missed, even some of the letters and documents from the safe ... they go to news media scattered all over the world. I can't tell you where the material is because I don't know and, in some cases, a secondary or third person I don't even know holds it. I can promise you; it will never surface unless any of us die or disappear.

"You see, your story was very convincing, but the errors were easy for me to see before you started. The people who were desperate to keep the secret, desperate enough to kill, might see us as a threat that could be eliminated. I'm just a small town cop, but my father always said, 'If you stick your hand under a log and get bit by a snake you weren't smart, but you should have learned. If you stick your hand under there again, you deserve to die.' There's a lot of relevance in that saying to what's happening to us. You may be honest in saying you believe no one will harm us. You aren't everyone. You haven't said these people have been removed from power. Obviously, they aren't dead. Now, we'll all sign your paper, you'll give us the check we've more than earned, and we'll leave."

Jones looked up at my brother. The man's features were an odd combination of dislike and admiration. He remained silent for several seconds. Jones asked rather than look at his files. "You are?"

"Reading Partin."

"So tell me, what proof can you give me that these bits of evidence you have will never surface?" Jones asked. "You asked us to take you at your word. You'll have

to take me at mine." Reading nodded and added, "Just as you said nothing would happen to us, you'll see nothing gets released, and the secrets remain secrets."

Jones folded his arms, remained silent as he thought of some counter. Eventually, he asked, "Small town cop, tell me one item that you have that you believe is so incriminating we can believe you have the material you say you possess."

Reading smiled. I knew the look. It was something my brother had anticipated, and he was ready. "I have a picture. It is a picture of a Gestapo official, a very high official. He disappeared a few days before the war's end in Hitler's bunker and hasn't been seen since. Now, if I were to lay a picture of a very high ranking, and prominent US official, from one of your departments, next to it, the resemblance would be striking. The similarity in the genetic markers is astounding. The general shape of the head. The hairline. The eyebrows and their juncture with the nose are identical. The nose is interchangeable without seeing a difference. Deep-set eyes spaced identically, of the same color, with the same hardness. Both have very thin lips that turn down at the corners. Same cheekbone structure. Same bags under the eyes. Double points on a square chin." Jones' face paled as Reading spoke. "Even more coincidental, they share the same last name. True, it's spelled different, but Nazi leaders' arrogance is legendary. I made several copies of these along with a very detailed evaluation, and they're spread around. Would you like me to continue with that example or different ones?"

Jones held his hand up. "No more is required. I'll need some approvals. I'm sure we'll get them. Wait here."

Silence. Complete and utter silence. Jones left the room. Reading stood isolated; his eyes fixed on Naleeva's, hers on him. I knew something had passed between them. That was an easy guess. I remembered Naleeva saying she knew the face.

I wondered if Reading was telling the truth about what

he'd done with the artifacts he'd smuggled into the country. If he was bluffing, I hoped it was good enough to get the rest of the players to fold their hands. If not ...

My hand went up and touched the dog tags hanging around my neck without consciously thinking of them. Between the two that identified me was one that read:

Wilson Bernard T O pos 124-44-3256, USMC L Catholic

It was an insurance policy, not issued by Liberty Mutual, Progressive, or the Good Hands People. No one knew of it but me. Not even Reading. I decided to keep it that way.

Chapter 84

In the parking lot of Patrick Air Force Base

Reading and I stood waiting for the car to drive us to our duplex in Vero. We watched the car containing Naleeva and Mug travel the road to the gate. It was the first time we'd been truly alone for four days.

Reading was tired but at peace. He turned to me and said, "Don't look so relieved. Until we walk through our front door, I won't believe we're there."

"We'll make it." I reached up and kissed him on the cheek. "That was quite a speech. You sure got everyone's attention." He grinned but said nothing. I asked, "Was it all true or was it all BS?"

"A little of both." He shook his head. "Don't ask. It's best that I'm the only one that knows what the truth is. Hope you never find it out, because if you do, it means I'm dead."

I looked at him. He smiled and shook his head and mouthed, "no."

"You don't know what I was going to ask. It wasn't about where everything is hidden."

He shrugged his shoulders. "Okay, what?"

"The bit about the pictures and genetic markers. I know you got that from Naleeva, but who was it? It changed everything in that room." I doubted he'd answer me, but I thought I'd give it a try.

"One of the most prominent men in Washington, I can tell you that." I could see that Reading was struggling with the urge to tell me. "How do you think it would go over if people learned it was probable that one of the most powerful individuals in our government's law enforcement agencies was the son of the Nazi head of the Gestapo?"

Chapter 85
**Chessie & Reading's Duplex
Vero Beach, FL**

"This place never looked so good," I said.

Reading closed the door behind us, and walked straight to the thermostat, to cool it down from the 82°. "Kind of looks like a royal palace."

"I hope my Jeep starts, I don't feel like cooking, do you?" I hoped he didn't. Anything that was in the refrigerator was likely to be questionable.

"If your Jeep starts, and you want to drive and get something, great." Reading unbuckled his belt and kicked his pants off. "If I remember correctly, there are seven cans of Coors left in the door, and they're something in the refrigerator that won't spoil. While you go to Pizza Hut, I'll inspect the inside of a couple of those beers and be sure the tube and my recliner still work."

"What about something besides pizza? I could go to Yin Chen's. How's beef lo mein sound?" I knew that was Reading's favorite Chinese dish.

"Hell yes!" he said as he headed toward the kitchen.

I went to my bedroom and plopped down on my bed. My bed! There is nothing that is more secure and comfortable than returning to sleep in your very own bed.

I sighed enjoying familiarity and the solace it provided after three months plus of living on the edge. After a few minutes of enjoying doing nothing, I went to my bathroom to check my makeup. I shook my head and said, "That damned maid didn't show again." My panties and bra hung on the back of the door, the bath mat was on the floor in front of the shower, and a bath towel hung from the curtain rod. I really knew I was home. It would save time, so I called Chen's and placed my order. The girl said, "Ten minute, it be ready." When I hung up, I started humming, "There's no place like home." My Jeep keys were on the dresser. I picked them up and headed for the living room.

Reading was settled in his recliner watching *Jurassic World* on the TV for at least the tenth time. He was caressing his Coors can as I walked around his feet, picked up my bag and headed for the front door. I hadn't got halfway there when he yelled, "Whoa, girl. You forget what you have in your purse? You'd better leave them here."

I stopped, was confused for a few seconds then remembered that two government checks were in the bag I held in my hand. Each one had very nice things written on them: Reading and my name were on one each and $175,000 on both. It would be better not to go hauling those things around town. I took them out of my purse, walked over to Reading, and handed them to him. "Tomorrow, first thing, we take them to the bank."

"You got it, Sis!"

~ ~ ~ ~ ~

By the time I pulled out of the strip mall that housed Chen's restaurant, I needed lights. My jeep seemed to purr like a freshly stroked kitten. I passed a T-bird convertible and wondered if that was something worth spending money on. I quickly concluded, no, there were other more practical things. I laughed and said out loud, "Damn Chessie, you're getting more like your brother every day."

As I retraced my route home, I made my first turn. I noticed a car ran a caution light to stay behind me. That registered on my mind, so I kept checking my rear view mirror. The black car stayed fifty feet behind. I made another turn. So did the black car. I began to be concerned. The third turn really bothered me when the car stayed on my rear bumper. I called Reading on my cell.

"Hey, Reading, I think someone is following me," I told him.

"You sure?" he asked.

"Pretty sure. They made the last three turns I have, and they made a real effort to stay with me."

Reading said, "Don't stop for anything unless you have to stop for a light. Don't let them cut you off. Run a light if you have to. I'll be outside waiting for you."

I slowed as if I was going to turn, put my turn signal on, and checked the mirror. The black car's turn signal came on. Instead of turning I speeded up and went straight.

The car did too. I was certain someone was after me. I reached the last turn before I'd be at our duplex. I turned ... so did my tail. Reading was standing outside our front door with one hand behind his back. That hand would be holding his automatic. As I slowed to turn into the parking lot, the black car mirrored my action. As my Jeep rolled to a stop, I expected to hear a gunshot.

"Welcome back neighbor!" it was the man from the other side of our duplex. After some pleasantries, Reading and I went inside.

"I feel foolish," I said.

"Don't." Reading put his arm around my shoulder.

"Is this the way life is going to be from now on?"

"We'll learn to live with it, Chessie."

"That's bull shit!" I wasn't happy at the thought of being constantly vigilant.

Reading looked at me and shook his head. "We went swimming with sharks. It will take some time before we stop seeing their fins."

"Two-legged sharks." I took a deep breath. "You know I've always been a people person. I don't know now. The bones from my digs are looking better all the time."

"Give it time, Chessie; things will settle down. It will go back to normal."

"I hope you're right."

"I'll be right. I don't want to even consider the alternative."

The End

DL Havlin is an eclectic author whose varied experiences and background provide him with a memory chest full of material for writing his novels. He graduated from the University of Cincinnati and attended pre-law at Rollins.

His life has been as varied as his novels. Havlin's occupations have included tasks from systems analyst to worldwide customer service director and from licensed boat captain to football coach. He's in demand as a speaker and seminar presenter for relationship and writing skills.

Havlin's passion for fishing, hunting, Florida's wilderness, and its historical heritage, frequently appear in his writing and his speaking engagements. His tales are just as likely to be set in Kiev, Singapore, London, Sachsenhausen or other places in the over eighty countries he's visited. Their people and customs resonate in his novels. Known for creating memorable characters, his interjection of humor, and his carefully crafted plots, reading a DL Havlin book is always a pleasurable experience.

Books by DL Havlin

A Place No One Should Go

The Bait Man

Blue Water Red Blood

Bully Route Home

The Cross on Cotton Creek

Deadly Development

Escaping Skeletons

Finding the Nancy Lynn

The Hangin' Oak

September on Echo Creek

Story Time-R

Turtle Point

All books are available on Amazon and Kindle